PRAISE FOR
AUDREY CARLAN

"FIVE STAR REVIEW! I recommend this book to anyone looking for a sweet, fierce love story. It takes a lot to write an original story that takes twists and turns you won't see coming."
~**Abibliophobia Anonymous Book Reviews Blog**

"Damn Audrey did it again! Made me smile, made me laugh & made me cry with her beautiful words! I am in love with these books."
~**Hooks & Books Book Blog**

"A sensual spiritual journey of two people meant for each other, heart and soul. Well-crafted and beautifully written."
~**Carly Phillips, New York Times Bestselling Author**

Fate

A TRINITY NOVEL

Fate

A TRINITY NOVEL

WATERHOUSE PRESS

WARNING

To my soul sister Carolyn Beasley.

Without you, there would be no Kathleen Bennett.

*As this series comes to an end, my fondest wish is that like Kat,
you too find your happily ever after.*

With all my love and friendship for life.

BESOS

Bound - Eternally - Sisters - of - Souls

CHAPTER ONE

KATHLEEN

Regrets are wishes unfulfilled. After thirty years on this earth, I have more regrets than fingers and toes, and most of them are connected to one man. The one I pushed away. And now I'm alone. No man, no children, no hope for more.

They say loneliness is a choice, and I guess that's true. People flit in and out of my life like buzzing bees sipping the nectar from my sweet spot, leaving emptiness behind. He used to fill that space with joy, laughter, and what I thought was love. Believed in it, even. Until it was gone. Now, there's nothing left but an empty husk, a shell of the woman I used to be. A woman I wish I could be again.

My therapist says I have PTSD from the fire and resulting injury, and maybe he's right. Everyone else seems to have the answers to my problems, but I'm the one stuck in hell. I'm the one who wakes to pain shooting up my side, down my right arm, and out my fingertips each and every night. And that's when I realize, once again, how alone I truly am. There's no man to wake up and hold me close, murmuring sweet nothings in my ear until I relax and fall back into a peaceful slumber.

The days I could count on a man to hold me within the

warmth of his embrace are over. One of my many regrets. Still, I wouldn't change my decision. He's better off without me. Or at least the broken, hollow shell I've become.

Not that it matters. He didn't love me when I was physically and mentally perfect. He definitely wouldn't be able love me now. So why can't I let go? Free him from my mind, my heart, and my life. Why does my happiness hinge on the one that got away?

Three years is a long time to pine for someone you purposely forced out of your life. Three long years of burn treatments, grafting, rehabilitation, and therapy. Therapy. Such a joke. Dr. Madison can't fix me. Nothing can. Every new procedure gives me hope I will look and feel like I did before the night my entire life changed. They never do. Sometimes I get patches of smoother skin. A little less scarring here, a little more there. The grafts leave their own scars, but those are better hidden. Still, I'm not *me*.

Kathleen Bennett, the real Kat, was figuratively burned to a crisp in the fire. Everything that made me the woman I was, the person I was proud to be—happy-go-lucky, in love with life, in love with Carson Davis... That woman died. In her place is a bitter, scarred woman with a chip on her shoulder and an unquenchable desire to disappear.

Maybe my answer is to leave, become someone else. But I could never leave *them*. My soul sisters are my lifeblood. They are the roots that grew this tree into something I was once proud of. Now, this tree of life feels like a shriveled-up mess of dead leaves and scrawny, unattractive branches. Still, the roots binding me to those three women go deep, far deeper than an outsider could imagine. Our connection was born of love, laughter, sacrifice, hardship, pain, and rebirth. They understand me, even the screwed-up version I am today. And they won't stop trying to bring back the person I used to be—the one hiding under the abraded flesh.

Three years and I haven't been able to find her. I worry I never will.

"Kathleen, are you ready?" rumbles the voice I've come to count on. The one person I've been able to be completely honest with, Chase Davis, my soul sister Gillian's husband, knocks on my bedroom door. "Are you decent? We're going to be late if you aren't ready."

"Hold your horses. And yes, I'm decent. Come in." I sigh and fluff my bangs. Not that it matters. Nobody will be looking at me. And if they do, all they will see is a disfigured monster.

He enters just the threshold of my bedroom, pushing open the door. His navy suit is tailored to fit his frame perfectly. I made sure of that. My new men's line is coming together nicely. The only thing in my life actually going well, considering I'm unable to use my right hand for more than squeezing a stress ball in therapy. I will concede the hand is getting stronger, but I'll never be able to do the detailed work I was known for in my past life as a costume designer. That ship has long sailed, never to return again.

"Kathleen, you try my patience." Chase lifts his arm and taps his Rolex silently.

I smile and grab my purse from the nightstand with my left hand. "And your wife and children don't?"

His brow furrows, but his lips tip up at the edges. Speaking of Gillian always makes Chase smile. He can't help it. My feisty redheaded bestie and their adorable twins rule his world, and he loves every second of it.

He puckers his lips, a small smirk still present. "Be that

as it may, we have to go, or we'll be late for the test results. I'm eager to hear what this new technology has to offer."

Chase Davis, my optimist. Ever since the fire, he's made it his personal responsibility and goal to fix me. Well, not just me, but all of his wife's soul sisters. He helped Bree with her yoga studio and Maria with her apartment for the first year, until she hooked up with Eli. But for me he's been more. My own personal hero, though I've never said those words to him. For the most part, I pretend what he's doing is putting me out. Then I don't have to cop to what I really feel.

Relief.

He's there in ways I can't accept from my girlfriends. I don't know why. Chase has wormed his way into my broken side, and for him I allow the invasion. With the girls, no way. I need them to see me as the strong woman they think I am. The illusion of strength is one of the only things I have left.

In the beginning, when I was first released from the burn center, I refused Chase's assistance, wanting to do it all on my own. Until I realized I couldn't. He stopped in to visit me at my ramshackle apartment across town after my second set of treatments. Thank God he did. He found me on the floor, unable to move. The pain in my arm and side was excruciating. I had been fading in and out of consciousness. Turned out one of my grafts was infected. He pulled me off the floor, took me to the hospital, and stayed with me until I was discharged. Upon release, I found out Chase had pulled a fast one. He'd moved me into the building across the street, where he had planned to move Maria after her apartment was trashed by her ex. The apartment she ended up not needing because she moved in with her new husband, Elijah Redding.

Chase Davis, billionaire, alpha, and ferociously protective

of those he considers "family," had put the smackdown on my life. He was not leaving me to fend for myself. The new place came with a shiny new set of in-home nurses who stopped in several times a day to dress and redress my wounds, masseuses for muscle therapy, and weekly appointments with Dr. Madison, my shrink. The same psychiatrist Gillian and Chase had gone to during their own ordeal with the madman who put me in the position I'm in today.

"Really, Chase, they aren't going to say anything we haven't heard before. The tissue is too damaged. *You've had too many surgeries. There's not much left to work with. Blah, blah, blah. More tests, more trials...*" I mimic a person talking using my good hand.

Chase grips my elbow and leads me out of my apartment, down the elevator, and into the waiting limo with a firm, unrelenting hold. He's irritated. Big whoop. Nothing new here.

"Hey, Austin, how goes it?" I ask the bodyguard holding open the door of the pristine black stretch limousine.

"Perfect as a peach, Ms. Bennett," he says in his kind southern drawl, tipping his head formally.

I chuckle and slip into the car, sliding over to the side so Chase can get in.

"Where's Jack?" I ask.

Chase adjusts his cuff links and tugs the cuffs of his dress shirt. "With my wife. Playdate."

I snort-cough. "You sent your wife and toddler children with the *linebacker* to a playdate?" I can barely hold back the bubble of laughter forcing its way up my throat.

He turns his head, a dark-cappuccino-colored lock of hair falling handsomely over his forehead. Reminds me of the blond ones I used to brush off Carson's brow. Chase's blue eyes sear mine with a dose of sincerity. "This surprises you? Even after all these years?"

I shake my head. "Not really. It's just, there hasn't been a threat to any of us in years, and yet you act like we're always under siege."

He lifts a long leg and crosses it over his knee. His Salvatore Ferragamo black leather shoes are polished to perfection. Even his socks are lush.

Socks. Hmm. Maybe I should pair socks with suits so that men can have a perfect match? I pull out my voice recorder and click it on. "Match socks to suits. Look into fabric and colors for the current line."

Chase's lips twitch as he focuses on his phone.

"You know, you don't have to go to these appointments with me. It's not your job, nor am I your charity case anymore. I'm making top dollar on my clothing designs, and being in business with Chloe has changed my career for the better. You've really done enough." This is the same argument we've had at least ten times before.

He pockets his phone, inhales loudly, and cocks his body to the side. He stretches one of his long arms over the back of my seat. "Kathleen, you are not my charity case. You are my friend. Aside from Carson, my best friend."

Carson. Even the mention of my former boyfriend and love of my life makes me wince.

"Besides, I made a promise I intend to keep," he adds solemnly.

I frown. "A promise? That's the first you've ever mentioned any promise."

His lips shift into a flat line, and he turns back, facing the front of the car. "No matter. We are moving forward and seeing this through."

I grab his biceps. Hard as steel. Damn, the dude works out. He's not huge like my soul sister Maria's Eli, but he's definitely built to please a woman aesthetically and physically. And since he's knocked up my best friend once again, she obviously appreciates those attributes regularly. Lucky girl.

"Tell me about the promise."

He quirks his head toward me. "Maybe one day I will. For now, let's just hope for the best—"

"And expect the worst. Yeah, yeah. I know. You've said it a hundred times over the past three years. Still, it never gets any easier to hear that I'm going to be deformed for the rest of my life."

Chase grips my right hand softly and closes his eyes. It's comforting that he's not afraid to touch me, even in the platonic way a brother would. Like the girls, he's not afraid of my scars, nor does he see me any differently. Nevertheless, he knows *I* see me differently, and that's what he's committed himself to setting right.

"You know, one day you're going to have to accept what happened to us. To Bree, Phillip, Maria, your wife, your mom, you. None of it was your fault. Danny McBride was a sick and twisted individual who hurt all of us in ways we can't ever change. But he's dead, Chase. Dead."

Chase sighs. "Along with Thomas, the yoga intern, and a host of others from the bombing. I know I didn't make him obsessed with my wife and her friends, but I understand why he was. I have the same obsession with Gillian. I'd do anything for her and our children."

I smile, knowing his brand of adoration runs deep. "Love is the healthy form of obsession, and you have it in spades. But you can't blame yourself for the actions of another."

"Had I been able to stop him sooner..." he starts, but this time I cut him off by squeezing his hand.

He looks down at our clasped hands and smiles huge.

"Chase, stop it..."

"I felt that," he gushes, cutting me off. "You just squeezed the hell out of my hand!" His blue eyes twinkle with excitement.

I glance down and realize I'm still holding his hand. My scarred one is gripping his golden, flawlessly manicured one.

This time, I grin. "I did, didn't I?"

He nods. "You sure did. See, the day is already getting better. Gillian is going to be thrilled."

I let his hand go, lift my arm up, and squeeze my hand into a fist. The skin stretches unnaturally tight over the sunken-in holes and bumpy grafts, but I've made a complete fist. First time in three years I've been able to do that.

"My mobility has improved."

"Looks like the oral treatment that rebuilds tissue, joint mobility, and muscle strength is working. Good news indeed."

★ ★ ★

The good news kept coming too. The doctor told me I'd improved mobility by twenty percent in the past six months on the new medication. I may never have the fine motor skills I once had with the limb, but things like holding a glass of water, being able to grip a plate and put it into the dishwasher, and holding a baby are all on the horizon—things I wasn't able to do before, things the average person takes for granted. Every time I had to shoo away Gillian or Bree passing me their children, I was reminded of what I'd lost. And now, now I may have that chance back.

"Amazing. We need to celebrate." Chase opens his phone. "Baby, Kathleen's got some great news to share. Tell Bentley to set dinner for the crew."

I place my hand to his shoulder and shake my head. "Just us tonight. Okay? I don't want to get the girls' hopes up." I pat his forearm.

Chase's shoulders drop down. "Make that an extra plate for one. Yes, Kathleen will explain when we arrive. No, she doesn't want Maria and Bree called. Not at this time. I know they'd enjoy hearing good news too, but we're going to let her handle this news as she deems appropriate..." He glances at me, squinting.

I know he's unhappy that I don't want to celebrate. This is good news. It is. But we don't know enough about it to truly spread the word. Bree and Maria would be more than ecstatic, and I can't handle another letdown. Not now. Not when Maria just got married and is blissfully enjoying the honeymoon phase of her marriage, and Bree and Phillip are focusing on their home design.

"Gigi for now, the rest later. Okay?" I whisper.

Chase nods curtly at me and then speaks into his phone. "We'll be there momentarily."

When Chase hangs up, he presses his thumb and forefinger into his temples. "Kathleen, I do not understand this need to distance yourself from everyone. It's not only hurting you, it's putting undo pressure on my wife. In her condition..."

"Her condition? She's pregnant, not dying." I remind him, "This is my life, Chase. Mine. Not yours. How you handle a situation may differ from how I do, but this news is mine to tell or not."

He sighs. "You have spent the better part of three years pushing everyone you love away. I've been there, done that. Not only is it unhealthy, it just makes you miserable. And you are miserable. I can see it every time I look into your eyes. You miss him. You miss them." His words are rough and grating, hitting right on their mark.

I tighten my mouth and clench my teeth. "You have no right to bring him up. You promised you wouldn't."

"Well, like you, he's fucking up his life." He lets out a long breath of air.

"What do you mean? What's going on with Carson?"

My heart starts to pound a mile a minute. The mere thought of something being wrong with the man who owns my soul is enough to send me straight into a fully loaded panic attack. I inhale and exhale, pushing down the pressure building in my chest that's slowly squeezing my heart one centimeter at a time.

Chase doesn't realize my distress because he's looking out the window, scowling.

"If you hadn't left him, pushed him away repeatedly, he would have never put himself in this situation. I blame you."

I blame you.

"Excuse me?" My ire fires right alongside the panic, squashing it down.

"Something's off about the woman he's seeing now. Really off." Chase shakes his head.

I roll my eyes. "He's had women before. He'll get past it like he always does."

Chase huffs and clenches his jaw so hard a muscle in his jaw ticks. "I'm not so sure you're right."

"What could be so bad about a woman Carson is fucking?

He's a virile man. Believe me, I used to be the recipient of all that virility."

He tightens both hands into fists on top of his knees. "I'm telling you, Kathleen, I've got a bad feeling."

"So talk to him about it." I groan and flick my hand. This topic is killing me one word at a time. Imagining Carson with any woman is like deliberately driving a stake through my own heart.

"I have," he says between clenched teeth. "He's avoiding me. Avoiding everyone. Pulling a *you*, actually."

I sigh long and loud, letting my own frustration out. "There's nothing I can do."

He scoffs. "Sure there is. You can stop this shit you have going and take back your man. And don't pretend he's not the man for you, because I call bullshit. Before the fire, you two were the happiest any of us had ever seen you."

"Chase..." I warn. "Bringing up the past does not help the future."

"That's asinine, and you and I both know it. Tell me you don't love him still."

"I don't love him," I state instantly. I've gotten so good at this lie, it comes out fast with absolutely no hint of emotion.

"Liar," he growls. "You're going to regret not winning him back."

"I already do," I admit with a drawn-out sigh.

"Then do something about it."

With a heavy heart, I focus on the destroyed flesh of my hand, the same destruction that goes all the way up my arm, over my shoulder, and down my ribcage. I'll always be severely scarred. The grafting options and skin-smoothing surgeries are complete. They've done what they can. Now it's all about physical therapy. Getting back additional mobility in the arm and hand. Applying copious amounts of lotion across the rippled flesh to keep it soft and pliant. Staying out of the sun helps but won't make the scars go away. My body is no longer one a man wants to touch, to run his hands over in the throes of passion.

I shake my head. No, he doesn't deserve to have his eyes accosted by the reflection I have to face in the mirror every day. It's disgusting, and I'd rather him remember me the way I was. Beautiful, unmarred, pristine in mind and body.

"No. He's better off without me. I can't be what I was. I'm not the woman he cared for."

"That's not true. You are the same woman you've always been. A beautiful, talented, kindhearted woman with so much to offer a man. I am a man. I'm also Carson's cousin and best friend. I know what he wants and needs—it's you. The you then, now, and what you'll be in the future. Trust me on this. Your scars do not matter. When love is involved, those flaws become a part of what your man loves about you. Gillian's stretch marks from our children? I love them. I kiss them all the time. They prove my children were there. My son and daughter are alive because of those scars. I encourage her to wear them proudly."

"You're not a woman. You don't get it."

"No. I'm a man who loves his wife. Every part of her is mine. Scars and all. And Kathleen, she has many from before me I'd love to erase, but they show the path she's taken to get to me and our life together. To her they are precious, and to me they are proof that sometimes you have to go through hell to get to heaven. She taught me that."

"The love you have with my best friend is beautiful, but

Carson and I never had that." I swallow down the lump forming in my throat.

"You did once."

I blink, close my eyes, and flatten myself against the back of the limo seat. "You see, Chase, that's where you're wrong. Carson never loved me. He never once said it. Even though I said it all the time." I laugh dryly. "He even requested I say it to him over and over. Adored hearing it from my lips. Would ravish me with kisses and more every time. But not even once did he say it to me. And when I asked why, all he could muster was 'I can't. Please don't ask me to.' So there you go."

"So, you gave up?" The accusation is thick in his tone.

"Yeah, after everything, what I had to offer, repeated treatments, painful surgeries, and long recovery times... If he didn't love me before, he could never love me after. I took a calculated risk and it failed. Every single time I pushed him away, he never once uttered those three little words. I begged him to say them. All he did was cry, break down, and shake his head no. I can't be with a man who refuses to tell me he loves me."

"I know he does though," he says softly and with intention.

"Words, Chase. I needed the words. He didn't have them. I no longer have them for him. I have to move on. Obviously he has."

He sighs and runs his fingers through his hair. "What can I do?"

I cover his other hand with mine. "Move on. I have."

"Have you?"

"Yes." A bald-faced lie to one of the kindest, most loving men I know.

"You really need to talk to Dr. Madison about this lying

trait you picked up. I'm not buying it and neither are your friends. Regardless, I'll let you have your play...for now. We got great news today, and it's time to celebrate."

The limo pulls up to the curb in front of the Chase Industries building, where he and Gillian live on the top floor.

"Bring on the bubbly." I plaster a fake smile on my face, knowing I need to put it on for Gigi. She'll worry if I don't.

Chase helps me out of the car and leads me through the building and up the elevator.

Gillian is waiting at the entrance with Carter on her hip. Claire bolts into her father's arms the second he steps off the elevator.

"Daddy! Daddy! We have news too!" She grabs Chase's face and forces him to look directly at her.

"Oh yeah? What's that, baby?" He looks into Claire's crystal-blue eyes, her red curls so like her mother's auburn locks bouncing around her shoulders. "Auntie Ria says I'm going to get a bruh-ver! You hafta to take him back!"

Chase laughs. "You didn't go to the doctor without me, did you, babe?" He poses the question to Gillian.

"Nope. But I did have lunch with Maria, and she did her voodoo hand trick and says it's a boy. She was right last time, so anything is possible." Gigi shrugs.

"Another boy, eh?" He grins, his chest puffing out in pride.

"Auntie Kitty!" Claire realizes I'm standing next to her father. "I'm getting a bruh-ver. Do you want it?" She crinkles her sweet little nose.

I pet her cheek with my good hand. Under no circumstances do I touch the children with the disfigured one. If they were scared of me, for any reason...

A shiver slinks up my spine. I'd never survive that. My

pseudo-nieces and one nephew are my main sources of joy nowadays. "Honey, I can't have your new brother."

She frowns. "But I ask-ted for a sister. This is not fair." Her little pink lips shift into the cutest pout.

"Honey, life isn't fair. It really isn't."

In more ways than one.

CHAPTER TWO

CARSON

One month earlier...

The San Francisco sky is dark, cloudy, and foreboding. The gloom of the weather fits my current mood. I sit in my truck, drumming restless fingers along the steering wheel. The clock on my dash reads five fifty-five. She should be arriving any time.

I just need a glimpse.

Somehow, I feel if I can see it with my own eyes, the truth of the situation will make itself known. I just need to see *her*.

A blue Honda pulls up and parks along the curb across the street. Her blond hair pops against the navy jacket she's wearing. She runs her hand through her hair and enters the building.

What seems like eternity drags on in the minutes I wait for her to exit. When she does, I watch closely, taking in every feature, from her blond curls to her blue eyes. Even at this distance she's beautiful. Yet a sense of uncertainty slips across my heart.

If she were meant to be mine, wouldn't I feel it? Know it deep down from within the very depths of my soul?

Perhaps not. I felt that way once before, and it didn't last. Crashed and burned more like it.

Maybe the thing people talk about—unconditional insta-love—only happens when you've known the person from the very beginning? The thought saddens me as I watch her settle into her car, pull into traffic, and leave.

The end result is that I need to be sure. Just because she's told me it's fact doesn't mean it is. I've been taken advantage of in the past in business, not to mention the gold-digging whores who think they can sink their filthy claws into me by opening their legs and showing me a good time. Those women I scrape off like gum on the bottom of my shoe. Unwanted and annoying.

There's only one woman who's ever had her claws in me, and she's the only woman I wish had never taken them out.

Still, I need concrete evidence, or I'll never believe what she's saying.

Decision made, I put my truck in gear and head across town to the shady bar I formerly had no plans to ever enter again.

When I arrive, the parking lot is mostly empty except for a handful of wayward Harleys and off-brand motorcycles. It's only six thirty. Not exactly party time, and this is not the type of establishment that promotes happy hour or half-off drinks for the regular after-work office crew.

The building itself is off the beaten path and made up of all wooden planks. It's shocking the damn thing hasn't been bulldozed for being a hazard. Structurally, I'd swear a strong wind off the bay could flatten it, but there it stands, as it has for over twenty years.

I park my truck and head to the entrance. The Honda

isn't here yet. I didn't expect her to arrive that quickly. She told me she starts work at seven most days, so here I am, ready to confront her about her confession last month.

If I were being honest with myself, I should have already touched base with her. She could fuck up my life royally if she can prove what she claims to be true. I, honest to God, have not been able to give credence to her claims. Not even for a moment. It's beyond comprehension and preposterous. Definitely not something I ever thought could happen to me. I've always, *always* been careful.

Since that night three weeks ago, I've been hiding out. Only Chase knows I'm seeing someone new, although labeling it as *seeing her* is a tad far-fetched. I couldn't very well tell him the truth. Not yet anyway. Not until I'm one hundred percent clear she's not pulling a fast one on me.

Misty Duncan.

I didn't even know her name when I fucked her over two years ago. All I knew was that she was blond, beautiful, and available during my drunken haze of need. And now it's all coming back to bite me in the ass. Hard.

The bartender approaches warily. He's probably not used to seeing clean-cut guys in this establishment. I've just come from a business meeting downtown, and my suit and tie make me stick out like a sore thumb.

"What's your poison?"

"Beer. Cold. Whatever you've got on tap is fine."

He scratches his long scraggly beard and nods.

I scan the room, making sure I can see the front door from my seat. There's a couple of rough-looking guys playing pool, each with a two-bit floozy dangling on their arms between shots. One of the guys slides a hand along his girl's thigh, brazenly copping a feel before putting his entire paw all the way up her leather skirt until she tips her head back and moans in delight.

Ugh. Why does Misty work here anyway? She seems like a nice girl. Pretty, great body. The girl could work anywhere. So why here?

The bartender sets the beer on the counter and foam overflows down the side of the glass. I don't complain or say a word. This is not the type of place to lodge complaints.

I spy a stack of napkins in the corner and reach over and grab a few, sopping up the worst of the mess, when the door opens. The woman of the hour enters in a flourish.

I check her out while she tosses her purse behind the bar, grabs an apron, and ties it around her small waist. Staring, I try to find reasons to be attracted to her, but sober, I just can't. She may have blond hair and brown eyes, but she is *not* Kathleen. There's no subtle grace in her walk, no twinkle in her eye, no dimple in her cheek, and she's small. Pint-sized, even. She pales in comparison to my girl. No, my Sweetcheeks is long and lean with a stunning body. Misty has short legs, big hips, and far bigger breasts. Cosmetically enhanced breasts.

What the hell was I thinking banging her that night?

Not knowing what else to do, I suck back my beer in a few swallows and give a chin lift to the bartender. He grabs my glass and pours me another.

"No tabs here, suit. Just cold hard cash," he says, placing the glass down with a little less bravado than before.

I pull out my wallet and set down two twenties. "Got it."

He nods, approval in his gaze.

"Hey, Carson? What are you doing here?" Misty smiles and walks over to the opposite side of the bar where I'm sitting.

"Figured it was time we talked."

She licks her lips and pushes a lock of hair behind her ear. "Yeah, okay." She glances around, noticing there are really no patrons needing assistance. "Do you, uh...want to do it here? Right now?"

"No time like the present," I answer dryly.

"Okay. So, you've had some time to think about what I told you." Her voice turns into a whisper, even though no one's paying attention to us. There are fewer than ten people in the place, including us.

I nod. "I have."

"And?" She's nervously biting her lip.

"I want a paternity test," I declare flatly and with no room for argument.

Her eyes widen. "That's fine. I, uh, don't have medical coverage or anything..."

"No worries. I've got a friend who owns LabCorp Genetics. He's agreed to come over this week and fast-track the results."

Misty swallows and cants her head to the side. "You don't believe me, do you?" She shakes her head so hard her hair sways back and forth with her movements. "Of course, you don't." Her lip trembles and her voice cracks.

I set my hand on her shoulder. "Honey, it's not that I don't believe you. It's just a really big fucking surprise. Three weeks ago, I came in here because I needed a beer after a shitty day. I never thought in a million years I'd be walking into a dive bar I visited over two years ago and come face-to-face with a one-night stand."

She winces.

"I mean, uh, how do I say this without sounding like an asshole?" I run my hand through my hair.

Misty tightens her lips and blinks a few times.

"Look, there's no reason to sugarcoat this. We hooked up. For a night. I come back in here over two years later and am hit with a story, told by a woman I don't even recognize, that I could be someone's daddy."

"But you are..." she says desperately.

I hold up my hand. "If that's the case, it won't be a problem to get a test done. Right?" I soften the last word, attempting to make sure she doesn't crumble into a ball of tears right here on the spot. As it is, it could still happen.

She puts her hands on her hips and straightens her spine into a rigid line. "But I'm not lying. I wouldn't do that!" Her eyes water, as if she's on the verge of tears. "Do you think this is easy for me? I was just as surprised as you are when I found out I was pregnant. I didn't know your full name or anything about you. There was no way I could ever contact you. This entire time I've been raising our child alone, and it hasn't been easy, Carson. Not even a little bit. And I'm doing it all on a waitress's salary? I've had to get my neighbors to babysit just so I could work...and..." Her voice is getting louder and louder as fear and anxiety become prevalent in her posture.

I set my hands on both her shoulders and dip my head down to be level with hers. "Hey, hey. I'm not saying you're lying, and I don't even pretend to know or understand what you've been through all this time without assistance. But right now, I need to protect myself as much as my potential child by proving paternity. Can you understand that?"

She sniffs and looks down at her shoes. Her shoulders are down and curving in as her entire being seems broken and small. Instead of responding, she nods.

"My friend will be in touch with you this week. We'll work

out a time for both of you to get tested as well as me. Results will be fast-tracked and then we'll know."

"And then what?" Hope fills her tone with a sincerity I can't return. Not until I know.

"Then we'll deal with the outcome."

"Meaning what?" She sighs and twists her fingers together in front of her.

"Well, if this child is mine, I'm going to be a father. A real one. Not this Disneyland-dad bullshit. I'll want regular access."

Misty inhales and the tears finally fall. "You're going to take my daughter away from me." Her hand comes up to her chest as if her heart physically hurts.

Now this I can't handle. I do not do well with women crying. The poor thing is positively shaking in heels too high for the job she has. I stand up and pull her into my arms in what I hope is a comforting hug.

"God, no. Misty, relax, honey. I'd never do that to you or to anyone, but that also doesn't mean I won't want to be in my child's life. Shared visitation. That kind of thing."

Misty curls her fingers into my dress shirt. "But she's only a baby. She can't be away from her mother. I'm all she's ever known."

Fuck. I knew this would be bad, but Jesus Christ, I had no idea my heart and mind would take such a beating.

I run my hands up and down her back until her body stops trembling.

"No one's taking anyone away from anyone. We'll work it out. I promise you this. You're not going to lose your child. If she is mine, we'll work together to do what's best for her. Sound like a plan?"

Misty sniffles and pulls back away from my chest. She

huffs out a tortured breath and wipes at her eyes with both hands.

"It's going to be okay. I swear it." I make the promise, not sure how or if I can even keep it.

★ ★ ★

"Why are you being so secretive about this woman of yours?" Chase leans against the arm of his white leather couch in his high-rise office overlooking the Pacific.

I sigh. "Brother, I'm not. It's complicated."

He takes a sip of his scotch and swirls the liquid around, and the ice cubes clink against the glass, sounding overly loud in the wide open space.

I take a sip of my own drink, letting the liquid burn a trail of fire down my throat. I welcome the prickling heat. At least it's better than the alternative, the endless reminders of what's been running rampant through my mind the past week.

Chase taps his lip. "Women are always complicated. Now tell me why this woman has your balls in a vise."

As much as I want to spill my guts all over his pristine couches, I hold back. I'm not ready to hear the chastisement in his tone when he finds out I may have gotten a woman pregnant, and worse, not have known it for over two years. Chase is the epitome of a family man, though people wouldn't know it with the no-nonsense way he runs his empire. But when it comes to Mrs. Davis and their twins? He's a whole different man. His wife and kids are his world, and Gillian's pregnant again, which means the Papa Bear side in him is out in full force. When it comes right down to it, I'm not sure he'd understand the predicament I'm in right now.

The truth is, I don't know how to tell my cousin about this. Until I know if the child is mine, I'm not opening Pandora's box.

"Look, let's just say I'm in deep."

Chase's eyebrows rise into his hairline. "Interesting. How so?"

I cringe. "Not that it's any of your business, asswipe."

He smirks while finishing off the last of his drink. "Another?"

I slam back the rest of mine. "Fuck yes."

"The fact that you won't discuss this woman does not give me the warm fuzzies."

"Warm fuzzies? Who are you? Did Gillian rip off your balls and replace them with pink fuzzy dice again?"

Chase lets out a warm chuckle. "Too right. Shit, she's already trying to do too much with this pregnancy. She's driving me positively insane. The caveman in me wants to keep her locked up in our penthouse, barefoot, pregnant, and taking care of our twins. In the grand scheme of things, is that so wrong? Really?"

"Man, let her be. She knows her body."

"I know it better," he deadpans, not even a hint of humor in his tone.

I grin. "*Touché.*"

He lifts his full glass in a salute before refilling mine with another two fingers of Macallan 24.

"Seriously though, what's her name?"

"Misty."

"Sounds...uh, young." His words are an accusation.

"Not too young."

"Tell me about her."

I groan. I knew coming here today was a bad idea, but I'd been blowing him off for three weeks. If I hadn't hooked up with him he would've sent out a search party.

Chase comes around the couch and sits across from me. He pulls one ankle up to the opposite knee and stretches out his arm in an open-for-discussion gesture.

"Carson. You've never been so tight-lipped about a woman before. This is me. Your best friend, your blood. You know you can tell me anything. Hell, how many times have I confided in you?"

I smile. "Really? Because I don't remember getting an invite to a spur-of-the-moment wedding in Ireland three years ago."

"How long are you going to hold that over my head? It's been years. Give it up."

Chase's blue eyes look like they could pierce through mine, like daggers of truth sticking me straight through the heart.

"Fine. Christ, I'm sorry. Okay, here's the deal. She's a woman I had a one-night stand with two years ago."

Chase frowns. "Two years?"

I can almost see him doing the math in his head. "When you were trying to get Kathleen back?"

The second tumbler of whiskey goes down far easier than the first while I mull over his words. "Yeah, I met Misty immediately after the last time I tried for a Hail Mary."

"You mean after I had to pick your drunk ass up at a random shithole motel?"

I nod. "That would be the night."

"Fuck."

"Exactly."

"You never mentioned a woman."

"I vaguely remembered her, man. Apparently, after I fought with Kat and she kicked me out the last time, I got shitfaced, took Misty to a nearby hotel, fucked her, and passed out."

Chase shakes his head.

"Yeah. Not my best moment. Worst of it is, I didn't even remember her name. She was gone before I woke up."

"Well, I can only say we all have times in our lives we're not proud of."

I run my hand through my hair and pull at the roots, wishing I could be honest but knowing I'm not ready for the backlash. The sting of pain in my scalp brings me back to the present moment. "It's just random that I'd catch back up with her." What's more ridiculous is that the one night of sin might turn into a lifetime of service, but I keep that tidbit to myself.

"So, there's a spark?" he asks.

I want to say no, there's no spark, not a single flicker of excitement when I think about her, because the only firecracker I've ever felt was a tall blonde with a chip on her shoulder who continues to deny us a happy ending.

"You could say that," I lie.

Chase twitches his lips and squints. He knows I'm lying. Luckily, he doesn't call me on it.

"I did say that. Does this mean you're seeing her?"

"Uh, yeah. I'm seeing her." For now, I want to add, but choose not to. If it turns out this woman is the mother of my child, I'm going to be seeing a lot more of her.

God, this is a clusterfuck of epic proportions.

CHAPTER THREE

KATHLEEN

I glance around my costume closet. Black clouds of smoke billow along the ceiling and push through the bottom of the single closed door. The room is in the basement level of the San Francisco Theatre and is closed off from the rest of the production team. The show transformed the area because of the exorbitant number of necessary costumes, and it's definitely not the safest place to work.

Getting up fast, I head for the window and stand on a chair to reach it. For some reason, it's blocked with what looks like wooden boards that weren't there yesterday. I pound on the window, trying to open it. No dice. The smoke around me gets thicker.

Grabbing a scarf, I place it over my mouth and nose and breathe through it. I don't know much about smoke, but I do know fire sucks all the oxygen out of the air and that smoke is harmful to breathe. Going over to the only door, I grab the handle and scream as the heat from the metal knob sears the center of my palm. I back up and get my bearings, ignoring the throbbing pain in my hand.

I'm starting to feel light-headed. A tightening around

my chest adds pressure to my upper body as though someone is stepping on me one foot at a time. I wrap a scarf around my blistered hand, wincing and blinking away the pain. Then I grab another piece of clothing near the door and use it to turn the handle. I have to get out of here!

Right before I grab it, the smoke alarms sound. I clench my teeth and hold my breath, trying not to suck in the fumes coming up from under the door. Finally, I yank the door open with my right arm, and I'm blasted by a wall of fire. Pain rips up my right arm and over my side as I use another piece of clothing to smother the fire licking against my skin. The scent of charred flesh pierces my nostrils. My mouth waters.

"Help me! Please help me!" I scream before I kick the door shut.

Tears fall down my cheeks, wetting my face. My eyes burn from the smoke, and I can barely breathe. The air in the room is as thick as a Bay Area foggy day, only hot as hell.

"Help!" I scream at the top of my lungs, but no one hears me over the alarms.

A pounding sound comes from the window as I fall to my knees, the lack of air suffocating me. I gasp like a fish out of water, looking up toward the window. A speck of black night comes into view. Fingers yanking and then bare feet smashing against the window. My eyes roll back in my head.

"Help..." I whisper as I fall face first to the floor. "Help me."

★ ★ ★

"Wake up! My God, Kat, please wake up." Gigi's voice breaks through the fog and haze of my nightmare.

I jump back, my arm throbbing and aching. I groan and

cradle it protectively.

"Kat, Jesus! You scared the hell out of me!" Gigi cries, petting my arm and head.

"Us. She scared the hell out of us," Chase clarifies from his perch against the wall. He's shirtless, wearing nothing but a pair of silk pajama bottoms and a frown, his arms crossed over his chest.

Shit. The nightmares.

I blink away the fear still clawing at my psyche and press my fists against my eyes. "I'm sorry, guys. Uh, just a dream."

"Honey, you were screaming for help. Over and over." Gigi places her hand at her throat, a worried gesture if ever I've seen one.

Taking a deep breath, I shake my head. "Again, I'm sorry." I start to shift my feet and push the covers back. "I can go home. Really."

"No, no, no! Chase!" Gigi's voice is pleading.

"Absolutely not. You'll stay here with your family. But I am upset you didn't mention you were still having the nightmares."

Like a balloon deflating, all the strength I'd built up about this secret seeps out of me. "I have them every once and a while." *Lie.* "Seriously, they are not a big deal." *Lie.* "I've already forgotten what I was dreaming about." *Triple lie.* I'll never forget that night. It plagues me daily.

What if they hadn't broken through the window?

What if Maria had come alone and passed out too?

What if the bodyguard hadn't been able to pull us both out?

Chase scowls. "Kathleen, you can lie to us all you want, but it never works."

Totally not true. That shit works on the girls all the time.

Just not on Chase. He's always been able to see through people.

I ruffle my hair out of my eyes and pat Gillian's hands. "Honey, I'm fine. Really. I'm sorry I woke you guys up. It was just a nightmare. I'm fine."

Gillian stands up, placing a hand over her small bump. She's only four months, but she's already showing.

Chase moves over to his wife and places a hand over hers. "Baby, you both okay?"

She nods silently.

"Go on to bed. I'll make sure Kathleen is comfortable and meet you in five, okay?"

"'K," she says sleepily. "Love you, Kat. Good night."

"Me too. Good night," I say, watching her leave, her long silk robe trailing behind her. The woman looks like a nineteen fifties Hollywood film star in her lush off-white dressing gown.

"You've got one classy broad there. She always sleep wearing satin and silk?"

Chase grins. "Unless she's naked and under me, yes."

I crinkle my nose and make a gag sound. "Dude, she's my best friend."

"And I'm certain you know far more about our sex life than you should. She is not shy. Now, back to the nightmares. When did they come back? And don't bullshit me." His tone is hard and biting.

"Come back?" I huff with a laugh. "Chase, they never left. Some nights are worse than others. Tonight, I relived the fire in its entirety." I ran my hand down the knotted, bumpy tissue of my right arm. "Can still vaguely feel the burn of the flame."

He sucks in a harsh breath. "Dr. Madison tomorrow?"

"Fine. Yeah. Whatever."

Chase comes over to me and rests his hand on top of my

head. He messes up my hair like a big brother would. "We'll get through this."

I want to laugh at the absurdity of his optimism, but I don't have the energy. Lethargy is setting in, and I need to sleep. Even with the nightmare, I sleep better here than I do at my place alone. Something about being in a home where I'm loved makes it easier to slumber peacefully. Well, except for the pesky recurring dreams.

"Thanks, Chase."

"Anytime, Kathleen. Anytime. You are always welcome here." He turns to walk back out of the room.

"I know," I whisper.

He stops and leans against the doorjamb. His golden bare chest is on display, looking mighty fine. Reminds me of Carson. If I squint a little, I can almost imagine Carson's wheat-colored layers and the enticing patch of blond curls, which trail down his stomach to one of my favorite parts of him.

"Do you?" Chase asks softly. "Do you know how much we welcome you in our home, our lives, our hearts?"

I grin. "You getting all mushy on me, Davis?" I use his last name whenever I want to make light of something.

"Guess so. Just want you to realize how much you matter to this family. And that is what you are. Family."

"Believe me, I know." If I didn't love them and the rest of the girls so much, I'd have left a long time ago.

"Good. I'll have Bentley make your favorite tomorrow. Crepes."

"And cookies?" I joke.

"Of course." He grins wickedly.

"That's your favorite, Chase. But I love a good crepe."

"Huh." He blinks a few times and rubs at his chin. "You

know, you're right. It is." He winks and then taps the door before closing it.

I shake my head. That damn man. Always poking his nose in my business.

You love it, Kat. At least you know he cares. And having him as close as you do is the closest you're ever going to get to having Carson again.

I roll over, tuck the extra pillow against my chest, and think of the man I lost. The raw emotions the dream brought back and the sweet and gentle nature of Gillian and Chase bring on tears. They slide down my face and wet the pillow below.

When am I ever going to find myself again?

"Good night, Sweetcheeks." I hear whispers through my psyche. His whispers, the only voice I long to hear.

★ ★ ★

I open my eyes to red curls and blue eyes. Claire is lying right next to me, her head on the pillow level with mine. Her nose is only a few inches from mine.

"Auntie Kitty, you need to take a boy out of my mommy's belly and hide it." Her eyes get big as she whispers conspiratorially in her three-year-old voice.

I chuckle and kiss her nose. "Honey, I can't do that."

She scrunches up her entire face, looking distraught. "But you wike boys. You wike my bruh-ver, Car Car."

If my arm worked better, I'd grip her around the waist and tug her close so I could snuggle her. Man, I wish I could do that. I choke down the sorrow the thought brings and focus on the very serious-looking Claire.

"What's so bad about boys? You and Carter have a great time playing together."

She pouts. "Yeah, but he won't pway dolls and Barbies and doesn't wike to cohwor wif me. A sister would."

I tap my chin. "This is true. But it just means you get all the dolls and all the Barbies to yourself. You get to keep the best color crayons and markers. You know how your brother presses too hard and messes them up?"

Her expression turns thoughtful. "Yeah. He does that!" she says loudly, as if it's just dawned on her.

"If you have another sister, she'll want to touch all your stuff, play with all your toys, wear all those pretty dresses I made you..."

Claire gasps. "But those are fer me!" Her eyebrows draw together.

"Very true. And you know how cousin Anabelle and Dannica fight about their stuff?"

Her little mouth opens in a tiny O.

I can already see the wheels spinning in her mind.

"If you have a brother, he'll want all of Carter's stuff. Not yours."

"You fink?" She squints at me, disbelief rife in her gaze.

"I *know*."

"Auntie Kitty?"

"Yes, honey."

"Don't take my new bruh-ver. I decided I want him."

I lean over and kiss her face and blow raspberries against her neck, making her giggle like mad. Man, I adore the sound of a child's laughter. If someone could bottle it up, it would cure the entire world's ailments. Definitely mine...for today.

"You gonna get up now?"

"Yeah, honey." I sit up without thinking about the fact I'm only wearing my camisole and a pair of undies. The sheet falls, and my entire arm is out in the open, visible to very impressionable eyes.

Claire sits up and points at my arm. "Ouchy boo! Auntie. You hurt!" She leans closer, slanting her head to the side.

My heart is about ready to pound out of my chest, and sweat prickles against my hairline.

No. Please God, no.

I try to pull the sheet back up and over it.

Claire grabs it, pulling it away. "Wemme see!" She moves closer.

Tears sting the back of my eyes, and I wait for the disgust and fear to show on her beautiful face. My niece is going to hate looking at me, or worse—be afraid of me. Bile rises up my throat as I wait to hear how she'll reply.

In true Claire fashion, she reaches out her hand, and her little fingers caress the gnarled skin from shoulder to wrist. "Hurt?" She's gazing up at me. There's not even a hint of discomfort on her face.

I shake my head and swallow through the cotton coating my throat.

"Wooks wike it hurts." She is matter-of-fact.

"It doesn't, honey."

She nods and caresses it one more time, running over the bumps and valleys with a featherlight touch. It's the most I've ever let anyone other than a doctor or one of my best friends touch the scarred skin.

Claire inspects it for a few more seconds, dipping her tiny fingers into the puckered holes and back out. Then she completely and utterly blows me away with her grace, love, and compassion.

She looks at me with her crystal-blue eyes, the same as her dad's, leans toward my arm, and kisses my biceps right over a nasty patch of scars.

I close my eyes as the tears slip down my face.

"I kissed it better." She smiles, proud of herself.

"It worked, honey. It's all better." My voice cracks, and I clear my throat so she can hear me.

She smiles wide. "Mommy magic." She is referring to something I've heard Gigi say to her countless times when the children hurt themselves. She'd kiss their boo-boos and hurts and say those two words too.

"Yes, your mommy is magic, because she gave us you. I love you, honey."

"I wuv you too, Auntie Kitty. Now I need cookies and a new bruh-ver." Claire scrambles to stand and bounces on the bed until she flops to her bottom and slips off with the exuberance only a child can muster.

The laugher bubbles out of me, free and weightless. The first time I've felt lighter in months.

★ ★ ★

The second I enter the kitchen, Gigi rushes to me, her arm around my waist, pulling me out into the hallway.

"I did not invite him here. Apparently, they already had plans to discuss some business venture over breakfast, but I swear to God on my children's lives, I didn't know he'd be here." Gigi's speaking so fast she has to lean over and catch her breath when she's done.

"What are you talking about?"

"It's not my fault." She wraps a hand around her belly.

"What's not your fault?" I'm confused.

"There you two are. Come on, breakfast is already set," Chase says while putting an arm over his wife's shoulders and kissing her temple.

I walk around them to the kitchen. "Gigi was just apologizing to me for something—" And the words fall right out of my mouth when I see who's sitting at the kitchen table eating a cherry-filled crepe.

He stands, looking like a tall drink of water. His blond hair falls across his forehead in sexy layers that say, *I don't give a fuck what my hair looks like,* but it always looks amazing.

His scent wafts across the room. I'm surprised I didn't smell it when I entered the hallway. Only one man I know smells of hay and the sea. A man who surfs as often as he rides his horses. Living directly on a swath of farmland bordered by the Pacific Ocean will give a person that unique scent. I must say, even now, it hits every single last one of my nerve endings from the roots of my hair down to my toes. Pleasant tingles of awareness and desire sprinkle out each pore, putting a static energy in the room anyone within a ten-foot radius could feel.

Carson's eyes are crinkled around the edges. More lines haloing those baby blues than I like to see. He's tired, worn out...but why?

"Hey, Sweetcheeks, didn't expect to see you here, but always a pleasure." His low, rumbling tone zips through me, calling back memories of making love, laughing until the wee hours of the morning, and whispered vows we've since broken.

Sweetcheeks. His nickname for me. Silly name from a silly man, but he loved my ass and told me as often as he groped it. I just loved him. Still do.

"Carson, it's been a while." I clench my teeth and batten down my emotions.

He nods, comes around the table, and stands before me. The entire room ceases to exist when he's in it. As if everything around me has gotten smaller, farther away, and all I'm capable of seeing is him. The man I love. The man I'll always love but can no longer have.

Carson lifts a hand to my face. With his thumb, he traces a path from my temple down to my chin and lifts it up. He leans forward and places a soft kiss to my lips. I gasp. He hasn't made that gesture in two solid years. I'm so shocked by his nearness and the sheer connection pumping between us, I don't move a single muscle. He brushes his lips along mine again. I lick my lips and just the hint of our tongues touch. He groans, and I pop back at the sound.

I lift my hand to my mouth and then shuffle around him. "Um, yes. So, uh, what are you doing here?" Sizzles of recognition and excitement whip along the surface of my skin.

Neither Chase nor Gillian have said a word. Both are standing quietly across the kitchen, leaning against the cabinets. Gigi looks like she's been stunned stupid, whereas Chase has the biggest shit-eating grin on his face.

Jesus. Now he's never going to stop hounding me about his cousin.

"Business concept we've been volleying back and forth."

I nod and make myself busy by getting a cup of coffee. Without thinking, I go to grab the carafe with my right hand. I barely get the pot out when it starts to drop. Carson's fast, though. He wraps a hand around mine holding the handle. Shoot. I haven't tried to use that hand for something that heavy in a long time. His presence has knocked me off-kilter.

"Let me get that," he says, plastering himself against my back. Carson never did have space issues, especially when it came to me. *The closer the better*, he always told me.

Together we pour the liquid into two cups I imagine were left out for us. He leans firmly against my behind. I can feel the outline of his pelvis and package against my ass and the warm strength of his chest against my back. God, I've missed this. Being close to him. To a living, breathing person. I close my eyes, soaking in every ounce of his presence and committing the sensations to my memory. I'll need it later.

Once he puts the carafe back in the coffeemaker, he inhales deeply against my neck. Shivers ripple along my spine, and a long-forgotten fire smolders between my thighs.

"Christ, Sweetcheeks. I've missed your scent. Only it's different...sunshine and..." He shifts my hair over to the side and rubs his nose along my neck.

The hairs on my nape stand at attention and my knees weaken. I brace myself up against the counter, fingers clenching the granite. He wraps both his hands over mine. The second he touches my scarred flesh, I stiffen.

He breathes against me, as if touching my scars doesn't faze him. Stunned, I stand unmoving.

"Coconuts. You smell of coconuts."

I bite into my lip and pray he steps back before I internally combust, or alternatively, burst into a puddle of tears. "Coconut oil. It's good for the scars."

"Mmm, I like it. Suits you." He trails his nose up my neck once again and kisses my temple. Then he grabs his cup of coffee and backs away. I can hear his footsteps getting father away until the sound of chair legs skidding across the floor registers. He may be ten feet away now, but the impression of his warm body still resonates against my backside.

I close my eyes and calm my raging heart, allowing my brain to come back online.

Gillian comes over to me, plops a teaspoon of sugar into my coffee, and pours some of the homemade vanilla creamer Bentley makes especially for her into my cup. The spoon tinkling against the sides of the glass brings me back to reality.

"Over him, are you?" Gigi accuses.

"Yes," I hiss and sip my coffee. The soothing vanilla and hot coffee ease the lusty beast inside me as I stare at Carson and Chase laughing it up while digging into their breakfast.

"What are you going to do?"

I jerk my head back. "Nothing. It's over. We're over." I remind her as much as myself.

Gigi's eyebrows rise up into her hairline. "You could have fooled me with the way he was pressed up against you, sniffing you. My God, that was so hot! Scenting you like that." She fans her face dramatically.

I shake my head and hide behind my cup. She leans her shoulder against mine. "He's yours for the taking, you know."

If only that were true.

"It's not meant to be," I say with finality.

"Only because you won't let it."

CHAPTER FOUR

CARSON

"Goddamn, goddamn, *goddamn it!*" I pound against the steering wheel of my Range Rover until all the frustration seeps out of my bones in miserable heaps of negative energy.

"Why the fuck did she have to be there? Today of all days." I blow out a harsh breath and lean my head on the steering wheel. Anxiety and desperation flow through me and out my fingertips with every breath.

Just when I think I'm getting over her, I see her again. Christ, she was a vision, too. Her golden hair is shorter, barely hitting her shoulders now. She had a long-sleeved shirt on, so I couldn't see how the injury on her arm was faring, but her hand looked a little better. Her neck seemed great, the long column completely smooth. I wonder if the doctors have been able to fix the patches of burned flesh near her ribs and breast?

"Stop it, Carson. Just, stop it!" I chastise myself, pressing my fists against my eyes to relieve the instant ache.

Stop thinking about her as though you have the right to care.

Kathleen has spent the better part of three years pushing me away. Hell, that's three times longer than I was with her, yet

I can't get the woman out of my mind. I've loved her since the day I first laid eyes on her. The night we met at a charity event on a blind date, set up by Gillian, sealed my fate. The moment I got my arms around her on the dance floor, her scent, essence, and very spirit seeped deep inside my soul. To this day, I have not been able to break free from it. But I have to. She's made it clear she no longer wants me in her life.

Then why did she respond the way she did when I touched her?

I don't know what came over me. Maybe it was because the lab's receptionist had called to tell me the expedited test results would arrive via courier this afternoon. The thought of losing all freedom lit a fire within me, which had been dormant until I saw my Kathleen. And an hour from now, I'll find out the results for good. I swallow and tighten my hands on the leather steering wheel.

How could I have fucked up so bad? Loss and grief is why. The death of the most important relationship in my entire life is what happened. Made me stupid, incapable of thinking straight. I drank too much and fucked the wrong woman.

Most of that evening over two years ago is still a total blur, except for the fight with Kathleen. The night has gone down as one of the worst of my entire life. The night I lost the woman I love forever.

★ ★ ★

"Carson, I don't know how many times I have to say it. We're over. There's nothing you can do or say that's ever going to change the situation. I'm not the woman for you."

"Bullshit, Kat, and you know it as well as I do!"

Her arms are crossed over her chest protectively. A shawl hangs over her shoulders, covering the worst of her burns. She never lets the skin see the light of day. Well, not in front of me anyway. Her hair—a golden array of blond, light brown, and copper—is long, hanging down to the middle of her back and flowing all around her upper body. Her eyes are the most beautiful color, reminding me of caramel candies. The intensity within them shows determination and sadness in equal parts. Both of which I hate, because I know what that look means.

I loathe seeing this look in her eyes, knowing it's for me. Usually, her focused stare would bring men far stronger and bigger than me down to their knees. In a single moment, she's cut me apart, letting me bleed out until there is nothing left.

"You can't want me to go. It's always been you, Kathleen. Always."

Her voice breaks into a sob. "Why can't you leave me alone? There is no you and me. We've been over for a year now. Please, please, stop trying to convince me to see things your way."

In a handful of steps, I get to her and curl a hand at her nape and the other around her hip. I don't dare hold her by the arms.

"Kathleen Bennett, I adore you. Want to marry you. Have children with you. Grow old by your side..."

She shakes her head violently. "No. Stop. I can't." The tears pour down her cheeks.

"I don't know why you insist on pushing me away. I don't care about your scars! I don't fucking care if you can't stand to look at yourself, because it doesn't matter, sweetheart. I see you. Me! The man who would do anything for you. The man falling at your feet to keep you." I hit my knees, wrap my hands around her hips, and push my face against her abdomen.

"You have t-to g-go..." Her voice splinters as she holds on to her convictions and pushes me away.

I shake my head against her belly and rest my chin there while looking up into the most beautiful face I've ever known. I've kissed those pink lips until they were so swollen they'd turned red. I've nibbled that jawline, teasingly, lustfully. I've stared into those brown eyes and whispered my dreams for our life together. And it was heavenly. The most perfect life. I know beyond a shadow of doubt this woman is my be-all end-all. She is my fate.

"Carson..." She runs her fingers through my hair, her voice so lost I can barely hear her. "You deserve more, more than I can ever give you. I'm not me anymore. I'm not the woman you fell for."

I close my eyes and kiss my way up the center of her chest until I have her lips. I cup both cheeks and take her lips with mine. Our tongues battle, fighting a war I am determined to win. She tastes of salty endings and the hope for new beginnings. With my heart in my hand and my lips on hers, I show her love—gut-wrenching, mind-altering, earth-shattering love.

Kathleen runs her hand up my chest, and with her scarred hand over my heart, I think maybe we can start again. But I am holding her close and she is shoving me away. Eventually, my mind clicks with my body and registers her struggles. She isn't trying to get closer and take more. She is scratching, clawing, and pushing me away. In an instant, I let her go.

I let her go.

She stumbles back several feet, shaking her head. Her cheeks are a mess of tears and mascara. I don't care. My Kathleen is a diamond in a sea of rocks. When she is happy, she sparkles so bright. Only, her tears are not joyful ones of reconciliation but rather distress and self-loathing.

"No. Carson, no. I'm done."

I grip the roots of my hair tightly, wanting to feel the sting of pain as I pace her apartment. "This isn't over."

Her voice breaks. "It is. Forever."

I stop and suck in a harsh breath. "Look me in my face and tell me you don't love me."

A torturous grimace falls across her features. She opens her mouth and then closes it again.

"Tell me you don't love me, and I'll go," I roar, rushing to her.

She bites her lip as tears run in a river over her cheeks. "I can't ever say that."

"Exactly," I grate through clenched teeth. "Then we're not done. One day soon, you're going to regret this decision. You're going to think back to the one man who adores everything about you." I point at her heart. "You."

"I'm not me anymore."

My lips hurt from pinching them together so tightly. "If you keep telling yourself that, you're never going to find her. Maybe you don't want to. You seem happy to hole yourself up in this dark apartment, never letting the light in."

"There is no sunshine anymore."

"Open your eyes, Kat." I cup her cheeks. "Open your fucking eyes. Let in the light. It's there, waiting for you. I'm standing in it, holding my arms open for you, baby. Let me help you get there," I plead.

Jesus, I'd strip myself of everything I know, jump into the fiery pits of hell, if she'd give me half a chance. The golden-caramel color in her stare fades, darkens, and with it, the glimmer of hope flickers out. I know she's made her decision.

"Be happy, Carson. That's all I've ever wanted for you. Find someone to share your life with. Let me go." Her words are a whisper, but they could have been shouted through a bullhorn for the way they smash into me.

I take one last look at her and touch my mouth to hers. I will never forget the taste of sorrow on her lips.

"You're going to regret this."

She closes her eyes, distancing herself even more. "I already do. Now go."

"You love me, Kathleen." My own voice is so rough I wouldn't be able to recognize it as my own if played back to me on a recorder.

Her eyes remain closed, her black lashes long and wet, tears still clinging to them.

"I know. Sometimes, Carson, love isn't enough. Please...go," she begs, desperation so thick in her tone it slices a fissure in my heart.

★ ★ ★

The woman I love had chosen to be dead to me, and there was nothing more I could do to bring her back. Even two years later, it hurts as much as if it had happened yesterday.

I shake my head as I drive through downtown San Francisco, leave the city, and head toward my beachfront home located on a ranch bordered on one side by the Pacific. Visions of the bar I went to when I left Kat's apartment after our fight flash across my vision as I drive back to my place.

★ ★ ★

Six shots of whiskey, lined up one after another on the table in front of me.

A blond waitress with pretty brown eyes hitting on me.

The blonde leading me across the street to a hotel.

Paying for a room.

Falling back on a bed. Kathleen stripped naked on top of me.

Not Kathleen...the waitress.

The blonde riding my cock, my fingers digging into her hips.

I need the release so bad.

Wanting the pain to go away.

Pounding into the wet heat of my Kathleen from behind.

Blond head tipping back, screaming out in pleasure. Hair the wrong shade.

Grinding my hips and pumping my release into her.

Falling back on the bed.

Waking up alone and hungover.

★ ★ ★

I had no idea that night had the power to get any worse. For over two years I'd pined over Kathleen. Sure, I saw a few women. Mostly to scratch a sexual itch. No one can go forever cut off from physical touch. Unless that person is Kathleen Bennett.

Chase tells me she's not so much as dated a man since breaking it off with me six months after her first rounds of burn treatments. Back then I still had hope. And then, all of a sudden, I see her again. I haven't laid eyes on my girl in what feels like forever. And she responded like the old Kat would have. Shy, sweet, unafraid of my touch. Yearning for it, even.

It took everything I had not to get stiff seeing her again, smelling her, feeling the softness of her skin at her nape. I'd always loved the way she smelled, especially near the hairline behind her ear. My secret spot and an erogenous zone on her. I wanted so badly to kiss, lick, and nibble that patch of skin, sink my teeth in and never let go.

Fuck, my dick is getting hard thinking about it. I even touched her scarred hand. She stiffened, but she didn't run away. The first time in years she hasn't run away. There were no tears, no harsh words, almost as though a peacefulness had come over her. Much like the woman I once knew and loved. Still love, even after these last couple of years. Seeing her again...

Christ. What the hell am I going to do?

Nothing.

Until I find out the results of the DNA tests, there is nothing I can do. But what a thrill it was to see her respond to me. Kissing her, even briefly, brought back everything I'd ever felt for the woman. Years later, and she's still capable of bringing me to my knees. If Chase and Gillian hadn't been there, I would have pushed harder. Thank God I didn't. I have no idea what's going on in my own life right now. At least I know she's doing well.

Chase has begrudgingly kept me apprised of her life—otherwise, I wouldn't know a thing. Bastard. He's become close to her. At first, per my request. I made him promise he'd take care of my girl. I even went old school and made him spit in his hand and shake on it. We've always been more than cousins. More like brothers. When he came to live with us at such a young age, his mother in a coma, my mother having just died, we bonded on a brotherly level that could never be broken. Now he's the only link I have to her. If I'd been able to say those three fucking words, maybe things would be different.

Even at the risk of losing her, I still couldn't say them.

I love you.

I love you, Kat.

I love you, Kathleen.

Over and over I tried to tell her. Proved it every day with my actions. Bent over backward to help her heal, but it wasn't enough. She wanted those three words, and I couldn't give them to her. Every single time I'd attempted to utter them, move the breath past my lips, I'd remembered the last time I said them, and the pain and heartache would come back, stealing the words from me once again.

After all this, I'm not sure it would have mattered. If I'd said them that night, maybe... She'd asked time and time again if I loved her. And of course I'd tell her I did, but she wanted to hear it. I wanted to hear it. All the time, I made her tell me. Needed it from her, but what she gave, I couldn't give back. Maybe that was the nail in the coffin of our relationship. Still, it was hard to fathom it would end the way it did.

I treated her well, like the goddamned goddess I thought she was. Nevertheless, once the fire happened, she lost something. As if the fire had taken away her ability to live. She gave up. Nothing seemed to work to pull her out of her funk, and with each painful treatment it got worse. A little bit more of the woman I loved withered away until I could hardly recognize what was left.

I pull up to my house and the massive black wrought-iron gate begins to glide open. As I'm waiting, a white LabCorp Genetics minivan pulls up behind me.

Seeing the van makes the skin on my arms prickle, and a layer of sweat coats my pits and forms at my hairline. I take a long, slow breath and get out of the car. Whatever happens, I'll deal with it. One step at a time.

The driver is a young college-age kid. Couldn't be more than twenty years old. He's wearing his company hat backward on his head and his unbuttoned shirt reveals a tie-dyed shirt underneath.

"Hey, man, how goes it?" the courier asks, ruffling through a big bag.

"Fine. You got something for me?" I ask.

"Totally, dude." He pulls out a nine-by-twelve-inch envelope. "Here you go!" He slaps the envelope into my hand with more exuberance than the situation warrants. At least he likes his job.

"Thanks," I mumble under my breath.

"Yo! Wait up. Need your signature, or my boss will have my balls. And she's a total tight-ass wench." He grimaces.

I chuckle, remembering the days when I had to answer to someone. Owning my own business affords me the luxury to come and go as I please and work when I want to. I'll never go back to working for someone else.

The kid holds out a clipboard. I scrawl my name across it and give a salute before I make my way up the steps.

He zooms out of the circular drive, off to deliver someone else's bad news, I imagine. I shake my head and move through my house.

It's huge. Not as big as the mansion estate I grew up in, but way too much for a single man. I'd hoped to one day move Kat in here, marry her, have a few kids. Growing up, I knew I wanted a big family. Had I not had my brothers, sister, and Chase, losing my mother would have been even more devastating. Because I had them, there was always something or someone to keep the tone in the house a little lighter. Push the darkness away.

Once I reach the bar, I pour three fingers of scotch. I'm going to need it to get through whatever this report says.

Taking my time, I go out back and keep walking. Past my pool and the horse stables and directly out to my ocean-view patio. When I bought the land, I had a deck built near the back of the cliffs, the ocean still a safe distance away but with a perfect open view. I'd even piped out speakers, lighting, and built a gazebo so that I could enjoy the ocean no matter what the weather was like. Today the sun was bright and the temperature a perfect seventy degrees. If only my heart was as light.

Sipping my drink, I watch the waves crash against the shore and wonder what it would be like if Kathleen had never been in the fire. Too many times I've recounted ways I could have changed the outcome of that evening. She was supposed to have been with me, except her work ethic wouldn't let her leave until the finishing touches were complete on the last piece she'd been working on.

I should have pushed her to be with me. Told her I needed her. Fuck, I always *needed* her. She was everything to me. All women paled in comparison to her beauty, heart, and talent. I remember watching her work in her tiny apartment until late in the evening. Heck, sometimes I'd fuck her until we both passed out, and then I'd wake in the middle of the night to the sound of the sewing machine whirring. When I'd find her, she'd be working on something magnificent.

Since then, I've heard she's been designing clothes, working in partnership with my sister, Chloe.

Now my sister is a sore motherfucking subject. She refuses, absolutely *refuses* to talk about Kat in any way. Even work-wise. Says it's putting her in the middle and making her choose family over her work and her friendships, and she won't do either. Truth be told, it's put a huge wrench in our relationship. One I should fix, since I'm the one constantly pissed off at her.

I flip the envelope back and forth until I finally rip the seal and open it. I pull out the report. It's several pages, most of it black boxes lined up along other black boxes. My name is on the left and Cora Duncan's is on the right.

While I scan the documents, so many emotions rush through me, beating me to a pulp the same way the waves are battering the sand. It's all a bunch of garbled scientific nonsense until I get to the last page.

A letter from my college buddy, Bradley Grover, who owns LabCorp Genetics, rounds out the packet explaining exactly what I need to know.

Carson,

I've personally ensured that my top geneticist ran your swabs against Ms. Cora Duncan's DNA three times. During the PCR analysis, or polymerase chain reaction process, we compared twenty-one genetic markers by multiplying twenty-three paternity indexes derived from twenty of the genetic loci we test.

Based on the testing results included within, the probability of paternity is 99.9%.

That means eighteen-month-old Cora Duncan is in fact your biological child.

Call me if you'd like to discuss. Carson, I imagine this is an intense time, but I'm here if you need a friend.

Brad

Bradley Grover

Chief Executive Officer
LabCorp Genetics

Fuck me. I'm someone's father. I have a child. A daughter. Cora Duncan.

Even her first name starts with a "C," as is tradition in my family.

What the hell do I do now?

CHAPTER FIVE

KATHLEEN

"Ugh, what I wouldn't give to have a doughnut right now," Chloe grumbles and sips on a wheatgrass smoothie.

I watch her suck down the disgusting concoction and fight my gag reflex. "Still on the paleo diet, I see."

She bites down on her straw as if drinking the stuff is hurting her as much as it is helping. "A few more days, and then I can work up to a twelve-hundred-calorie diet again."

My eyes practically bug out of my head. "Work up to it? What are you eating now?"

"Five hundred," she says while pushing papers around her desk.

I've just given her the designs for the new menswear line I want to start my team on.

"Sounds...er...practical," I say, the lack of sincerity in my voice betraying how I really feel.

Chloe rolls her eyes. "We both know I'm basically starving myself so I can look incredible in the gown you've drawn up for Paris Fashion Week."

I chuckle. "You could just take a couple of Bree's yoga classes."

"And look at that hot bitch while sweating like a pig and falling on my ass in a position God never intended a woman's body to be in in the first place?" She stares at me, blinking rapidly.

That does it. Laughter pours out of me, and I flop back against my own chair in the master office we share. "God, you're good for me." I wave at my now overheated face, trying to cool down.

"Well isn't that the truth." She sucks on the green smoothie, grimaces, hacks, and tosses it half-full into the trash before grabbing a foil-wrapped treat off my desk. "How many calories do you think are in just one of these? Like ten, right?"

I snicker. "Try seventy-five to a hundred."

Her eyes widen after she plops it into her mouth. "Your numbers are jacked. I'm going with ten. That means I can have nine more of these suckers." She winks and then picks up one of the designs.

"What's this little L-shaped thing here?" She points to a section of my work.

My penmanship with my left hand has gotten better, but actual designs don't always fare as well. Usually, I take advantage of the super savvy voice-activated computer Chase had crafted by his tech geniuses. The software records what I speak, and with a finger I can scratch onto a tablet display to get my designs down on paper.

"It's a pair of socks." I smile.

Chloe nibbles on another Snickers bar. Mentally, I plan on taking out an inch on the dress I've designed for her without mentioning it. What are friends for, anyway?

"Socks? Since when did we get in the business of sock making?"

"Well, it's something I wanted to chat about. I was with Chase last week and noticed he always tries to match his socks to whatever shoe color or pant color he's wearing. What if we design socks to match our suits? We can even create an entire line of ties that can be sold with each suit and sock set to make it even easier for the customer."

"As if being a man isn't easy enough?" she deadpans.

I wait. Finally, a hint of a smile curves her lips at the edges. "Clo..."

She waves a hand and opens another candy. "No, no. I'm seeing it. Totally seeing it. We could call it *Men at Ease* or something like that. Make it easier for the men to get dressed in a given week. Everything can be interchangeable. It's brilliant as usual, Kat." She smiles.

"I thought so." I waggle my eyebrows.

"Let's meet with the creative team about it later in the week. Sound cool?"

I nod. "Yeah, works for me." I push the button for our shared receptionist. "Jen, can you schedule a meeting for both of us to meet with creative for a new product powwow? We'll probably need a good two hours. Make it over lunch, and we'll order in."

"Nice. Good idea." Chloe gives me a thumbs-up.

Once I hang up, Chloe lays out her new concepts for our women's line. "I'm not feeling that strap and bodice together. Something's not quite right."

I focus on the design, and it reminds me of the sequined dress I wore to Carson's father's birthday party all those years ago. I run my scarred finger down the design. He was so handsome that night and happy to show off his new girlfriend to his dad. That was also the night Chase proposed to Gillian.

Seems like forever ago...

"Earth to Kat. Hello? Cut the strap or leave it?"

I shake my head, and a few drops fall down the slope of my nose and onto the paper below. I glance away, wiping at my eyes.

Chloe gasps and puts a hand on my shoulder. "Kat, what's the matter?"

I sniff and lift my head, trying to blink back the unwanted tears. "Nothing. Uh, the design just reminded me of a better time, that's all."

She sighs and leans against my desk, sitting on the edge. "Lay it on me."

I clear my throat. "There is nothing to lay on you."

She sits on my desk and crosses her ankles and her arms, obviously planning to hold out for the long haul. The woman is ruthless if she wants something, and right now it's whatever has me crying over her designs.

Stupid men.

"Does deflecting usually work for your best friends?"

I shake my head. "Not usually, no."

"Then what makes you think it will work on me? Kat, we've been partners for two years now, working together for almost three. I know when your head is not in the game. Usually, I don't care, as long as your heart is in it. But crying over a design? If you hate it that much you could have just said so." She holds a serious stern look until she can't any longer, and her lips tremble with laughter.

On instinct, I elbow her thigh. "Shut up."

"You shut up. No, actually that would be the opposite of what I requested you to do. Blonde moment." She conks her own head.

"Stop trying to make me laugh."

"Stop avoiding the question."

I inhale a long, slow breath. "I'm fine. The design reminded me of a better time is all."

"Ah, I see. My guess is something having to do with my brother?" Her eyes soften.

I shrug. "Yeah. I saw him last weekend."

Chloe pounces and with a nudge to my shoulder spins my chair 180 degrees. Before I can right it, she spins me the rest of the way and gets in my face.

"You saw him? When? How? Why? Are you getting back together?" Her words come in a jumbled string.

I lean back in my chair, giving myself some space. "He was at Chasé and Gillian's the morning after I spent the night."

"Fucking bastard cousin of mine. I'll kick his ass for putting you on the spot."

"Cut it out. He didn't plan on having me spend the night, and he did plan on having Carson there. It was fine, actually. Nice, even. I hadn't seen him in a full year. He looks good."

Really. Fucking. Good.

Drop-dead gorgeous.

"So, what happened? Did you talk to him?"

I stand up and pace the room, trying to get my thoughts together. "Not much. We chatted. He kissed me. We had coffee and a quiet breakfast, nothing more."

"Whoa, whoa, whoa. Back the truck up. Put that shit in reverse. He kissed you?" Her voice croaks as if she's holding back her excitement the way a kid does when parents tell them they are going to Disneyland but not for another week.

"Yes. Kind of the way he used to, just after the accident. Softly, barely even anything. Still, something was definitely there."

"My God! Oh my freaking God. Does that mean you're going to get back together?"

I groan and let my head fall back as I look up at the ceiling. "No, it doesn't mean anything of the sort. He's with someone right now."

"Not if you said you were available. The man has been pining for you for three years, Kat. If you say you're ready to take him back, he's going to be there with bells on."

"Not true. He's been living his life just as I have," I counter.

She makes a noise that sounds like a cross between blowing air out through her mouth and spitting. "I wouldn't call what either of you have been doing as living."

"Really? Even after all we've accomplished?" I shoot back, my tone laced with a hint of acid.

"All work." She waves her hand in the air. "Work, yes, you've been doing *a lot* of that. And very well, I might add." Her tone softens considerably.

"Thank you."

"But all work and no dick makes Kat a crotchety bitch," she states plain as day.

I open my mouth and close it a couple times. "No dick?"

She nods. "You said it, sister."

"No, I think you did." I chuckle, the hilarity of the conversation starting to hit me.

"Okay, so what's the end result of this meet-and-kiss between you and my insanely handsome brother?" She bats her eyes prettily.

I roll mine. She does not lie. Her brother is the most beautiful man I've ever known, inside and out. I can't deny there was a hint of something there between us. Maybe we should talk about it? Ugh, I don't know. It's been so long. I'm still disfigured, though not nearly as badly. My work life is fantastic, so I can support myself even against all the odds and despite the nerve damage in my hand and arm. My relationships with my girlfriends are strained, but I'm working on that. Will work on that. Perhaps that's where I should start.

"I'm not sure. We left on civil terms, and for now, I'm happy about it."

"Will you concede there could be more?"

"Between your brother and me there will always be a history. I just can't say if there is going to be a future."

"How's about while you figure it out, I'll be hopeful for the both of you?"

"Deal."

Chloe grabs for another candy bar. I smack her hand away. "Put down the candy and pick up an apple!" I warn.

She frowns but lets go of the candy bar. "Thanks." She looks at the candy longingly.

"Paris Fashion Week," I remind her.

"Paris Fashion Week." She turns on a toe and sighs.

★ ★ ★

I push open the door to my favorite pub. After spending all day going over new designs, making fabric deals with suppliers overseas, and checking in with my head seamstress on how the designs are coming together, I'm positively beat. Multicolored lighting hits my eyes as I take in the familiar surroundings of my go-to eatery on a Friday night. I had been invited to hang out with Maria and Eli, but I declined. Why, I don't know. Tonight, I just need to be away from it all. Allow myself to get lost in my thoughts.

Thoughts of him.

Carson.

All week I toyed with the idea of calling him up, suggesting we get coffee. I don't even know why. Just over two years ago, I pushed him so far away I would never have ever dreamed we could go back. Then I saw him, and everything rushed in like a tidal wave breaking onshore. Just the sight of him obliterated my heart and destroyed the walls I'd built up in my mind. The ones preventing me from ever going there again.

Why now?

I've been asking myself this same question all week. When he touched me in Gillian's kitchen, it was as if his touch had never left me. It felt so...right. Perhaps it's time to, at the very least, be friends again. There's no harm there. I care about him. I know he cares for me. Hell, I still love the man, although I'm positive he's moved on by now.

Then why did he kiss me the way he did? Touch his tongue to mine? That single touch shot a bolt of electricity so strong through me I have yet to forget the spark.

Shaking my head, I glance around the hopping pub and don't see any open tables. Until my gaze lands on a pair of blue eyes in the very far corner. A pair I'd recognize in a sea of a hundred blond-haired, blue-eyed people. To me, they are the most unique eyes. Sky blue with a gleaming golden rim around the iris, as if the gods knew he'd need a halo surrounding him at all times.

Quickly, I glance down and away, heading toward the bar. What do I do now? Maybe he didn't see me.

I wave to the bartender. He gives me a chin lift, knowing what I want to order without me having to yell over the crowd.

I've been here so many times, it's my own personal Cheers.

Before I can ascertain if there are any individual seats along the bar, I feel a warm hand land on my shoulder.

"Hey, Sweetcheeks. Thought it was you," Carson says while urging me to turn around.

I move, matching the momentum of his pull, a smile plastered to my face. At first, I think it's going to be forced. I'm so used to wearing the mask that keeps everyone and everything at bay. My smile stays in place as I take in his shaggy blond hair—he must have run his fingers through it too many times—and the light stubble along his strong jaw after a full workday. The polo shirt he's wearing has his company logo positioned right over the heart.

"Hi, Carson." That's about all I can manage to say, my tongue having swollen, choking off my words.

Be cool, Kat. Be cool. It's just Carson.

"Busy tonight," he offers while pushing both of his hands into his pockets and rocking back on his heels.

"Yep. Usually is on Fridays. I'm not normally this late." I glance down at my watch once more, taking in the hour as past seven, far later than my average five thirty Friday night, early dinner alone.

He squints. "Oh, meeting someone?" He frowns, the simple gesture piercing my psyche.

I'm quick to allay his fears by shaking my head and looking down shyly. "No. I often come here to eat on Fridays. It's kind of become my routine since it's so close to my apartment."

"Kitty Kat!" The bartender yells his nickname for me over the crowd of people, obviously not caring who he bothers in the process. He's holding up a tall, beloved Poor Man's Stout, more commonly known as a Black Velvet. My drink of choice.

"Add it to my tab. Thanks, Robbie!" I tip the drink back and swallow a large helping. The crisp notes of raspberry cider and thick coffee bean taste of Guinness mingle into perfection in my mouth. "So good."

"I'll say," Carson mumbles under his breath and looks away.

I take a few more sips of my beer, not knowing what to say or do. I've never been at a loss for words when it came to Carson. It's odd, almost feeling as though we'd just met for the first time. I guess after not having seen one another for so long, it's hard to bring back the casual banter we once lived off of.

I'm just about to say something when he gestures to his table.

"Eat with me?" His voice is hopeful with an edge of grit to it.

I weigh my options. I could pretend like I didn't plan on eating here tonight, which would be a lie—and I've been trying not to lie lately, especially to people I care about. And even though Carson and I are no longer together, I still care about him a great deal.

"Um..." I glance around, looking desperately for a place to go to on my own.

Carson clasps his hand over my scarred one. I flinch but don't remove it. My therapist encourages me to allow people to touch me platonically so I get used to human touch again. I resist the urge to remove my hand and instead squeeze his in return, sincerely wanting him to feel me. His eyes widen briefly and a smile breaks out across his face, making him impossibly handsome. I'd walk through hell and back just to see the smile on his face. I hadn't seen it focused solely on me in so long, I'd forgotten how much I missed it.

"It's been a long time since we've spent time alone together, Kat. Break bread, have some beers. We're still friends, right?"

"Are we?" The coy note in my tone surprises me as much as I think it does him.

He smiles again, those beautiful teeth and blue eyes hitting my heart with a one-two punch. "Yes. Most definitely."

"Okay. I did come to eat."

"Me too. Right this way." He lets go of my hand and guides me in front of him, his hand securely planted on my lower back the same way he used to guide me around before.

I close my eyes, imprinting the warmth. Last week at brunch was the first time I'd felt his touch in over two years. Hell, felt any man's touch. Just as I've memorized the heat, it's gone when he pulls out the chair at a table.

Once he sits across from me, he pulls my good hand up onto the tabletop and holds it with both of his. "Tell me what you've been up to. I want to know everything." There's a gleam in his eye I remember so well. When this man gives his attention to someone, he gives everything.

I laugh. I can't help myself. Carson has always had the exuberance of a small puppy. Every moment in life to him has always been one to rejoice in and take advantage of. He's not the type of person to ever let any bit of happiness he can glean go to waste. I'm thrilled to see this part of him has not changed.

"Well, you know I've been working with your sister, Chloe."

"Yes. And I understand your clothing lines are killing it overseas and doing pretty well in the States too."

I nod and go to lift my beer with my scarred hand. Just as I get it up, the weight of it becomes too much for my injured nerves. Carson, like last week with the coffee pot, grabs the glass and settles it into my other hand. He didn't even flinch, make a comment, or look put out by my disability.

Huh.

"Killing it overseas...the States," he encourages, bringing us back to the question he asked.

"Oh yeah, uh, yes. We're doing well. Working with Chloe is a dream come true. She's so talented."

Carson leans back and taps the table. "If I remember correctly, so are you, Sweetcheeks."

A noise between a huff and laugh slips from my lips when I hear that tried-and-true nickname. "Sweetcheeks. Still?" I raise one eyebrow.

He grins and leans closer. I can smell the distinct odor of the sea wafting off his skin, reminding me of far happier times splashing in the ocean off the private beach on his property. The memory and scent combined send a zip of recognition down between my legs, where I clench, staving off the impending desire. The ache that happens in my sexual organs when my brain tells my pussy its mate is close and ready for a good time is hard to ignore, especially with Carson so close. I slow my breathing, trying to bank the flames.

"Sweetest cheeks I ever had the pleasure of seeing." He waggles his eyebrows suggestively. "At least if my memory serves."

I shake my head. "Not since the grafting surgeries. Not so sweet anymore." He doesn't know what I've had to deal with. The skin of my ass isn't so perfectly smooth anymore. I can just barely feel the slight change in the topography from where the doctors removed healthy skin to cover the worst of my burns. My inner thighs suffered the same fate. As if I wasn't scarred enough. *Let's add some more spots on her body we can damage.*

"I'd like to be the judge of that." He grabs my hand once more and runs a finger from my elbow to my palm, where he swirls that single digit around the middle of my hand. "Always so soft."

Heat nips my hand, and electricity travels up my arm in a blazing trail. My nerve endings prickle and my pulse waits for even a hint of his next touch. My heart starts to hammer in my chest.

"Carson..."

"Yeah, honey." He says this as if we've just catapulted into another time and place. More than three years ago, to be exact. The surroundings are similar, the feelings the same. Lust. Heat. Desire. All wreaking havoc on my psyche. Am I ready for this? For these feelings?

Chancing a glance at him, he must be sensing it. His eyes are heavy-lidded and at half-mast, his teeth biting into his bottom lip as if he's preventing himself from saying something inappropriate.

Slowly I pull my hand away from his, breaking the contact and severing the insta-lust permeating the air around our little table.

Blessedly, a waiter I've known for years pops over to our table. "Hey, Kat. Sorry it took so long. You two want to order?"

"Yes." I'm instantly thankful for the respite from the hammering of unexpected feelings slamming into me, all hyperfocused on the wall of man sitting two feet away who has his eyes leveled on me.

"Okay, do you know what you want?" The waiter asks me, but Carson responds instantly.

"I abso-fuckin-lutely know exactly what I want." He stares unwaveringly at me. "Something I've been craving for a long, long time," Carson growls.

His words hit me like a wrecking ball, and I gasp. The connection, the sexual energy we've always had ignites in Carson's presence, barreling to the surface.

The desire.

The need.

The ache.

The want.

All of it spears through my body, mind, and soul as if it has always been there, lying dormant, waiting until its mate came back to claim it. I am so fucked.

I know, sitting across from him, his eyes darker than normal and hyperfocused on me, things are going to change tonight. I could never have anticipated how much.

"I'll take a shot of Patrón, please," I mutter, needing something far stronger than a beer.

"Make that four for the table. We need to take the edge off." Carson smirks, grabs my hand, and toys with my fingers while ordering a couple appetizers. He traces a circle on the center of my palm with his index finger.

I flush with heat, remembering just how good those fingers were against other areas of my skin. "Oh, God." I bite my lip and glance away.

"Already calling out to God, Sweetcheeks? It's a little early in the evening. The festivities haven't even begun yet." He brings my good hand up to his lips. His stare is mesmerizing as he places a soft, purposeful kiss to the top of each fingertip.

I swallow the dry lump of regrets I've had for the past few years. The ones scratching their way up my throat since I spotted him tonight. I'm at a loss. I have no idea what the hell to do or say. He's got me utterly speechless and so turned on I can hardly see straight. I haven't allowed any man to flick this switch inside me in years, and all Carson has to do is sit across from me at a table for two in a busy pub, kiss my hand, and I'm jelly.

"What the hell has gotten into me?" I whisper under my breath.

"Nothing as far as I can tell. But that's going to change tonight."

The waiter stops by and sets down the shots before shooting off to other thirsty patrons.

"Drink up, buttercup. You're going to need the liquid courage." He hands me a tequila shot and a lime wedge. "To what could be." He lifts the glass between thumb and forefinger, the shot looking positively miniscule in his large hand.

I dumbly follow along with his movements and shoot it back. The liquor provides the scalding sensation I need to continue sitting here and not run away like a scared kitten.

Carson lifts the second shot. I grab mine and follow his lead. The willing marionette.

This time he changes his toast. "To what is *meant* to be." His words are laced with promises I'm not sure either of us are ready to keep.

Nonetheless, I once again follow his lead. He raises his hand and holds up four fingers to someone behind me.

"Are you trying to get me drunk?" I tilt my head, bite my lip, and narrow my gaze.

He grins huge at what I'm sure he sees as a familiar gesture.

"If that's what it takes."

The waiter places four more shots on the table. "Food's coming soon," he says and is off like a rocket to the next table grappling for his attention.

"What it takes for what?" I lift the third shot, already feeling the burn of alcohol in my gut from the first two on an empty stomach. Each drop of liquor is slowly spreading out through my limbs, making me feel looser and more relaxed. Mostly just making me *feel*. For the first time in a long time I feel good. *Alive.*

Then again, the feeling could be attributed to the man smiling like a loon across from me.

"To get back in you." He lifts the shot and tosses it back. I follow him, not exactly understanding what he said.

"Wait... What?" I blink several times. The room is starting to blur a bit around the edges. The music is pounding out a rhythmic beat, and I sway in time to it in my seat.

Carson licks his lips, and I'm fascinated by the small movement. I want nothing more than to put my lips on his and taste the tequila directly from his tongue. God, those were some good times. Drinking and fucking. But that was all before the accident. Before I lost the body he loved. Before I lost myself.

"You are so beautiful, Kathleen." He smiles and drops his chin into his hand.

"I miss you." I admit it under the influence of the alcoholic truth serum I just shot back times three.

He grins. "You don't have to miss me." His tone is coated in lust.

"Why is that?" I pick up the last shot. Where is that waiter, anyway? I need more of this awesomeness.

"Because you've always had me." He lifts the glass and shoots it back.

I do the same, searching his eyes for even a hint of bullshit.

I find none.

"Fuck." I swallow around the feelings that bubble up, not knowing how to deal with them in my inebriated state.

"That's the plan, Sweetcheeks." One strong eyebrow rises. "I plan to fuck you all night long."

CHAPTER SIX

CARSON

She tastes like heaven and hell mixed together. I dip my tongue in for another sip as I plaster her body against the door of her apartment with mine. She mewls her desire as I hold her in place, every inch of her curves pressing against me as God himself intended.

"Fuck, Sweetcheeks. It's been too damn long," I say in a bit of a drunken slur.

I hadn't intended to drink so much, but once we were sitting across from one another, after years of not being together, I needed something to take the edge off. The feelings between us were battle-ramming me into the past, and I wanted to focus on the moment, the present. On her.

My girl was finally, *finally* spending time with me. Talking to me. Laughing. Enjoying a Friday night out just like old times. I was fucking elated, beyond thrilled.

And now, now I have her exactly where I want her. I lick my way down the column of her swan-like neck. Fucking brilliant.

She moans and presses her pelvis against mine. My dick throbs and aches with every punch against her softness.

"Honey, touch me. Please just touch me. I need your hands all over," I confess in a moment of true, honest weakness. But just like it was before, there is no reason to feel weak. Kat knows my need inherently, for she too feels it.

Her good hand pushes between our bodies, and she plucks at the button of my jeans with the precision only a clothing designer could have. She shoves down the zipper. A second of bliss almost topples me when the air touches my bare cock, and then her warm little hand cups my girth and tugs.

Nirvana.

Pain and pleasure spike through every nerve ending from my groin to my chest, where I push out the longest sigh of relief history has ever heard.

"God, honey, I love your touch," I whisper, licking the place behind her ear that makes her knees wobble and her pussy wet.

She groans, getting a better grip on me, using her wickedly talented hand to stroke up and down, rubbing the crown with the moisture she finds there. Her thumb is spinning me into a haze of beautiful oblivion. My mouth waters and her scent invades my nose. Sunshine and coconuts. The coconut is new but equally stimulating.

While she plays, I use both hands to lift her flowy knee-length skirt until I find the tiny scrap of lace attached to her hips.

"Hope these weren't your favorite," I grumble into her neck, biting down on her succulent skin as I shred both sides of her panties and tuck the scraps of lace into the back pocket of my jeans.

"Jesus, Carson. What has gotten into you?"

Desire flares higher with her words. She tugs hard on

my length, and I arch into her hand and moan. It's as if all my pleasure has zeroed in on my cock and her magnificent hand, which is perfectly stroking me into a ball of knots.

"It's *me* who's going to get into *you*. Into this sweet cunt. Fuck me." I cup her sex and rejoice in the wetness that coats my hand. I roll my fingers around her clit and dip two fingers into her welcoming heat.

I feel her body tighten as she closes her eyes and presses herself against the door behind her. She no longer has ahold of my cock, focused only on her own pleasure. I love making her crazy and greedy. It's been far too long since I've had a woman respond to my touch the way Kathleen does. As though her life depends on it.

She's my everything. My one. The only woman I know inside and out. The only woman I want to know in that way.

I thrust my fingers in and out of her. "You like that, honey? Me fucking you with my hand?"

Her perfect teeth are biting into her lip, her eyes closed, her nose crinkled in concentration. "Shut the hell up, Carson. You know I do." She gasps when I push deep, rewarding her honesty.

I bring my body as close to hers as I can while steadily moving my fingers in and out of her. I press our foreheads together. The zap of connection holds me there and makes me crazy with the need to please her. "I'm going to make you come so many times you'll never forget how good it is between us."

Her body jolts, and her mouth opens on a silent cry. I give in to the temptation and lick around her kiss-swollen lips, tasting tequila, lime, and my girl. Magnificent. My balls react, drawing up tight, feeling heavy and full, needing some action of their own.

I rub my lower half against her as I finger her fast and hard. Pops of arousal slither along my spine as she starts to tremble and shake. I place my thumb over her pert little clit and swirl in fast circles.

Her hands come up to my neck, and she hangs on as the orgasm rattles through her violently.

"Fucking beautiful," I whisper against her lips, watching every emotion flit across her face before taking her mouth in a deep kiss while rubbing at her clit slowly until she comes down off her high. "That's it, honey. Nice and easy."

Kat hums, licking into my mouth and leaning most of her weight on me. In a quick move, I swoop her into a princess hold and walk through her apartment until we get to her bedroom. When I hit the bed, I let her body slide down mine and push her skirt down until her bottom half is bare. Kathleen gets her footing and looks at me lazily, running her hands up my polo shirt, helping me to lift it up and off. Her gaze is rapt on my chest and abdominals.

"You've changed," she says in awe.

Three years ago, I was lean and fit. Since losing the only woman I ever loved, I spend all of my time at work and in the gym. I've put on a solid thirty pounds of muscle and taken off any additional fat I used to have.

"Being lost and alone changes a man," I say, wishing I hadn't when she winces and looks away.

Before she can let the shit of our past creep in, I wrap my hand around her neck and use my thumb and forefinger to tilt her face back to mine. Without saying a word, I kiss her, putting everything I am into the kiss. The loss of us, the waste of time not spent together, years of longing, lust mixed with intense amounts of need. I don't let her pull away. Instead, I hold on.

Sucking her tongue, nibbling on her lips, my desire taking the driver's seat in the heat of the moment. No way am I going to let her doubt and fear sneak their way into this homecoming.

Eventually, we both pull away, needing air. I take that time to shove off my jeans, kicking off my sneakers and toeing off my socks.

Her caramel eyes look like melted dark chocolate in the moonlight. She stands there, her chest lifting evenly with each breath. It's as if she's centering herself, calming the vivid swirl of emotions centering around both of us.

I go to lift her shirt by the hem, skimming her luscious hips, when she places her hands over mine, stopping me. I can only see her bottom half, but it's close to what I remember. Leaner now, a little less curve, more toned. Looks like someone else has been working her body while being alone as well.

Seeing the golden strip of hair at the apex of her thighs makes my mouth water. Again, I pull at her shirt, lifting it to just her waist when both of her hands stop me and her entire body goes rigid.

"No. Leave it." The words leave her lips on a whisper.

"I want to see you bare, honey." I push my cock against her belly, and she whimpers.

"P-Please leave it..." Her broken tone catches my attention.

I focus on her face, the moonlight glinting off the wetness in her eyes. I lift my hands and cup her face and her beautiful smooth cheek and neck. For a few moments I just stare at her, wanting her to see what I see.

But when a single tear slips down her cheek, and then another, followed by her plea, "Please..." I lose the battle.

I pull her into my arms and hold her tight. Her face

plummets into my neck, her arms around my shoulders. I run my hands down her back to her bare ass. With slow movements, I pet the rounded globes I so adore. She was right. I can feel the slight pebbling of the skin, but it doesn't deter me one bit. Dipping my body lower, I lift her by the cheeks and hike her up. Instantly, she wraps her long legs around my waist.

Carefully, I lower a knee to the bed and bring her down to her back, hovering between her parted thighs. I brace my weight with my hands on either side of her head and focus on her gaze. The shimmer in her eyes coats the love, fear, anxiety, and the heaping dose of want she can't hide.

She's scared of what I'll see of her body, and the last thing I want to do is put her in a position to fear me.

"If you want the shirt on, it stays on. I can work around it. There's a whole lot more of you I want to get reacquainted with." I kiss her neck and she sighs. Enough said.

I run my hands over both of her breasts, pushing down the cups of her bra through the shirt. It's tricky, but where there's a will, there's a way. The nipples I want so badly to wrap my lips around poke behind the surface of her gauzy shirt. I wrap my mouth around her right breast through the material, soaking it with my saliva.

Her upper body arches as she moans and grips my hair. I nibble on the peak through her shirt, making sure to bite down hard enough to excite, not hurt. Kat's legs rub up and down my sides, her pussy getting wetter by the second.

When I can smell the musk of her arousal wafting up between our bodies, I thrust my cock against the slickness.

"Oh God. So good," she murmurs, moving her head from side to side as I make my way down her body, both of my hands tweaking her perky nipples.

Every nuance of her body hits me like a blanket of desire. When I reach her upper thighs, my own limbs are trembling. I want so badly to split her legs open wide and power drive straight into the heart of her...but I won't. Not until I've tasted every inch she will allow. My drunken brain reminds me this could all end tomorrow. She could regret what we've done, push me away. I need to make her see and feel things... Give her what no other man can. Me. All of me.

My dick feels like it's going to explode as I move down her body, feeling only the cool cotton bedsheets until I encounter the edge of the bed. In a calculated move, I kneel, grab my girl's ankles, and tug her down until all I see is pink, wet, juicy pussy.

Her scent assaults me, forcing an animalistic growl past my lips.

"Carson..."

She gasps when I hold both of her thighs wide open, spreading her before me in a graphic display of her womanhood and my own control over my mate.

"Jesus Christ, I missed you," I tell her pretty cunt before licking from slit to clit.

Her hands fly to my hair, but I don't—no, won't—allow her to control this moment. This is all about me reconnecting with what's fucking mine. To what will always be mine, if I have anything to say about it. I grasp both of her hands and force them flat against the inside of her thighs, giving me the ability to control her hands and also hold her legs wide open to my desire.

My dick punches against the bed as I lick and suck her tasty pussy. Copious amounts of precum drip from the tip of my dick, and I don't care as I rub it against her girly sheets. I'll leave my mark there too.

I swallow down her arousal as she rides my face, her hips thrusting wildly, reaching for the effervescent goal. The beauty of my girl is she is multi-orgasmic. In the past, I've clocked her at ten orgasms in a night. If I weren't hurting to get inside her heat, I'd go for surpassing that record.

I flatten my tongue and rub it all around the hard kernel of her clit. She's howling like a wild banshee, completely lost to her pleasure.

"That's right, honey. I eat you. Me. Carson. Has any man touched my pussy since the last time?" I ask before I stick my tongue as far as it will go and lick deep. Sizzles of ecstasy pour over my consciousness, puddling at my hardened cock. Man, I need to get inside and soon before I lose it against her sheets.

She shakes her head furiously.

"No? I want to hear you say no man has touched my pussy," I grumble through clenched teeth, not knowing what the fuck has come over me.

All I know is my dick is raging hard, my ass cheeks are locked tight, and my heart and mind are out of control, lost to the haze of lust and greed.

"No man, honey. Only you. Oh God, right there. Don't stop, Carson. Please don't stop!" She screeches and I double my efforts.

Her body is squirming all over the place until I hold her down, curling my hands around her thighs so she can't move. I can no longer reach her pussy, but her clit is prime, red, and protruding from its hood like a homing beacon for my mouth. I lick a circle around it, press my lips to the edges, and suck. Hard.

Kathleen screams as her orgasm bulldozes through her. The hands I released are now gripping my hair, forcing me to press harder against her tight bundle of nerves.

I almost come against her fucking shin as she loses it. When she softens, I let go of her legs, open them wide, and swallow my reward down.

No woman has ever tasted like sweet heaven the way my Kathleen does. I think men are destined, predisposed to need their woman's release as if it's the nectar of the gods.

"So good. Fuck, honey. I need to get inside you."

I crawl up her sated body, rejoicing in the fast lift and fall of her chest as she comes off her high. I place my hands under her arms and position her head up at the pillows.

Just as I'm about to crawl back down her body, she stops me with two hands on my hips and a lift of her head. Before I know it, her mouth is wrapped around the weeping head of my cock.

I slam a hand to the headboard and hold on, my knuckles turning white with the effort, while my woman tends to my swollen dick. It's red, angry, and bursting for attention.

Kat licks and sucks, humming in the back of her throat when she takes me deep. No woman has ever done that. Used the back of her throat to tickle and tease the head of my cock by humming. It's unique to her and so fucking good I could spurt down her throat right now, but that wouldn't satisfy either of us. I need inside.

This evening I've been inside her mouth and tasted her pussy, but now I want into her heart. I want to pound my way back into her soul and burrow so deep she'll never be able to push me away again.

"Stop, Sweetcheeks, or I'm going to come down your throat."

She hums again and takes a long suck, dragging her lips up

my length until the head pops out of her mouth with an audible slurpy plop.

"Go ahead," she says, knowing I love it when she swallows. Every man does. It's primal and utterly gratifying to know that my woman has a load of my hot release in her belly.

Fuck. The thought has me crazed, fucking her face, one hand wrapped around the headboard and the other gripping the roots of her hair at her nape. The end of my cock slips a little farther down her throat, where the muscle constricts around the crown. My head swims, stars flickering in my vision as I fuck her throat, going deeper than I ever have. She takes it. Takes it all. Even when she gags, she doesn't stop—rather, she holds the flesh of my ass, allowing me to deep throat her.

Welcome home indeed.

I'm gonna lose it. My balls swell and lift, feeling like two giant boulders hitting her chin as I go deep.

"Fuck!" I roar and pull back as though I've been burned.

The head of my dick pulses and throbs. I swear I can feel my goddamned heartbeat at the tip of my dick.

"Need you. Need you so bad, Kathleen." I mumble, sliding down her body.

She opens her legs with a gleam in her eyes so beautiful that wetness hits my eyes. There've only been two times I was overwhelmed enough to cry. The day my mother died, and the day I saw my girl wrapped in bandages from a fire that almost took her away from me.

I'm so gone for this woman.

I sit back on my haunches, centering my cock between her thighs. I curl a hand around her ass cheek for leverage and cup her face with the other. With my eyes glued to hers, I sink home.

Tight.

Wet.

Warm.

Home.

When I'm all the way in, wrapped entirely around in the only woman I have ever loved, I flatten my body over hers.

"Push up your shirt. I want to feel your skin touching mine everywhere."

Tears spill down her cheeks as she bites her lip and nods. Then she wiggles her hands between us, and I help her pull her shirt up and off. She uses her good hand to reach between her breasts and undo the clasp of her bra. Again, I help her free herself from the constraints.

I don't look down when she's completely naked. The last thing I want right now is for her to feel as though I'm inspecting her scars, the things she sees as grotesque.

Instead, the second her breasts are free from her bra, I plaster my chest to hers. Every inch of my skin that possibly can is touching every inch of hers. My cock flares within her depths.

"I need to move."

"Then move." She swallows.

"I need to show you." I lift my hips back until just the tip is in and slam back home.

She gasps and tilts her head back. I take the offering of her neck, sucking and biting the white expanse. At her right shoulder I can see the marred skin. No longer does she have the delicate rounding I used to nibble and bite while making love. Seeing that saddens me briefly, until I switch sides. I take her left shoulder, biting down on the cap until her hands fly into my hair.

"Yes!" she hisses. "Show me."

Wrapping both hands around her shoulders, I curve my back and fuck her good and hard for a few blessed thrusts, giving my cock exactly what it needs.

With every penetration, I touch the end of her pussy, wanting more, needing to go deeper. I want to imprint so far inside her she'll never forget how perfect our connection is.

"Don't ever forget this, Kathleen. Don't forget how good we are." I pound into her.

She raises her thighs up and wraps them high around my ribcage, tilting her hips up as she does, working with me.

The nails of one of her hands dig into my back while the other just holds me. "I could never forget you. I never did. God, Carson. I never could," she whispers against my mouth before kissing me.

This kiss is different than the lusty ones from before, where we just needed to taste and feed. This kiss is more. So much more.

Our tongues dance while I press into her over and over. On every thrust in, she moans. Every retreat, she whimpers.

The joining of our bodies is beautiful. Perfect. We're meant to be. It's us.

Fate.

I know the moment it changes for Kathleen, because she moans low in her throat. A keening sound, which speaks of desperation, of need. My cock responds to that sound. It's time. Kathleen's body starts to tremble, her limbs locking down where she wants me to stay. She clings to me, focused solely on her release, on me, on this power building between us. It will rock our worlds.

When the moment hits, it's unlike anything I've ever

felt. My entire body is slammed with sensation so bright it's blinding. So good it's unearthly. My mind is blown. Kathleen screams out as it takes her over, her entire body locking me down so tight I never want to leave the confines. It's as if her soul has wrapped its entire essence around mine, uniting us in a way that will change our lives forever. We're bound. Our souls have made the decision for us. There can no longer be a Kathleen and Carson. It's decided. Our souls have spoken. We're mated. For life.

My entire body burns white-hot as I let loose with a gut-wrenching battle cry. Over and over I pound into the only woman I ever want to be with.

She accepts me within her body as I pump hotly into her. My seed shoots up my cock and bursts, filling her with life, love, and me.

When the last of our orgasms fade, I lift up on one arm and cup her cheek. Her caramel eyes are bright and shining with tears that fall unchecked. She's allowing me to see deep inside her. The hurt, the longing, the need to be with me.

"I love you, Kathleen," I say for the first time.

Her eyes widen and the tears slide down her cheeks, wetting my hand as she gasps. I pet her moist bottom lip, my thumb pressing the drops of her tears against her pretty lips before I share her feelings by tasting them on my tongue and kissing them away.

I lift just far enough so she can see me. To believe every word. In this moment, I'm opening myself, giving her my all.

"I love you so fucking much it's tearing me apart." I choke out the words, not having said those three little words out loud since the very day my mother died.

Those were the last words I said to my mother before her

life seeped out of her forever, and now I'm giving them to the only woman who's deserved them since.

"I'll always love you, Carson," Kathleen says, just before I again take her mouth with mine.

CHAPTER SEVEN

KATHLEEN

Last night was magical. There are no other words to describe it. After three years of pain, anguish, and sorrow, I feel free. Free to be a woman in love. Free to see the light at the end of the tunnel. Free to believe there is more out there for me. I'm not damaged. Just because I'm scarred, marred in a way I barely tolerate, it doesn't mean I'm gone. I haven't disappeared. Last evening, Carson proved it to me. It's what my soul sisters have been harping on me about. It's what Chase has said time and again.

I am not my scars. They are a part of me now. A part I can never erase. In the last discussion with my medical team, they said we've gone as far as we can with the attempts at making them aesthetically pleasing. My arm, ribcage, and just the very side of my right breast will remain deformed. It is what it is. I can no longer change that. The time has come to accept what happened to me and move on. Stop living in the past. Stop wishing for a different body. I am who I am. This is the new me.

I'm not a monster. I'm Kathleen Bennett. A survivor.

I survived a horrible fire. I lost my will, and with it, the desire to hold on to happiness. Somehow, I twisted myself into believing my injury made me ugly, unlovable—something to despise. Mostly because that's how I felt when I saw the scars. Every time I removed my clothes and met my reflection in the mirror, I didn't recognize the person staring back at me as me. I guess that's how all people feel when they get older or gain a bunch of weight. With time, everyone changes. Some changes are for the better. Others are thrust upon us, and we have to make do. It's what I've been doing for the past three years. Making do. No longer am I going to push my needs and desires into a corner so I don't have to look at myself—or worse, so no one else has to.

I deserve to be happy.

The thought flickers through my brain like a kaleidoscope of monarch butterflies flapping their wings at the same time.

Happiness is a choice.

For the past three years I chose not to be happy. Sure, anyone in my position would have gone through a grieving process. And I did grieve. For the loss of my ability to sew. For the loss of my strength and mobility. But most of all, I grieved for the loss of Carson. I didn't believe a young, virile man with his entire life ahead of him could love or want to be with a disfigured woman. I put so much into my looks and our physical relationship, I threw away our mental and emotional connections as if they were day-old news. Somewhere in my mind I believed I was not worthy of having someone so beautiful care for me and see me through a dark time. Instead of coping with the changes and challenges, I made the worst decision of my life.

I pushed Carson away. I did that. My scars didn't. That was all me.

I love you, Kathleen.

He loves me.

During the heat of the moment, Carson Davis said the three words I'd always wished he'd say. *I love you, Kathleen.* Technically, four words. And what beautiful words they were. The moment he said them, something inside me clicked. Healed. Without Carson in my life, I was lost. Going through the motions in black and white. My life no longer had color. He brings color to my world.

Wheat-colored hair.

Sparkling sky-blue eyes.

Straight white teeth.

Golden-brown skin.

All that beauty is mine.

We didn't speak of our situation after making love last night. No, once we'd cleaned up, we were all shared smiles and sweet caresses. Throughout the night, Carson woke me and made love to me again. Three different times. He said he was making up for lost time.

When I think about it like that, we will have a lifetime to make up for lost time.

Turning on my side, I watch him sleep peacefully. Each little puff of air through his lips lifts a lock of hair that has fallen down his forehead.

How many mornings did I wake alone, scared and afraid to face the day without this force to fill me up and make me a whole person? I get now why people call their soul mates their other half. For me, Carson always filled all the empty spaces inside me. When I pushed him away, bits and pieces of his essence fell away too, leaving gaping holes within my heart and mind where his essence once lived.

I haven't been happy the past three years. Each and every

day, I woke up and thought *I can make it through today*. Just put one foot in front of the other.

Why should anyone have to "make it" through a day?

Dr. Madison, my therapist, said it was depression and I needed to work through those thoughts in a healthy manner. Fill up the holes inside me with something else. The only problem? Nothing worked. It was only ever Carson. He'd dug those holes inside me in the first place and burrowed deep until he had his place. He's the only one who could piece me back together. Last night went a long way toward that happening.

Parts of me feel more put together now. There's a lightness to my heart I've been missing for years. An ease I hope to enjoy for longer than a single night.

Will he want to see me again?

I blow out a long breath, fluffing my bangs up and away from my forehead. *Kat, be reasonable.* He told me he loved me. Wanted me to never forget how good it was between us. As if I ever could. Does it mean we're automatically back together?

Do I want to open myself back up to loving this man?

Of course, I never lost my love for him. It was the one single constant I could count on through my therapy and the mental anguish that followed a life-altering injury such as mine. At least I'd had love and lost it. Most people don't even find it once. I figure I was lucky. I *am* lucky.

But what happens now?

A ringing phone cuts off my silent musings.

Carson blinks his eyes open. I stay where I am, holding my breath, staring at the beautiful sight of him lying in my bed for the first time in years. He lifts his lips into a beautiful smile.

"Morning, Sweetcheeks," he rumbles, tugging me around the waist and dragging me closer to his naked warmth.

The instant my bare legs touch his, the comforting warmth seeps deep into my bones. He didn't bother to put any clothing on last night. Out of force of habit, I'd put on a long-sleeved nightshirt after our last round of lovemaking.

The phone stops ringing as Carson rubs his scruffy chin against my neck, sighs, and inhales my scent. The sound reverberates against my neck and flows down into my soul.

Carson is in my bed. In the flesh. Holding me.

I love you, Kathleen.

In my mind, I hear those words over and over. They give me the ability to snuggle into him and just breathe. Enjoy the moment for what it is. The morning after.

Only this time, it's the morning after with the man I love.

I love you, Kathleen.

He'd said the words, and I believed him.

The phone rings again, ruining my good vibes with its persistence.

Carson groans, scowls, and then turns flat on his back, digging around on the floor. He's so tall and his arms so long, his reach is incredible.

He pulls the ringing phone up and glances at the display.

He frowns, narrows his gaze, and punches the "ignore" button.

I couldn't be sure, but I think the name of the person calling was Michelle or Missy or Misty.

Then it hits me. What Chase said last week. That he didn't think the woman Carson was with was right for him, or something of that nature. Honestly, I wasn't paying too close attention, because if I had, I would've spent weeks hating myself all over again for letting him go.

Carson's body is rigid when he turns back to his side. The

second his pretty eyes hit mine and that smile comes back, the phone rings a third time.

He sits up, groaning and letting the sheet fall around his lap. God, he's sexy, all tanned skin and tight brick-shaped abdominals. I want nothing more than to roll over and lick them to prove there is indeed an indented outline around each one.

"Fucking hell!" He smashes the accept button and turns to the side of the bed, curling over to listen.

"I told you I'd call when I was ready." His voice borders on angry.

Not exactly the happy-go-lucky man I am used to, especially after a night of smokin'-hot sex and reconnecting to lost love.

Carson's entire body visibly tightens, the muscles of his back bunching up and engaging.

"Jesus Christ. Is she okay?"

Abruptly he stands, leans over, grabs his boxer briefs, and shimmies into them. If I weren't so focused on the heightened breathing, the worry taking over his entire form, I'd have ogled him. Instead, I sit up and watch him silently pace. He pushes his hand into the mop of sleep-mussed hair and tugs. It is definitely a Davis male move. Chase does the same thing all the time. I've even seen Carson's dad do it a time or two.

His face is a mask of irritation when he turns to pace toward the bed. "Uh-huh. You what? No, I'm not home." His head flings up, eyes alert and on me. He cringes. "Nowhere."

God, something must be really wrong.

"How is that even possible? No family? Friends?" He shakes his head, fumbles with his polo, and pulls it over his head in jerky movements. "Fuck. I'll figure something out. I'll be there in a half hour."

Carson sits on the bed, grabs his socks, and holds the phone to his ear with his shoulder. Not easy to do with an iPhone. He could just put it on speaker. I secretly wish he would. Then the fear and anxiety pumping off him and coating me would be relieved.

"Yes, thirty minutes. Where am I? That's none of your concern." He peeks at me from the corner of his eyes before rubbing at his face. "I said I'll be there, and I will."

Without even a goodbye, he hangs up on whomever he was talking to.

Moving slowly, I crawl over to his side of the bed and lay a hand on his shoulder.

His entire body jerks and then settles when he realizes it's me.

"What's the matter?"

Carson licks his lips and glances away, his head falling down to view his shoes. "Uh, nothing. I gotta go."

He finishes tying his shoes and then stands.

"Who was that on the phone?" My voice rises along with the dread filling my heart.

"No one," he deadpans.

I tilt my head and cross my arms. "Didn't sound like no one. Carson..." I'm about to tell him what we had last night can't go forward if he can't be honest with me. Instead, I follow my heart. "Talk to me," I urge.

He swallows and his chest rises and falls. "I can't. Not yet. I...I have some things I need to figure out," he says cryptically.

I crawl across the bed and stand in front of him. I lift my hand to his cheek, and he leans into it briefly before closing his eyes.

"What things? Let me help you. I can see that you're angry or confused. Just talk to me."

He cups my wrist and brings my palm to his lips, where he lays a warm kiss. "Kat, last night was everything. More than I could have ever hoped for, but I gotta go. Can we please talk later?" Something in his eyes reveals his genuine need. He's struggling with whatever it is he's not saying.

"Later?" I swallow down the instant emotion bubbling up my throat.

"Yeah, uh, maybe tonight or tomorrow?" I hear equal parts hope and distraction.

Without waiting for a reply, he moves out of my hold and locates his wallet and keys. He shoves his wallet into his back pocket and frowns. His hand shifts behind his back and then he brings it around with lace dangling from his fingertips.

The frown marring his beautiful face dissipates, and he lights up with a giant smile, clears his throat, and coughs. "Yeah, I'm so keeping these." He waggles his brows and it almost dissolves the icepick digging into my heart.

I try to grab for the undies, but he jumps back just in time. "Give them to me. They're ruined!"

"Don't care. Still want them. They'll be my good-luck charm for the day," he declares while backing up through my hallway and toward my front door.

I giggle and follow him. "Um, last night..." I try, but he cuts me off with a hand to my neck and a quick, hard press of his lips.

"I already told you. Last night was everything. I just have a situation I have to deal with. Can you understand?"

"Why won't you tell me what it is? I'm sure I can help. I want to help you with anything." My voice is laced with worry and regret. Too much time has already passed between us, and now he's running off to handle something that has obviously made him very agitated, and he's pushing me away.

"This is not something you can help with. I'm sorry. I really have to go. A, uh, friend"—he settles on the word "friend" as if it's foreign and sticky on his lips before continuing—"of mine needs me."

The fumble with the word *friend* sends a fire alarm clanging in my head.

"You know, we never did talk about whether you were seeing anyone before we hit the...you know." I gesture to the bedroom.

"She. Is. Not. My. Girlfriend." His response is instant and adamant.

"Okay, but you are going to help a woman. Someone who asked where you were. That sounds more than casual."

He closes his eyes and his nostrils flare. He doesn't move for a few heartbeats. "I can't talk about this right now, Kathleen. I just can't. I have to go. I'll call you."

Carson kisses me swiftly before he's gone in what feels like a flash.

"He'll call me," I repeat to the closed door, feeling cold and alone all over again.

I shake my head, thinking I very well may have stepped into the Twilight Zone. There's only one thing I need now.

Reinforcements.

★ ★ ★

"¿Ahora lo que dijo?" Maria's screech is so loud I have to hold the phone away from my ear to avoid losing an eardrum.

"Ria, English, please."

"*Lo siento*. Sorry. He said *what* now?" she repeats.

"He said he'd call me." I close my eyes and press my thumb and forefinger into my temples. It sounds like a stupid blow-off, even to me.

"And this wasn't a booty call?"

I sigh. "Maria, I haven't had sex in three years. The last time I had sex was with Carson. This was *not* a booty call."

She hums as if she's thinking about what I told her. "And he blew you off?"

Another broken sigh slips from my lips. "Yeah. Now I don't know what to do."

"How did he sound when he took the call?"

"Agitated. Angry. It sounded like whoever called him wasn't supposed to. But that doesn't sound right either. If it was the mystery woman Chase mentioned last week, she should be able to call him. Right?"

"*Si*. But if he was angry, maybe he broke up with her recently, then met up with you, had the night of his life, got his Sweetcheeks back, and didn't want to deal with the other woman's skanky ass anymore."

I laugh. Leave it to Maria to make light of any situation.

"Maybe. God, I don't know. It was just weird. What do you think I should do?"

"As much as I hate to say it, wait it out. If he doesn't call tonight, you'll know something's up. He is a man. They do weird shit all the time. Just the other day I saw Eli walking through the house carrying a duffle bag. When I asked what was in the bag, he acted all put out. *Estupido*. You never act strange when a woman asks about something, especially if you don't want her to know."

I cringe. "What was in the bag?"

"Guns," she says flatly.

"Guns!" I scream into the phone and glance around my apartment as if the mere mention of the vile things could magically manifest in the center of my living room.

"*Si*. Keep up," she chastises me. "He was taking guns out to the shed to hide them for an old friend who was going to stop by because he owed him a marker."

He owed the "friend" a marker. I've watched *Sons of Anarchy*. Markers are always awful things scary dudes with names like Butch demand in return for a favor they once did for you.

"Holy shit, he owed guns to someone? Like a bad guy?" I gasp, placing my fingertips over my mouth.

Sometimes finding out the finer details of your friend's marriage to a badass bounty hunter is not all roses and chocolates. Guns? Jesus. Now I had two things to worry about. Carson being a weirdo after a night of what I kind of thought was us getting back together, and Maria and her husband hiding guns in a shed. What the heck is going on?

"*No se preocupe*. No worries. It's not a big deal. One of his FBI friends needed them for a raid. He'd gotten them from another raid himself, so they were going back to the feds. Still, it's off the books. You know, like when the Italians say, 'It fell off the truck,'" she says nonchalantly.

"The Italians?" I stutter over my words. "You mean the flippin' *Mafia*?"

"*Si, si*. Now you're paying attention. Kind of like that— only totally the good guys."

I rub at my now aching head. "Maria, how does any of this help me?" I want to say it's accomplished the exact opposite by giving me a heart attack.

"Basically, I'm saying, guys do stupid shit. They act like the world is ending, when really it's just putting guns into a shed for the FBI."

I blink a few times. This makes absolutely no sense at all.

"Uh, thanks, Maria. You helped a lot."

"Sweet, *mi gatita*." I roll my eyes at her "little kitty" nickname. "Call me and let me know what happens tonight? *Sí*?"

"Sure."

"Besos," she says.

"Besos."

I set my phone down on my lap. How the hell does hiding guns in a shed for the FBI relate in any way, shape, or form to Carson blowing me off, telling me he'd call me, and then running away to go help some woman he refused to tell me about?

Ugh. This is so frustrating. I don't even know how to deal with this. With him. I want to call him. Yell at him and tell him he's an ass for confusing me and making me second-guess everything that happened between us, past and present.

More than that, though, I want to call him, tell him I love him, and kiss him until it all goes away.

Maria down. Time for opinion number two. I debate calling Gillian or Bree. I glance at the clock and realize Bree will be between classes.

Bree...you're up!

CHAPTER EIGHT

CARSON

An anger inside me simmers so strong it is as though I am a volcano ready to blow. I take the corner to her street as though my truck is a race car.

A fucking fire.

I had to see this shit to believe it. Fire ruined my life once before. It has to be like lightning. This shit can't strike twice. Could it?

The downtown street is poorly paved, with potholes littering the road like confetti. My four-wheel drive can handle it, but how can her shitty Honda scrape through on balding tires and a rotted undercarriage?

Yeah, I took in the details of her car since we last spoke. It's the vehicle my daughter is being driven around in. *My daughter.* Fuck. Those words will never get any easier to hear. It's such a foreign concept. Not something I ever thought I'd be dealing with. At least not like this. I'd always envisioned my life with Kathleen, married, and having children with her. Not jetting from the woman I love to the woman who has my daughter.

Sweat trickles down my back as I drive. This area is

notorious for gangbangers and drug dealers. Why the fuck is she living here?

When I get closer to her address I see the fire trucks and police cars lining the center of the street, preventing traffic from passing through, their blue and red lights flashing maniacally. I pull up in front of another dilapidated house and focus on the two blond heads sitting on the curb. Misty's brown eyes clock me the second I step out of my car.

She stands, a toddler clamped to her chest. My heart beats like a bass drum while I force myself out of the car. Every step I take closer to them sounds louder in my ears, as if my heart is going to rip right out of my chest and flop onto the cold, hard ground.

The little girl turns her head, and I stop in my tracks in the middle of the street. That heart of mine moves double time as I take in the chubby cheeks, the golden hair, and the cherub lips. She looks exactly like my sister Chloe did as a little girl. The likeness is uncanny. Had I seen her prior to requesting the paternity test, it wouldn't have been needed. There is no denying this child is mine.

My daughter.

Without even asking, I hold out my hands. Instinctively, my body yearns for its young. The baby smiles, her eyes lighting up with intrigue and what I hope is happiness.

"Carson, be careful with her. She doesn't like strangers," Misty warns. The second Cora's little body curls against my chest, every concern, worry, and disgusting thought I had about this situation flies out the window. I am holding my daughter, and she's perfect.

"Hello, baby girl. I'm your daddy." I stumble over the words and rub my nose against hers.

She giggles, and it lights up my entire world. I'm in love with her already. A single laugh is all it takes. I hold her close, inhale her sweet scent, and close my eyes, imprinting this moment in my mind. The sirens, the officers and firemen calling out commands—it all fades away as I connect with my own flesh and blood for the very first time.

"Cora," I whisper, allowing her name to sit on my tongue, becoming familiar, special.

She lifts her hands to my face and squishes my cheeks. "Dog dog," she says in garbled baby talk.

Misty smiles and pats Cora's back. "No, Cora, that's your dah-dee, not a doggie."

"Dah-dah, da-da."

I smile and kiss her cheek, holding her as close as I can get her. She smells of baby powder and the floral perfume I associate with Misty. "Yes, baby. Your dah-dah."

I suck in a huge breath of air and let this moment reach into my heart and implant itself there for eternity—the day I met my daughter. I start to look around. The firemen are still putting out the last of the fire. The building is a total loss. The entire structure is charred black.

"This was your building?"

Misty's eyes fill, and tears fall down her cheeks. "We lost everything." She gulps and pushes her hand to her mouth, a river of pain and wetness staining her pink tank top. "I don't know what we're going to do, where we're going to go. I can't afford a new place, and Cora needs diapers and a place to sleep and food..." Her voice rises, tinged with hysteria.

Cora's little body tightens in my arms, and she swings her head to her mother. "Ma-ma, ma-ma!" She reaches grabbing hands out to her. I don't want to let her go, but I'm proud of my daughter. Her immediate instinct when hearing her mother's sadness is to comfort her. Says a great deal about her character already.

Begrudgingly, I let go of Cora and hand her off to Misty.

"You will stay with me." I say the words before I really understand the ramifications of such a decision.

"But I don't know how long it will take me to earn enough money to get another place."

I tighten my hands into fists and focus on my daughter's angelic face. She will have everything. My girl will want for nothing the rest of her life. Silently, I swear I'm going to make her happy and give her the best life. In order to do that, she needs a home. Mine is practically empty.

"I will take care of her, and you, indefinitely. Right now, this means you will have food, shelter, clothes—all the necessities to lead a happy and healthy life. My daughter will never again go without. Her safety is my number-one priority." The truth of the statement shoots from my fingertips and out every pore, permeating every fiber of my being.

"What about childcare when I work? Your house will be too far to get to on time..." she says as I lead them to my truck.

"You're quitting your job. Your job is to take care of Cora right now. I'll find you something with one of my companies or with my family businesses. This area is history for both of you. Now where's that piece of shit you call a car? I need to get the car seat."

"It's gone." She cries, more tears pouring down her face as I open the passenger door of my truck.

"What?"

"It was parked in the back, right up against the building. All the cars next to the apartment building are toast. There might be something to salvage, but I don't know. We can't get to it to know for sure."

Her brown eyes widen in fear, a fresh bout of tears wetting her pink cheeks.

I close my eyes and grind my teeth. "Fine. Let's go to the nearest store to get her a car seat and some essentials for you both. Christ, this is such a clusterfuck," I say, not meaning to freak her out, even though it does.

"I'm sorry, Carson. I'm sorry. I know this is not the way you wanted to connect to Cora. You can see I didn't have any other option. She is your daughter. Yours and mine. I've been taking care of her alone for eighteen months. It's high time you helped!" Her voice breaks, and the volcano in my chest explodes.

She is right. Cora is my responsibility. Had I known about her earlier, none of this would have ever happened. She'd already be in my life, safe and protected.

I walk around the truck and get into the driver's seat. Misty holds our baby on her lap. Cora's being quiet, almost pensive. Smart little girl. She knows something's not right about the situation, and she's reacting in a calm way.

I watch her little hands play with her mother's long blond hair and rest her head against her chest. She stuffs a thumb right into her mouth, and I melt on the spot. What would it feel like to rock her to sleep, to give her a bath, to feed her a meal I made? Soon, I will experience all of these things. Far sooner than I ever dreamed possible.

★ ★ ★

The trip to Target was insane. First of all, it was only my second time in a Target. The last time was with Kat, over three years ago. Without sounding pretentious, my family had people who picked up the everyday necessities, and I do as well. My housekeeper purchases household items as needed.

Babies need an enormous amount of shit.

Even with Misty assuring me one cart was enough for today and that what we bought would get the two of them through the next few days, I'm beyond baffled. A few days? It seemed like we had enough shit for a year's stay. What the hell did I know? I had been happily living my life as a single man with no children when Misty had been busting her ass at a scummy bar, leaving my child to be cared for by God knows who in the interim. That would stop immediately. The only people who will take care of my child from here on out are her mother, me, a trusted member of my family, or a nanny from a reputable firm. And that will only be after several levels of interviews. For now, I'll take care of them monetarily, and the rest will come with time.

Once we get home, I bring all the bags in and drop them in the living room. I have no idea what I'm supposed to do with this stuff. Thank God, Misty dives in like a professional.

I watch her sort the diapers, wipes, baby wash, and diaper cream to one side. Then her own wash and bathroom essentials to another. Mentally I'm evaluating my extra bath. Will it be enough space for both of their things?

"I'm thinking you two should probably take the master bedroom," I announce out of nowhere, surprising myself once again with my lack of filter.

Misty smiles softly. "That's kind of you, but the couch will be fine. Like I said, we don't have to stay forever, but we can make do anywhere. We've done it before."

Her words grate on each and every one of my nerves.

"Misty, I don't think you understand. The second I put my arms around Cora, she became my daughter. I'm her father. She will have everything she needs from here on out. You, as her mother, are an extension of her. You will be taken care of too."

She swallows and looks away. "I tried to give her everything, you know." Her voice cracks. "I may not have a big house like this or the money you have, but I did the best I could." She sniffles, and her shoulders shake as she sobs silently.

Feeling like a major prick, I crawl over to where she's crying softly into her hands. I wrap my hands around her, bringing her into my embrace. I whisper against her hairline. "Hey now, it's going to be okay. I'm going to take care of everything. You did an amazing job. She's perfect, Misty. Look at her." Across the room, Cora is playfully pulling out all the books in my bookcase one at a time. I figure she can't get hurt and they're easy enough to put back. Plus, she's having a great time. Once a book falls out, she squeals in delight. "She's absolutely perfect. You did that. You."

A warm, small hand falls over mine as I hold her. "We did that, Carson. You and me. And you're right, she's perfect."

The moment feels strange. A tingling in my lower back prickles and then travels up my spine as I hold Misty, my daughter's mother. It's nothing like the all-encompassing peace that settles over my body and soul when I hold Kathleen, and yet it's definitely intimate. Clearing my throat, I push her back and move away a few feet.

"So, um, show me what all this stuff is and let me know what we still need." I genuinely want to know what these things are. If I'm going to be a father, I need to learn, and fast. "I already feel like I'm behind."

Misty reaches over and clasps my hand. With a soft smile, she says, "You're already amazing because you want her in your life. Everything else you'll learn along the way. And don't worry, I'll be here to teach you."

★ ★ ★

"I cannot fucking believe this!" Chase roars through the line.

I cringe and shut the door to my bedroom so that Misty and Cora can't hear my side of this conversation.

"Believe it." My tone is gritty and raw. A lot has happened today. Going from being warm and at peace in Kathleen's bed to changing my entire life within the blink of an eye is messing with my mind, not to mention my heart.

I told her I loved her. I finally said those words for the first time in my entire adult life, and now what? I don't know what's up or down, right or left. I have a child I have to take care of. And her mother. Remembering the way Misty placed her hand over mine sends a shiver of dread skittering through me. God, I hope she doesn't want me to be anything more than a father to our daughter. Just because I moved her in doesn't mean I'm going to be *with* her. I just want my daughter and her mother safe and off the streets.

How the fuck am I going to explain this to Kathleen?

Chase's aggressive tone startles me back to the here and now. "This is insanity! You have a daughter? An eighteen-month-old child you knew nothing about? Jesus, Carson. How is that even possible?"

I take a deep breath and allow his chastisement to hit me in the nuts. "I told you. That night, I didn't know. I was blitzed out of my mind. And then I never saw her again. Well, until I walked into the same haunt she works at now. Well, did work. She will not be going back to that shithole."

"This is...fuck! I don't even know what to say." After a few moments, he sighs heavily. "How is she? Your daughter?"

Leave it to Chase, Dad of the Century, to go right to the child. Pulling my hand back, I fumble with my phone. "Just a sec. I'll send you a photo. I snapped one while she was playing a few minutes ago." I find the picture I took, forward it to Chase, and lift the phone back to my ear.

I know the second Chase gets it. "Sweet mother, she looks exactly like Chloe!" He gasps. "My, the Davis genes are strong. She's beautiful, Carson. Really lovely."

My chest lifts with pride. It's an unusual but not unwanted sensation. "She is. But right now, I need your guidance. Not only do I need family around to help me through this, I need your assistance, man. As in, I need you to bring over something for my kid to sleep in. We picked up pajamas and a car seat, but your kids sleep in a crib. Cora was cranky and needed to rest so we came back home with the first round of loot."

"Her name is Cora?" His voice softens to the tone I'm used to hearing him use when he speaks to his wife or children.

I smile, feeling that same happiness filter through all the muck of the situation. The man can be a harsh businessman and an overprotective asshole when it comes to his wife and kids, but deep down, he's very old-fashioned and sentimental.

"Yeah. Fate, right?"

He inhales loudly. "Baby, we need to talk."

"Oh snookums, I didn't know you cared," I say, knowing

he's not addressing me.

"Carson has news." I hear him say this as if he's farther away but probably just holding the phone away from his mouth.

"What's going on?" Gillian's seductive timbre comes through the phone, concern lacing her words.

"I'll tell you shortly, sweetheart, but for now can you get the Pack 'n Play out of the closet in the hall under the stairs?"

"Sure, but why?"

"Soon, my love. Go on. And put on some casual clothes. We're going out."

He finishes his conversation with his wife. "Sorry about that, Carson. We'll be there in an hour. I'll pull together some essentials to get you through for a while."

An instant blanket of relief covers me. My family will help me through this. I'm not alone. I'll never be alone. "Thanks, man. And Chase...there's more."

"What more?" His voice hardens instantly.

I close my eyes and remember last night. The unbelievable rightness of being wrapped in Kathleen's arms. I remember distinctly how it felt to sink deep into her heat, how I finally was able to tell her I loved her. And now this.

"I was with Kathleen last night," I say in a forced rush of air. It's as though if I say it fast enough, somehow it will make it all okay. Chase won't be angry, I won't be dealing with being a new dad without planning it, and Kathleen and I can ride off into the sunset together.

"Excuse me?"

"Kat and I hooked up. I mean, no, not hooked up. We were together. I mean..."

"You fucked Kathleen last night?" Each word is a tongue-lashing I would expect to get from a parent, not a family member slash best friend.

"Well, yeah, man, I did, but it's more—"

"And now you have a woman and her child moving into your house?"

"My child, Chase," I remind him.

"This is so fucked up. What are you going to do about Kathleen?"

I sigh and grip my hair, tugging at the roots until the pain reaches my psyche. "I don't know. I left in a rush because of the fire and Misty and Cora needing me. I told her I'd call tonight, but how can I? I've got another woman in my home with my baby daughter, who needs me."

"Jesus, you've gotten yourself into a prickly situation, haven't you? I'll be there soon and we'll discuss. For now, get your head on straight. Start thinking about what your next steps are both with Misty and with Kathleen. She doesn't deserve this after everything she's gone through."

"And I do?" My anger rises and unleashes like a fire-breathing dragon. "I fell across her feet so many times wishing she'd take me back. Practically begging. Then finally, *finally* the universe decides to make it happen, and whammo! I'm tossed into a pit of poisonous snakes with no fucking ladder to escape. I don't know what the fuck to do. I'm trying to figure it all out, but the very last thing I need right now is you judging me! I didn't ask for this to happen. It was an accident. A stupid fucking mistake, but I'm doing my best to right a wrong. Okay? Give me a little credit for manning up."

Chase groans. "No, you're right. It's not my place to judge you."

"Cuz... Chase. You know how I feel about Kathleen. *You know.*"

A rumbling sound breaks through the line. "Yes, yes, I do." He sighs.

"Before I knew about all of this, I finally told her last night. I said the words she has been waiting to hear. And man, they felt so good."

"Stop. You're going to make me angry again." Chase's words are clipped and direct.

"Why?"

"Because I care about Kathleen. I care about her health, mental and otherwise. She has just barely started to come back to the person she was, and now this? You tell her you love her, fuck her, make her think life is hunky dory, and now you're going to lay this shit on her? I honest to God have no idea how she's going to handle it."

"Don't tell her," I say instantly.

"Unacceptable."

"Chase. This is my life. I have to tell her myself."

"And how, pray tell, do you plan to keep this from my wife? There's no way in a million years I'm going to lie to her. Not to mention, she's going to find out the second we arrive. You need her expertise in all this. Besides, she's going to lose her mind when she finds out she has another niece. My wife is ridiculous about family connections. Our family and her soul sisters are the only family she has. This is news she'll want to shout from the rooftops."

He is not kidding. Gillian is nothing if not nurturing and family-oriented. "I'll talk to Gigi. Just give me some time to handle this my way when it comes to Kathleen. I need to be the one who tells her. Otherwise, it will ruin any progress we've made. Okay? Promise me?"

Chase makes a rumbling sound akin to the sound a dog

makes when someone tries to take away his food when he's already eating. "Fine. But you have a week. I'm not holding my wife back longer than that. These soul sister relationships are touchy. You can't fuck with them. And you putting her in this position is not going to go down well."

"I'm sure you can find ways to get her mind off it." I add a joking laugh to lighten the heavy conversation.

"Are you suggesting I seduce my wife into submission?"

"What? Did you lose your touch? Having a little trouble in the bedroom now that you've got two kids and cooking up number three?"

"I won't even grace that with an acknowledgement. My wife is well satisfied. Always has been, always will be. I can't keep my hands off her."

"Then it shouldn't be too hard for you to earn me some time to figure all of this out before Gillian runs to Kat."

"Fine. I'll see what I can do, but I'm not forcing my wife to lie to her best friend. And I'm not touching that situation with a ten-foot pole. You're on your own."

"That, I'm used to." I grumble half-heartedly. Ever since Kathleen pushed me away, I've been alone. Now I have something small, perfect, and adorable to put all my efforts into.

"See you soon." I hear baby squeals coming from the other room.

"Indeed," Chase finishes formally.

CHAPTER NINE

KATHLEEN

To: Kathleen Bennett
From: Carson Davis
*I'm sorry I haven't called. You don't know how sorry I am.
I miss you.*

A fucking text? Is he for real? Three days, and nothing. Zip, nada, zilch. He neglected to call me, and after day two I finally broke down and called him, against Bree's advice. She said to blow him off until he came crawling back. Instead, I went against her better judgment. And for what? So he could ignore my call and send me an impersonal text instead?

I miss you.

"What the fucking fuck?"

My fingers fly against the keyboard of my iPhone.

To: Carson Davis
From: Kathleen Bennett
*That's all you have to say for yourself? After Friday night?
You said you loved me.*

I snarl and hit send so hard my thumb hurts.

Bastard. Who does he think he is to string me along? I glance at the phone. The three little dots signaling he's typing a message are hovering under my angry words. I roll my eyes and glance out over the busy San Francisco street. The scent of cinnamon buns and coffee is thick in the air, making my stomach growl. I'm sitting at my favorite little corner café bistro across the street from the park where Maria and Eli live. She should be here any minute for a morning pick-me-up. It's part of my plan to get back to *me*. The woman I used to be, or some two point oh variation of her. The main ingredient in the spice of finding myself is mending the ties that I've broken with my soul sisters. I'm definitely not me without them.

The phone in my hand beeps.

To: Kathleen Bennett
From: Carson Davis
I do love you. Give me time. I'm dealing with something.

Give him time? As if three years wasn't enough. I take a sip of my latte, and it burns my tongue.

"Fucking fuckity fuck!" I roar, slamming the offending thing down on the table. A dose of hot latte squirts out the top through the tiny hole in the lid and sprays all over the table in front of me.

"Seems as though I came at the perfect time." Maria holds her hands up palms facing out at me. "I'm unarmed. Don't spray me with your weapon of mass deliciousness." She grins, flips her long black braid over her shoulder, and sits down in the chair opposite of mine.

"Hey, Ria. I'm sorry," I mumble while burning with

embarrassment.

"Sounds like you were having a pretty fun time with your coffee there. Care to tell me what brought on the F-bomber? Not normally your speed, *gatita*."

I slump down into the chair and run my fingers through my shoulder-length hair. "Carson texted me."

She crosses her arms over her chest, the cool leather bomber jacket she's wearing molding to her arms and chest seductively. My best friend is sex on legs. Half Italian, half Spanish, a curvaceous dancer with a rack that makes men swoon, and legs for days. I pout thinking about how I can't even wear tight clothing like hers because it rubs against the tender skin of my arm.

"What did the prick with a dick say? *¿El se pidio discuplas?* Did he apologize?"

"Not exactly. He did say he loved me and he needed time. Said he was dealing with something."

She huffs. "Yeah, a two-bit whore he has to shake off." Her nose crinkles, and her face contorts into one of irritation.

I take a long, slow breath. "Who knows?"

Her head turns to me quickly. "Exactly. I know exactly who knows." She grins, a devilish excitement overtaking her features.

Suddenly, the light bulb goes on, and we both say the same name at the same time.

"Chase."

We laugh at our similar thought process until it dawns on me. I can't do that to Chase. Take advantage of his friendship. He was there for me when I wouldn't allow anyone else in. He pushed through all my barriers with a battering ram and helped bring me back from the brink of despair. He's not only my best friend's husband and my friend—he's my savior.

I shake my head. "No. Nuh-uh. I won't put him in the middle. It's not fair. This is my drama. I just didn't think I'd be dealing with it again. I mean, after three years to finally come back to the way we were was more than I could have ever hoped for. Maybe I should be grateful? He did set a fire within me that night."

Maria chuckles. "Yeah, a fire between your legs. *Bastardo. Eso no es cool.* Not cool. He shouldn't have started something with you he didn't intend to finish."

I lift my hand and set my chin into my palm while leaning on the table. "Maybe I should give him the benefit of the doubt? He did try to win me back for a full year after I ended it. It was me who ended it in the first place. Perhaps this is what I deserve."

Her head jerks back. "No way. Not even. You deserve to be happy, *gatita.* I know Carson makes you happy. Honestly, even though I'm pissed at him, I still love him too. For you. You're *perfecto* together."

I sigh and look out at the park. The sun is shining and the day is free of the San Francisco fog, but there's still a brisk chill when the breeze hits. Kids are running and playing, chasing after one another. There are some college-age guys kicking a soccer ball lazily back and forth while they talk. A mother and father are holding a child's hand and lifting him up every few feet as they walk along the sidewalk. And here I sit, wondering if the man I love is with someone else.

I pull out my phone and start to type.

"What are you doing?"

"Texting him back."

Maria rubs her hands together and grins wickedly. "What

are you gonna say? You gonna call him out on his bullshit?"

I shake my head. "Nope. I'm inviting him to dinner this weekend."

She frowns. "I'm sorry. How is this getting him back for blowing you off and texting you versus calling?"

"Well, he can't blow me off if he's having dinner with me, now can he?"

She rubs her hand over her chin thoughtfully. "*Cierto.* True. I'd rather you string him up by the *cojones.*" Her grin comes back looking extra violent.

To: Carson Davis
From: Kathleen Bennett
Then have dinner with me.

I wait with my heart in my throat as the three little dots pop up. It seems as if time stops or at least slows to a snail's pace. If he denies me this one request, a simple one, I'll know it's never going to work. This is too important to me, and after what he said while making love to me, he should know the truth.

To: Kathleen Bennett
From: Carson Davis
Where? When? You know I'd walk a thousand miles...

A half laugh, half sob leaves my mouth, and I cover it with my hand. I stare at the words so long they start to blur, tears having filled my eyes.

The Proclaimers.

"500 Miles."

He said it was his song to me. Every time it played on the radio or on his CD player— sometimes on repeat, he loved it so much—he would sing at the top of his lungs, pointing to me at the appropriate parts, making sure I knew how he felt about me. Together we'd sing the *da dut da, da dut da* part very loudly, sloppily, laughing and kissing in between verses.

Maria's hand covers my scarred one. Surprisingly, I don't flinch. Instead, I accept the gesture for what it is. Comfort. Something I badly need right now from my best friend.

"You okay?"

I nod. "Yeah, I think it's going to be okay. Maybe not today, or tomorrow, but he's worth the wait, Ria. He really is. I don't know what's going on with him, but he agreed to dinner."

"That's definitely a start."

"Yes. Yes, it is."

I lift my phone and text back.

To: Carson Davis
From: Kathleen Bennett
Your place? I'll cook.

I wait a couple seconds before his response pops up.

To: Kathleen Bennett
From: Carson Davis
I'll come to you. Your place. It's where it all began...again.

I smile and type back.

To: Carson Davis
From: Kathleen Bennett
See you Friday. 6 p.m.

To: Kathleen Bennett
From: Carson Davis
I'll bring the wine.

★ ★ ★

"And how does his evasion make you feel, Kathleen?" Dr. Madison stares at me over his spectacles as if he is analyzing my body language and every subtle twitch in my gestures.

I sigh and glance out his window. Darkness has fallen, but the moon is shining brightly, painting a beautiful path of light over the bay. "Uncomfortable. Lost. Forgotten."

The threads at the end of my sweater's sleeve fray even more as I pick at them.

"Why lost?"

I close my eyes and think about the last two years. "Because I don't want to be that woman anymore."

"What woman?"

"The one who doesn't care about herself, about others. The one who just goes through the motions to get through every day. I feel like now..." I shake my head, letting the emotions bubble up until I can't keep them contained as they pour out of me like a pot boiling over. "If I have Carson, if I allow myself to focus on the good we have together, I'll be me again. The real me."

Tears prick against the back of my eyelids. My arm throbs as I clench my hands too tightly into fists, pain rippling up each limb.

"Kathleen. Look at me," Dr. Madison says in his stern but soothing tone.

I purse my lips, let the tears fall unchecked, and focus

on his gaze. His eyes are kind, gentle in a way that shows he's loveable and honest. One of the good guys in the world. Maybe even an angel sent down from God to keep guard over lost souls like me.

"You have come a long way since your injury happened. You have gone through hell. You did that. Why is it after you have one night with Carson, albeit a life-changing one, do you connect that with your own mental healing?"

I cringe and think about his words. I have spent years coming back from the trenches of grief and loss. Carson wasn't there while I fought depression, anger, and fear.

He would have been had you not pushed him away.

My psyche isn't helping.

"Kathleen, I can see that this night you spent with Carson was a turning point for you, and one I'm happy to see. However, you cannot relate the success or failure of this particular circumstance to be the scale of where you are at in your progress. Regardless of this time with him, or the outcome, you are already different. Better. Happier. Wouldn't you agree?"

Happier.

"Yes, I suppose so."

"And you're doing better in your career than you were before your injury, even though there are hurdles to overcome with the way in which you craft your designs. Correct?"

"True. Chase changed my life getting Chloe to agree to go into business with me and fronting the initial expenses, which I paid back with interest, I might add..."

Dr. Madison smiles softly and nods.

"It changed everything. I'm now doing exactly what I want to do, aside from the sewing part."

He tips his chin and crosses one leg over the other. "And

the mobility has increased in the hand. To the point you can hold small objects."

I smile huge. "Yes." I rub my forearm and hand lightly. "The oral medication and physical therapy are finally starting to work. The doctors said I'll be able to hold my own children one day without a problem."

"That's excellent, Kathleen. I'm thrilled for you."

"Thank you."

"So now tell me how you are feeling about what happened with Carson. You had dinner, too many drinks, and had intercourse."

I nod. "It was more than that, Doctor. For the first time, he said he loved me."

"And are you afraid he said those words because he was under the influence? That he didn't actually mean to say them?"

"No, not at all. I've been inebriated with Carson more times than I can count, and he never once uttered those words. This time was different. It was as if he was finally able to say it. Almost as if he couldn't not say it."

Dr. Madison makes a note on the legal pad he has on his lap. "And how was the evening leading up to that moment?"

I smile and run my hand through my hair, thinking back to the joy and laughter we had at the restaurant. The kidding way he teased me. "Like normal. Like before. He tended to me the way he did when we were dating. Women walked by, beautiful women, and he didn't even bat an eye. His focus was entirely on me."

"And what do you think changed in you? Why did you agree to have dinner with him after all this time?"

I shrug. "Maybe I'm ready to be in a relationship again?"

"Which you could have started with anyone. Instead, you went back to the one man you claim you pushed away for his own good. What changed?"

What did change?

Do I look more like the old me?

Not really. Some of the scars have been removed from my neck, but my entire right arm from shoulder to fingertips is disfigured, as is the skin around my ribcage and the side of my right breast. It's not molten red, but it's discolored and nowhere near aesthetically pleasing to the eye.

The pain is still there. The nightmares too, although now that I think back, I didn't have one when Carson was there. Then again, it could have been because he woke me for additional rounds of lovemaking in the night. It's quite possible I didn't hit REM sleep and didn't dream.

I shake my head. "I don't know."

"Kathleen..." His tone conveys that he wants me to dig deeper. "Until you accept what has changed in you, how can you accept what has changed in him? He's been living his life for the past two years. There will inevitably be things that are different about him. Probably why he's evaded talking to you since the night of your rekindling."

"You think? Chase did say he had a new girlfriend, which Carson emphatically says he doesn't. But there's definitely a woman involved. Someone who called that morning led him to run off. She has to be the reason he's not talked to me."

"Perhaps. He may be dealing with his own situation. The connection between you two came back quickly. Your entire relationship changed in a single evening. It's possible and even likely he has things he also needs to tie up in order to be free to be with you. This could mean a woman, work, friendships, family, obligations... Without talking to him, you can only guess. And that, Kathleen, is unhealthy."

I can't help but pout. "I guess I always assumed when it was time for the two of us to be together again, he'd drop everything to be with me. It's silly. The hopeful wishes of a young girl, not a thirty-year-old woman. But what we had was the forever kind of connection."

"Kathleen, you pushed him away...for years. There are repercussions from every decision we make. This one has spanned a very long time. It is likely there are things he's going to tell you that you may not like. How you deal with those admissions and move forward is what matters most."

"So, what you're saying is, don't have a knee-jerk reaction like I did when he had to run out the other morning."

Dr. Madison smiles and touches his nose. "She can be taught."

I chuckle. "After three years, I'd hope so." Without looking at him, I sigh and tap at my lips.

Is Carson the same man he was three years ago when we were together? I know I'm not the same person, as much as I want to be. What skeletons does he have hiding in his closet now? Did we even go through them when we were together? The year we were together was the best year of my life. I'd never been happier. I had a beautiful, kind, and caring boyfriend who fucked like a stallion and treated me like a queen. He worked hard, I worked hard, and then we came together each night cuddling in our own little cocoon of pleasure. When we hung out with our friends we had the best time, until Daniel McBride screwed over everyone and eventually hurt me and my friends beyond repair.

Looking back, it's hard to come to terms with why I pushed

Carson away. Sure, I felt ugly and undesirable, but mostly I was broken. Mentally, physically, emotionally. I didn't want to tie him down with a woman who could potentially be damaged the rest of her life. In my mind, he deserved better. He still does. But I forgot one little thing. One very important facet to our relationship that could never be replaced by another person.

No woman would ever love Carson Davis with her entire being the way I did. The way I do. Still. The love I have for him fills up every crevice and pore. It's the reason I couldn't be with another man after him. There could never be another man for me, because he's my other half. When I made him leave, half of me walked out with him. Died along with our relationship.

It seems so stupid now. How could I ever be me again when my other half is missing?

And does he feel the same? Did he then? Is that why he fought so hard?

Once again, the tears pour down my cheeks and drip onto my hands clasped in my lap.

"What is it, Kathleen? I can see you're hurting. Let it out."

"How can you recover when you've lost your soul mate?" I choke out the words, pushing away tears as fast as they fall.

"He's not lost. I believe he's waiting to be found."

"What if someone found him first and he's coming to tell me we can never be?"

"I don't think he would have been with you intimately, nor would he have told you he loved you. I do agree there is something standing in the way. A man in love doesn't wait days after admitting his feelings. In my experience, a man would be consumed by it. Incapable of keeping away, which means there's a reason. And I fear, my dear, the reason may be hard for you to accept."

I shake my head furiously. "No. I pushed him away. It's my fault we're not together. Mine. I need to take responsibility for what I've done, the mistakes I've made." The determination and conviction I have in this decision weaves its way up my spine, splinters out across my chest, and wraps around my heart. If it means being with Carson again, having my other half back, I'm willing to work for it. "Whatever it is that's keeping him from being by my side, I'm going to help him through it."

"Sounds like an excellent plan. And, of course, I'm here for you whenever you need to talk or work through a difficult situation. Just remember, no matter what happens, you're stronger than you ever were before. Just take things one step at a time."

"One step at a time." I can do that. And maybe, just maybe, each step will get me closer to the man I love. The man I'm willing to fight to get back.

CHAPTER TEN

CARSON

"Da-dah, da-dah, dah!" An ear-splitting squeal accompanied by a wet smack to the face wakes me instantly. I sit up, hands flying to the squirrely bundle sitting on my chest.

"Sweet baby Jesus!" I gasp and grip on to Cora's little body.

"Da-dah!" Cora head-butts me as I grab her and pull her farther up my bare chest so I can see her better.

"Hey, baby girl. What are you doing in here?" I coo at my little girl. My little girl. It's all so foreign but becoming more familiar with every passing day. I've been a dad for a solid week, and as hard as it's been, it's also been the most rewarding and fulfilling experience of my life. The only thing missing is the woman I want by my side while I experience it.

"She wouldn't stop saying your name, and she's been up for two hours already. You slept a lot later than normal, so I figured it would be okay. I hope we didn't intrude." Misty's voice comes from the chair opposite my bed.

I glance over at her, and she's leaning against the chair in a purple cotton robe with white lace around the edges that falls mid-thigh. The robe is open, giving me a perfect view of her braless breasts and tight matching nightgown. Misty toys with the string that should be tied across her waist. She walks toward the bed slow and panther-like. I hold on to Cora and snuggle her neck, my eyes still on her mother. Once she gets to my bed, she leans her bare thigh against the edge.

"Uh, I was up till three last night, working." My voice is still morning-thick and gravelly.

Misty fluffs her hair. "Oh, it's no problem. I made breakfast and kept it warm for you. A big man like you needs to eat." She runs her fingertips across the mounds of her breasts and smiles softly.

The hairs on the back of my neck start to tingle, but I shake it off. She's just being nice.

"Um, okay. That's nice of you. Thank you." I lift Cora, hold her against me, and scoot to the edge of the bed. Thank God I didn't crash naked last night. Since I've had guests, I've been wearing pajama bottoms. Not the most comfortable, but it seems appropriate, given that I've got two women in my house.

"Anything to help. You've been so good to Cora and me. I just want to return the favor any way I can."

I stand up and cuddle my daughter close. Misty places a hand to my bare chest and gets closer than I expect. I can smell her flowery perfume and clean scent overpowering my baby girl's sweet smell.

"You know you can count on me for anything you need, right?" Her fingers flutter against my breast bone before she lets them slide down the expanse of my chest to my waist, where she curls a hand around the skin there. "A man has needs. And like before, I'm more than willing to satisfy those needs. In fact, I'd love to."

When she licks her lips and her pupils dilate, I shift

our daughter in front of her and step back. "That won't be necessary. I'm never going to take advantage of you, Misty. We're strangers, I get that. Just because you're down on your luck doesn't mean you need to offer anything in return. I take care of what's mine, and Cora is my daughter. She will have all that the Davis name holds, but you never owe anything in return. You get me?"

I know my facial features turn hard, because I can feel the pressure in my brow intensifying from how hard I'm frowning.

"Um...I, uh, yeah. I get you. Just, I'm here and happy to be here. With you. As a family."

A family.

Fuck. The one thing I'd always wanted in life, my own family. Now I've got it, but it's with the wrong woman.

"I'll just go make sure your breakfast is ready to eat," she says in a rush and turns around, her robe flaring behind her as she goes.

Cora twists her fingers in my hair and tugs.

"Ouch! Baby girl." I laugh and she giggles. "What are we going to do about your mommy?"

"Da-dah!" She smacks my face, leans forward, and lays a sloppy openmouthed kiss right on my mouth, and then moves to my chin and sucks on it.

I squint through the tickling and wetness, even though it warms my heart how quickly Cora has taken to me. It's as though she's never been without her dad, and vice versa. I can't wait until Kat gets to spend time with her. She'll fall instantly in love just like I did. Kat loves her nieces and nephew from Bree and Gillian. "I just know she's going to love you too, baby girl. And teach you how to sew and make you tons of pretty dresses."

One problem being I have to tell her first. How the hell am I going to tell her that when we broke it off for good, I fucked a woman and got her pregnant, only to find out two years later I'd fathered a child? Maybe I can just thrust Cora into her arms and let Cora win her over.

"That's a good idea. You want to meet Daddy's special friend? She's the only other woman I love besides you, baby girl. One day you'll meet my Kathleen, and the two of you will be the best of friends."

I take Cora over to my closet and set her on the floor to mess up my shoes, currently all lined up. If there is anything I've learned about my daughter in a week, it's if something is in order, she's going to disrupt that order at the speed of light.

As I pull out a T-shirt, she's already got two pairs of shoes off the rack and tossed them on the floor. I shake my head and smile at my girl. She may be a handful, but she's mine.

Once I'm dressed, I scoop her up and take her to the patio. When we go into the kitchen, Misty's already got my breakfast on a serving tray and is heading toward the slider.

"Wow."

She bustles over to the patio table and sets out my meal. A cup of steaming coffee is sitting next to a plate loaded with an omelet stuffed full of veggies and what looks to be bacon, fruit, and a side of toast.

"Thank you."

"I know how you like to eat right away when you wake up." She beams and pulls out my chair.

I sit down and put Cora on my left knee so I can eat with my right hand. She immediately grabs for the coffee cup, which I move out of her grasp and exchange with a piece of toast. The toast goes right to her mouth, where she licks and gnaws, making cute little "mmm" sounds.

"Thank you. This is unbelievable." I'm talking around a bite of omelet. The egg, spinach, and cheese topped with perfectly cooked crispy bacon is a taste sensation. "You really are a good cook!" I say, happily sipping my coffee.

"I want to make you happy," Misty says and smiles, watching me eat. It's strange and sweet at the same time. I don't always know what to make of Misty and the things she says and does. We're still getting used to sharing space, but so far it's been amazing. She loves to cook and does a great job of it. Our daughter is happy and healthy. But most important, they are safe and sound where I can keep an eye on them.

"While we're both here, I have something I want to talk to you about." I shift Cora and wipe at the crumbs that have fallen on my pajama pants. Good thing we're eating outside. No additional mess.

Another thing I never planned for. Kids are messy. Seriously fucking messy. Though Misty has made sure to keep the house spic and span, even going so far as to do my laundry. The only reason I know that is because my housekeeper complained there wasn't much for her to do.

Misty frowns. "What's on your mind?"

"Well, two things. But more importantly, the issue of Cora and her name."

"You don't like the name Cora?" Her hand flies to her chest, as if she's been struck with an arrow.

I laugh and put my hand over hers. She grips on to it as though I might turn weightless at any moment and fly away.

"I love the name Cora. You can't understand how much I appreciate that her name starts with a C. It's a tradition in the Davis family."

Her corresponding smile to my statement makes me realize just how sensitive she is. I need to use kid gloves with her, more so than I thought.

"Then what's the problem?"

"I want her to have the Davis name. Are you okay with me starting the paperwork with my attorney to have her name legally changed from Duncan to Davis?"

Misty beams. A full-on, no-holds-barred, all-gums smile. "That would be amazing!" Awe fills each word.

I'm not sure why she's so excited, but I'm thrilled this request isn't a battle. Then she grabs Cora's hand. "See sweetheart, your daddy loves you so much already. He wants to give you his name. Maybe one day I'll be so lucky."

Um, wait, what did she just say? Before I can ask, she stands up and grabs my coffee cup.

"Daddy needs a refill." Misty pops up, cup in hand. She practically skips when she goes into the house.

I spend a few moments staring out at the ocean and making sure Cora doesn't choke on her toast. "I'm not quite sure what just happened here. Regardless, I'm going to focus on the fact that I get to make you a Davis, baby girl. You want that?" I turn her around, lift her up, and hold her above me. She smiles and squeals with delight.

"Dah-da!" She smashes her buttery, saliva-soaked hand against my nose. "Dah-da!"

I laugh and kiss her chubby grubby cheeks. "That's right. I'm your daddy, and soon the whole entire world will know you're my daughter. Cora Davis. It has a beautiful ring to it, don't you think?"

"I, for one, do!" Misty says, setting down my cup. "What was the other thing you wanted to tell me, Carson?"

Misty is all smiles, soft touches, and eyelash flutters. Again, against my better judgment, I shake it off to get down to business. "I have a job for you."

Her face lights up once again. "Really? Already?"

"Well, it won't start for a couple weeks, and only if you think it will be a good fit. But my father, Charles Davis, has a personal assistant who is retiring."

"I'll take it," she says instantly.

"You don't even know what it involves." I frown.

"If you say it's a good job for me, I trust you. You're the man of the house. You take care of what's yours, isn't that right?"

"Well...uh, yeah, but Misty, you're not mi—"

"And it will give me a better opportunity to get to know Cora's grandfather." She claps her hands in front of her chest. "Goodie goodie gumdrop. This is going to be so great! Me working for your dad, helping out the Davis family." Misty stands up holding her hands like a trophy in front of her chest. "You are too good to be true, Carson Davis. More than we ever could have dreamed!" She places her hands on both sides of my cheeks and smashes her lips on mine.

Before I can pull away, she's licking and kissing my lips. Her mouth comes at mine like a face-sucking hoover. While trying to hold Cora and not fall out of my chair, I attempt to push her back. She takes the gesture as a move to pull closer. I try to push my head back and tell her to stop, but the second I get an inch of space and open my mouth to tell her to stop, her tongue is inside my mouth and she's kissing the daylights out of me.

Just as I get my bearings, she pulls off, jumps up and down. "This is so exciting! I can't wait. I'll have to get new work clothes. But I'll pay you back out of my first check!"

She's running her mouth a mile a minute. I can't get a word in edgewise.

"That's not necessary. Of course, I'm happy to provide for you—"

"Because you're the best man a girl could ever have. You hear that, Cora? Daddy got Mommy a big new job. Now we'll both be contributing to the family!" She spins on her toe in a circle, her robe coming open again, flashing me a lot more cleavage than I needed to see.

I close my eyes. "Maybe you should get dressed now."

She stops in her tracks and smirks. "Oh, I see how it is. You don't want anyone else seeing what's yours. I get it." She closes her robe tight and beats feet to the slider door.

"No, that's not it at all..." But it's too late. She's in the house and down the hall to her room.

"What just happened with your mommy, baby girl?"

"Ma-ma!" she says. She shoves a handful of bacon and eggs into her mouth.

"Shit! Are you allowed to have bacon?"

I watch carefully as she chews her big bite. Fear slithers from the base of my spine and up my back as I watch my child swallow. Sweat prickles against my forehead, and I hold my breath. Finally, Cora smiles and grabs for another handful of eggs.

"Oh, no, you don't, you little sneaky sneak! How's about we hit the ocean? I feel the need to connect to the elements and wash off this strange morning. You with me?"

"Wa wa!" She points at the ocean.

"Water is right." I smile. She's so smart already. I wonder if her vocabulary is further along than the average kid. I'll have to do some research or ask Chase about it. The man seems to be a damn know-it-all when it comes to all things kid related. Punk.

I stand up and take the stairs down past the pool and to our private beach. The second I get to the sand, Cora wants down. I let her down but stay really close, keeping an eye on the water and how quickly the waves come in and out.

She plants her butt in the wet sand far enough back she shouldn't get hit by any waves and shoves her hands right into the earth.

"Good idea, baby girl. Let's build a sandcastle." If anything is going to get my mind off what I have to do tonight with Kat and the weird things Misty said today, it's building a sandcastle for the first time with my daughter.

★ ★ ★

Kathleen is a vision when she opens the door. Her golden hair shines in the track lighting over her foyer, and she bites into her lip seductively. Jesus Christ, those plump pink lips. I lose it right then and there. Before she can even speak, I push my way into her apartment, kick the door shut with my heel, and pull her into my arms. My mouth is on hers, and all I can think about right then is home. She is home. Her sunshine-and-coconut scent soothes the raging nerves I've been carrying around with me all week. She dips her head to the side and opens her mouth enough so I can playfully lick at her tongue and teeth. The little groan of frustration she gives me when I don't deepen the kiss makes me smile against her mouth. I pull away just enough to sink my nose against her shoulder and neck to inhale her goodness and light for several seconds. This. It's everything. She is my peace, my serenity. The calm after the storm. I hadn't realized how stressed and ravaged my soul felt until just now. Being in her arms, having her essence surround me, soothes all that ails the beast within.

"God, I've missed you." I let out all the air in my lungs, holding her close, molding my form to hers.

Her hands run up and down my back in a loving caress. "I missed you more."

I smile and nibble on the smooth skin of her shoulder and neck. It's not the usual side I go for, but I'm trying to connect with the side of her she's comfortable with. When I get too close to the scars, she freezes up, and I don't want that for her or me. Right now, having her freeze up on me would destroy me. As it is, a week has been too long after what happened between us last Friday.

Kat runs her hands up my back once more until she tunnels her fingers through my hair, scraping her nails lightly against my scalp. She pulls far enough back she can make eye contact. "What's the matter, Carson? This isn't like you."

Without meaning to, the smart-ass remark flies out of my mouth unchecked. "And how would you know? It's been years, Kat."

Her entire body stiffens briefly, but she holds on. She doesn't let go, push back, or run away. Now that is a first and entirely unlike her.

She closes her eyes and sighs. "I guess I deserved that."

Hating I've hurt her—again—and knowing I'm about to hurt her more has put me on edge. "No, baby. I didn't mean it. I'm sorry. There's just a lot going on. Things have happened in the years we've been apart. Some of those things are not going to be easy to talk about."

Finally, I push back and move away from her first. I turn

around and see the table already set, candles lit, fresh flowers adorning the table. A bottle of wine and glasses are already set out, the wine uncorked and breathing.

"Shit." I shake my head. "You've made a romantic dinner for two, and I was being a selfish asshole." I grind my teeth and fist my hands at my sides. I don't know how to start this conversation, and it's eating me alive. Nevertheless, she's still my Kathleen, and she's gone to a lot of trouble to make me a meal. "Let's sit and eat what you've cooked up."

A soft smile lifts the bit of sadness weighing down the initial joy I'd seen in her face when I arrived. "I made your favorite. Lasagna." She walks over to the table and pulls out a chair at the head. "Sit."

I sniff the air and am assaulted by the mix of oregano, basil, fresh sauce, and garlic. My mouth waters and my belly rumbles. "Damn, it smells so good in here. Almost as good as you." I wink.

She chuckles and her cheeks redden as she flits to the kitchen. The apartment has a roomy, open-layout feel to it. Her cabinets are bright white with glass insets and backlighting to show her dishes. The countertops are a cool gray with specks of gold, black, and glittery-looking rocks running through them. Top of the line for sure. Of course, I wouldn't expect anything less in one of my cousin's buildings.

I look around at her apartment—really look—not like last time, when I had her up against the door and then in bed, before I had to jet off in the morning. I realize how little this place suits her. Sure, she has it filled to the brim with knickknacks, framed photos, original art, comfy pillows in various earthy tones, but it lacks something I was once used to seeing. Against one corner, she has a desk full of loose drawings, fabric swatches, and books on various designers and fashion trends. That's pretty standard. Another area has a large dark-purple couch, a replacement for the beat-up one she used to have when we dated. Actually, a lot of what she had when we were together is missing from the room, including from her bedroom, now that I think about it. When I was lying with her, nothing in the room around us felt the same as it did in the past.

Then it dawns on me. She'd gotten rid of almost everything she had in her apartment from before. The art hanging on the walls is different, the furniture, the pictures scattered around the room don't contain any of us together. The photos are all of her soul sisters and their children. Even trinkets, things I'd given her during our year together, were missing in action. It was the strangest thing. As I surveyed the room, looking for a scrap of the woman I fell in love with three years ago, I couldn't find her. It's as if she didn't even live here. Like she up and left. Walked out.

That's when it hit me like a punch to the heart. She'd removed anything remotely related to me and who we were together.

And I thought her kicking me out that night three years ago hurt. But this... Finding out she willingly, painstakingly removed every trace of what we had together, of me, from her life... Gutted. There's nothing else to describe the moment when a man realizes the woman he loved, still loves, has moved on so completely there isn't a trace left. And now I've opened a small window back into her heart and her life, and I'm going to break her all over again. She'll go right back to living without me, without us. She's done it for three years. What's to say she can't or won't do it again? And it'll be even easier this time since we only have one night to go on.

Fuck.

I can't tell her about Cora and Misty. Not yet. I need more time. More time to get her to fall completely and utterly in love with me again, or I'll lose her forever. A person only gets a second chance once. This is mine, and I'm not going to ruin it before I've even had a real shot. No way.

Kat comes back into the room with big red mitts on and a glass casserole tray that smells like virtue and sin mixed together with noodles and cheese.

She sets the dish down, removes the mitts, and pours the wine. Her left hand is a bit shaky, but for all intents and purposes, she's adjusted well to not having full use of her right hand, her more dominant hand.

"Thank you."

She sits and lifts her glass. "So, what should we toast to?" Her pretty brown eyes are swirling with excitement and a hint of mischief.

"There's nothing more important than us." *And an eighteen-month-old toddler with my blue eyes and a penchant for destroying order at every possible opportunity.* Kind of like what could happen if my secret comes out too soon. I keep that last part to myself and clink glasses.

We both take a sip, and Kat hums. It reminds me of how Cora makes "mmm" and "oohh" sounds while she eats, as if every meal is a surprise.

Kat dishes out the lasagna and salad, and I dig in, not sure how to go about winning her back and keeping her in my life in such a way the devastating hit of my family-man status won't hurt so bad.

"So, tell me what you've been dealing with this past week that's kept you from being with me?"

The question hits like a hammer, so hard a chunk of lasagna slides down the wrong pipe, making me gag and choke. I suck down a huge swallow of wine, which burns like acid against the tender tissue. Serves me right for lying.

Instead of admitting the whole truth and hoping she can understand, I stick to my guns and discreetly change the subject by grabbing her right hand—the scarred one I know she doesn't prefer to have touched—and run my fingers along the top.

"How's about you tell me what you've been up to the past two years. Let's start at the beginning and work our way up to the present." *Please God, let her buy it.* A pang of guilt pierces my heart, and I rub at my chest with the hand not holding hers.

She watches the move, her shrewd mind probably picking up that I've changed the subject. Just when I think she's going to nail me on it, she surprises me.

"Well, after things ended with us..."

"You mean after you ended it," I spit out, that wound still open at the top of my subconscious. I wince. "I'm sorry, Sweetcheeks..."

She shakes her head and pulls her hand away. "No, no. Once again, I deserve it. But if this has any chance of sticking long-term, Carson, you're going to have to find a way to let go of what happened between us." Her eyes seem to plead with me.

I nod. "I'll try. For you. For us. Go ahead. Continue."

Kat sips her wine and takes a bite of her lasagna. I do the same. The second bite of spicy Italian goodness hits my tongue, and I experience the taste. I'm ravenous, shoveling it in so fast I barely chew before putting in another bite.

She chuckles and dishes me out another serving without

even asking. I look up and smile, grateful she knows me so well. At least in this.

"As you know, I was in bad shape when things ended. I went down a shitty path. I didn't want anyone's help, and it ended up taking its toll. I'm not going to go into too much detail..."

Technically, she didn't have to. Chase had been keeping me updated daily on what was going on with her. I knew about the night he found her passed out with the infection, the hospitalization when once again she had refused to see me. I even had a hand in helping Chase move her things to this apartment. Lot of good that did, since she didn't seem to keep any of it. Something I definitely want to ask about.

"Basically, after so many treatments and going it alone, I got really depressed, pushed everyone away."

I can't stop my eyebrow from rising in question.

"Yes, it wasn't just you. I didn't talk much to the girls, refused to allow them to help me."

"But you let Chase." I forced the words through clenched teeth. It's been a sore spot for me and my cousin, but I trusted him too much to think he'd ever be inappropriate with her. Not to mention Gillian would have his nuts. But it did burn like white-hot fire in my chest when I thought about all the times he'd rush off to help Kat during her time of need. I wanted to be the only one to help her through. She was my responsibility but I couldn't be there, and it fucking killed me.

She twirls a lock of her hair and purses her lips. "Yeah, he was a godsend. That man pushed and pushed until I gave in. Now, I couldn't imagine my life without his friendship. He's been a confidant, someone who was a bit blind to my situation, unlike the girls. I didn't want them to see me as weak. Still don't." She frowns.

I reach out and rub her arm. "They would never, could never, think that about you. The bond you four have is unbelievable. Something to cherish. I'm not sure why you would think they'd see you as anything but the strongest woman in the fucking world. Surviving a fire, the injury, Phillip's explosion, the kidnapping, Tommy's death." I shake my head and bring my face closer to hers. "Honey, if you look up the word survivor in the dictionary, there is a snapshot of the four of you smiling. Seriously, I've never known stronger women. And you lead the charge."

"Thank you. It means a lot you see us that way." Her big brown eyes glisten with unshed tears until she sniffs and brushes her hair from her face with a soft smile, still holding eye contact.

"You, Sweetcheeks. I see *you* that way. No matter where I am, or where you are, I've only ever seen you."

CHAPTER ELEVEN

KATHLEEN

"Enough about me." I wave my hand in the air, sit back, and cross my arms. "I know very little about what you've been up to."

Carson wipes his mouth after finishing the second piece of lasagna, leans back, and rubs a hand over his face. He looks tired, ravaged by something he's not yet sharing. It's a hard pill to swallow that the man I've never stopped loving is holding on to something painful and not allowing me to relieve his burden. It's like the ghost of our bond is knocking at the door and neither of us is capable of nor ready to open it.

"Uh, as far as work goes, I've been investing in some new endeavors. Green resources, which could affect the state of California by reducing our carbon footprint in ways we haven't yet dreamed of."

"Oh?" Environmental concerns were always something Carson and I had in common.

"Yeah, the company I'm working with is mimicking the Swedish garbage-disposal system. They have a process where they can burn the non-recyclable garbage and produce steam from the moisture content in the trash. That steam powers a turbine that creates usable energy. Best part, the smoke it emits is ninety-nine percent nontoxic. It's really quite genius."

"Seriously?" I lean my elbows on the table.

Carson nods. "Americans are the leader in energy waste worldwide. This system could decrease landfill waste by forty-eight percent in the first ten years."

The provocative lilt of Carson's voice and the passion he exudes when he speaks of a new project has an electrical buzz of energy humming low in my belly. I've always been in love with his keen mind as much his body, heart, and soul. "Wow. That's incredible. And you're funding it?"

He shrugs. "Yeah, I've invested heavily. So have Chase and my father. We've got to do something, and this plan could give our state—hell, our nation—a new plan for two major environmental problems. Waste management and energy creation."

I run my finger around the lip of my glass, thinking about how this could also benefit his bottom line if he's invested in the initial creation of this product or system. "And I'll bet a lot of Fortune 500 companies need something stellar to invest in and put their green stamp on." I smile, getting to the bonus of this genius plan he's committing to.

The smile he returns breaks from ear-to-ear. "There is that."

Carson leans back and rubs his thumb over his bottom lip. What I wouldn't give to be that lip right now. Just sitting here is making my heart beat faster, desire pool low in my belly, and arousal wet my panties.

"You always were one smart cookie," he says.

I smirk, trying to ward off this needy ache building in my system. Being this close and having knocked back a couple glasses of wine has only increased my desire for him.

"I'm just glad you and your family are finding new and inventive ways to make the environment a priority and effect real change."

He lifts the remainder of his wine in the air. "Glad you approve, Sweetcheeks."

We clink our glasses together and sip. Instantly I'm struck with how easy it is to talk like this. About anything. Aside from whatever he's holding back, Carson has always been someone with whom I can discuss the complexities of my day, share in his investments, and both of us provide real, honest, well-thought-out opinions. It's refreshing.

"I miss this," Carson says abruptly.

I narrow my gaze. "What?"

"Just being with you. Having dinner. Ending my day with an insightful discussion. It's nice. I haven't had that in a long time." He twirls the stem of the glass from left to right and back.

He takes another sip of wine, his expression thoughtful as he gazes over the rim and focuses his attention on me.

"It is nice. But why haven't you had anyone to talk to? You can't tell me you've been celibate all these years." The space around my heart tightens with the thought he's had other women while I have been celibate. It hurts, but it's a part of our past I'm not able to change. The only important point is moving forward.

Carson sighs and adjusts his seat, moving closer, his hands now resting only a few inches from mine on the table. "No, I can't say I have. But you've got to know those women were scratches for an itch. I haven't had anything serious since you."

The sincerity in his tone surprises me. It's hard to believe this man—this handsome, honest-to-God supreme catch—didn't find anyone to commit to in the last two years. He's not the kind of man who hits it and quits it. At least he wasn't when I started dating him. "Really? No one special?"

Without even blinking, he grabs my hand and runs a devilish thumb down the center of my palm. Sparks dance up my arm from my hand. I gasp and bite my lip to prevent the moan aching to get out.

"Kathleen..." Carson dips his head closer to mine so we're close enough to breathe each other's air. "What we have only happens once in a lifetime. It's not something easily replaced. Not that I wanted to. Though it would have been easier to move on if I'd been able to get over you."

I clench his hand tighter on instinct. "And did you?" My voice is but a whisper, and barely enough air leaves my lips to make sound. "Did you eventually get over me... Over us?" I swallow the dry, scratchy lump that has appeared in my throat.

Carson abruptly stands up and tugs me against his chest. I slam into him, my breasts squashed against the powerful plate of his torso. Our hips are aligned, and I can feel him thickening, growing in the space between us. Without saying a word, he tunnels one hand into my hair, the other firmly cupping my ass and lifting me so I can truly feel every inch of his rock-hard length. It's comforting to know he's just as affected by me as I am him.

Then all thoughts are obliterated when his plush lips descend, and I'm gone. Lost to the hurricane of want swirling within me. He takes my mouth with his, and I taste the deep-red wine we had with dinner and a rich essence unique to Carson. I grip the back of his hair and pull him toward me, slanting my head and forcing him to take me deeper. More.

Just more. His tongue is tireless, tasting me everywhere. I'm just as greedy, sucking and licking with equal fervor. When he pulls away in a burst of air, he delves his head into the curve where my neck and shoulder meet. He runs his tongue up the entire column. Chills rush over my skin, and I squeeze my legs together, moaning at the pleasure the simple act affords.

"I'll never be over you, Kathleen. Not in a million years. Now it's time I prove it." He bites the tender skin of my neck.

I cry out, a mix of pleasure and pain I've missed for far too long.

In one swift movement, Carson has my legs up and around his waist. He takes the handful of steps needed to reach the couch and sits me on the back. I dig my heels into his ass, pushing his erection more firmly where I want it most.

He groans and palms my thighs, moving his hands over my waist and up to my breasts for a healthy groping. "Fuck, I've missed these." He squeezes them together through my shirt until the bulk of them spill out the deep scoop of my blouse. He fingers the buttons down the front, opening just enough to access the front clasp of my lingerie. Within a second, he's got my bra open, a tit in his mouth, and is thumbing the other perfectly. I sigh and hold on, allowing every nibble, lick, and suck to send me further into orbit.

I work myself into a tizzy, grinding my clit back and forth against his jeans. The friction is perfect through the thin material of my gauzy skirt.

"You think you're gonna dry hump yourself into orgasm, pretty girl? You've got another think coming," he growls before biting down on a slippery erect tip.

I mewl and move my hips in a delicious circle. "Please..." I beg. He loves it when I beg, and I have zero shame when it comes to achieving orgasm. Hell, I'll beg all night long if it means a handful of orgasms under my belt.

He wraps both hands around my ass, firming up our connection, moves his hips in a grinding, teasing motion, and then chuckles against my neck as I shake.

"Begging already, Kat? Oh, you know how much I like that. You're going to be rewarded." He plants small, piercing bites down my neck, each one feeling like a slap to my clit before he gets to the space between my breasts, where he sucks hard against a fleshy globe. He continues this blessed suction until he pulls away, smirking and looking very satisfied with himself.

I glance down and notice the strawberry-colored mark on my left breast. Before I can chastise him for marking me, he yanks me off the back of the couch, turns me around, and bends me over it. In what feels like no time at all, he's got my skirt up to my waist, my panties down around my ankles, and my ass cheeks in his hands.

"Jesus Christ, still the best fucking ass I've ever had the pleasure of touching." He runs both palms from top to bottom, where he squeezes the curve, digging his fingers in roughly. "I can't wait to fuck you here again, but not tonight."

While I step out of the panties, he pushes up my shirt and licks a trail from my tailbone up the small of my back. He may be able to see the scars from here but not too much. Not enough for me to stop what's he doing.

The sounds of him removing his shirt, fussing with his pants, and pulling down his zipper are almost as loud as the excited bursts of air leaving my lungs.

"Not going to wait. Gonna take you right here while looking at these awesome sweetcheeks!" He runs his hands down my ass again before tapping my ankle with his foot, forcing me to widen my stance.

Without warning, he cups my sex possessively, four of his fingers playing in the wetness he finds. "Always soaked for me. Do you think anyone else can get you this hot?" he murmurs in awe against my back.

I shake my head furiously. "No. No. Only you."

"Only me. And that's how it's going to stay, isn't it, Sweetcheeks? My pussy to touch, kiss, lick, and fuck. Isn't that right?"

His words are like kerosene on a fire. Lighting me up in a blaze of desire. "Please..." I urge.

"Back to the begging. Fuck yeah." He inserts two fingers deep into my slit.

The initial thrust of being filled by anything other than my battery-operated boyfriend is mind-numbingly good. My sex clenches automatically, wetness coating my outer lips with arousal. "Oh! God..." I let out the breath of air I'd been holding while shamelessly bucking into his touch. "Yes!"

"That's it, Kat. Ride my hand, pretty girl. Show me how much you like me touching you."

Greedy for more, I push back into his hand, bracing on the couch so I can maneuver to fit how I need him, tipping my hips up and back in a motion that will get me off fast. He plays me like an expert pianist, tickling and hammering my insides, making me moan and cry out in sheer ecstasy. It's always, *always* been this phenomenal between us. Mouthwateringly good each and every time.

Carson hums in the back of his throat and presses his dick against the crease of my ass. He's hard, thick, and weeping at the tip. I push back, wanting to jerk him and rub against his flesh. Touch him wherever I can.

He digs his fingers deep, powering in and out of me like he has something to prove. Whatever it is, I'm on board. With each plunge of his fingers, I push back harder. He's as deep as he can get with his hand, which makes me ache for his long cock.

"More..." I plead.

"You're gonna get more. So much more. But not until I say," he warns before the stinging smack of his hand brands my ass. Before I can truly register the pain, he spanks the other cheek and then the first again, alternating back and forth a few times. "Fuck this ass! Turning so pink. Marked by my hand." He crushes his dick into the crevice of my ass and dips those fingers high within me. The simmering heat around where he spanks me only adds to the ecstasy I'm going to feel when I finally soar.

I cry out when he spanks each cheek one more time, the burning skin of my ass and the warring orgasm coalescing into one another. Shivers erupt along my skin, and my blood rushes scalding hot through my veins. "Yes, oh yes. I'm going to come." I gasp once, the only warning that my world is imploding.

Just as the first tightening of my orgasm starts, he pulls his fingers out. I scream at the loss, needing him with every ounce of my being, ready to fight, beg, barter, and steal to have it back. But Carson is right there, and I didn't have to fear, because in a flash I'm jammed full of thick, hard, pulsing cock.

My mouth opens but no sound comes out, my pussy spasming around his length in vise-like pulses.

"There it is. Squeeze my dick. Fuck, it's so good." He whips my blouse over my head and my loose skirt follows it. Then he wraps me up with his strong embrace so that I'm hung up on his cock, my feet leaving the floor and my fingers just barely resting atop the back of the couch. His arms are around my waist and chest as he nuzzles my neck, breathing against it in harsh pants and gusts of air like he's run a marathon. I can't breathe or think. I can only feel. Feel his cock split me open wide, the root stretching the lips of my sex to the maximum point where the tiny burn adds to the overwhelming fullness.

The orgasm continues to wash over me, shaking me to my core until he rests me back on my feet, bends me completely over, pulls almost all the way out, and then slams home. A supernova explodes, ratcheting my pleasure to an entirely new plane of existence.

Carson burrows his hand between my chest and the couch, where he wraps his open hand around my neck, forcing me to stretch my neck out to his possessive embrace. His face is planted against my sweaty back, where he places a few tender kisses. "Gonna take you so hard you'll never ever think there's a possibly of getting over us," he promises before wrapping his other hand around my hip, pulling back, and ramming home.

He moves at a punishing rate of jabbing thrusts and succulent withdrawals. I'm in an effervescent sex haze as he contorts my body this way and that, ensuring maximum penetration.

The sex is raw, life-affirming, and messy as hell. I can feel drops of his sweat fall onto the small of my back as he fucks me harder than he ever has. I'm so lost in the ramming pleasure I don't even question it when he lifts my thigh up on the couch back so he can plow deeper. It's only when I swear he fucks my soul that I realize I'm crying, tears falling to my bare breasts. I'm stripped physically, emotionally...in every way possible. He's touching me everywhere, all the places that are his, or were his before, and are now his again.

The wet sounds of the plunge and pull of his sex seeps into the air around us, a delectable carnal melody. Carson ruts deep, making animalistic sounds, his pace becoming frantic and disorganized. Just the thought of him losing himself in me causes my clit to throb for attention. I run one hand down the front of my body and find the slippery nub, swirling it to the beat of each thrust.

"You're so beautiful, Kathleen." He runs a hand up my scarred ribcage, over my breast, and down my shoulder and along the abraded tissues of my arm. The tears fall in rivulets, as unstoppable as this life-changing moment. "I'm going to make you see this body the way I do. Beautiful. Sexy. And the only one I want to touch for the rest of my life."

The tears turn into pleasured sobs as he tilts his hips, hits the spot inside that defies all reason, and holds there, a battle cry of his own shooting from his lungs. The wide crown of his cock burrows deep inside, sending me into another tailspin of euphoria. He digs his fingers into my flesh as I scratch his thighs, forearms, and whatever I can reach as wave after wave of heaven batters us both into jerking, gut-wrenching rapture.

Eventually Carson slumps over my back, loosening his grip on my breast and thigh and kissing my sweat-dampened skin with soft, lazy presses of lips to flesh wherever he can reach.

"Together"—he lets out a long breath—"together, we've always been able to obliterate our surroundings and get lost in one another. Relieved to see that part of us hasn't changed."

I lick my dry lips and smack my chops. "Yeah, huh," is all I can muster, my brain so scrambled by what felt like two never-ending orgasms. Even my limbs feel like jelly. It's like my body has been hibernating for two years and has just returned from frolicking out in the sun after such a long respite.

Carson chuckles against my back and then slowly moves back. A combination of both our fluids starts to leak down my leg.

"Jesus fucking hell, that's hot."

I sigh and lift from my position hanging over the couch. "No, it's gross."

"Gross hot," he confirms.

"That's not a thing." I sashay as best I can down the hall to my en suite bathroom.

"It is a thing. It's a guy thing." He follows close behind.

"How are sex fluids a guy thing?" I flick the shower on and step into the tiled space. Carson removes his jeans, underwear, socks, and shoes. Damn, he looks like a golden god against the white tiles. I hum when I step in, and the water hits my chest and face before his heat hits my back. How did I go so long without this body pressed up against me in a shower? It feels like sacrilege now.

"You just said it." Both arms come around to embrace me from behind in a sensual hug. "Sex fluids. Ask any guy. The words sex and fluids in any conversation grabs their interest."

I push my wet hair back, ensuring it slicks against my scalp. "But how is it a hot thing?"

"Uh, sex and fluids. I'm not quite sure why this is a hard concept for you to grasp." His hands run up my sides and cup my breasts, and his hardening dick presses against my ass once more.

"Speaking of hard things to grasp?" I raise an eyebrow, lean back so he can kiss me, and insert my hand between our bodies where I can get a good handle on the pressing situation. "How can you be ready again? I mean, we just finished two seconds ago."

"Twenty seconds." He sucks the skin of my neck as I tug on his cock, wrapping my hand more firmly around it.

"Twenty seconds, then." I spin around and press his body against the tile wall. "That's still a fast recovery."

He grins and cups my head and my ass. "Sweetcheeks, I've been without you for too long. My dick even feels it." He pushes my body back a little so he can watch me jack him. "See, he's even weeping for you."

I laugh and lean into his chest. "So cheesy!"

He chuckles, which quickly turns into a moan as he relaxes against the tile. "Shit, Kat. I'd give just about anything to have your lips wrapped around my cock right now." That's one of the things I've always loved about Carson. He never shied away from asking for what he wanted, whether it was his preference for dinner out, a movie, or what he needed in bed. I never had to guess with him.

"Really? Anything?"

He grins, probably remembering the game we used to play for sexual favors.

He bites down on his plush bottom lip, and I kiss it away, sucking it into my mouth, mimicking what I could be doing to his cock right now. "Anything?" I ask him.

He sucks in a breath through his nose, his nostrils flaring. "Fucking anything." He curls a hand around my shoulder and presses down to get me to my knees.

I grin wickedly, grab the washcloth hanging over the rack, and put it under my knees for comfort. "It's going to cost you."

Carson's eyes are wild and have darkened with lust. Water drips down his nose and lands on the tip of his dick. I flick my tongue and lap at the droplet. He groans. "No price is too high."

I quirk an eyebrow, open my mouth, and suck just the tip in, swirling my tongue around the wide, knobbed head, and then let it go with an audible pop. "You sure?"

"Name your price, hellion." His fingers burrow into the wet strands at my nape, and he grips them tight.

"Breakfast tomorrow..."

"Done." He pulls my head closer.

I pull back. "And coffee."

"Fuck yes." He tries to bring me closer.

"In bed." I lean a little closer to where he wants me most.

"Fine."

I back up one more time. "And you have to serve me, all while naked."

His eyebrows rise in surprise. "Deal." He grins, and that grin turns into a pained hiss as I suck him down my throat in one big swallow. "My God, Kat. No one sucks cock like you."

I smirk and double my efforts.

CHAPTER TWELVE

CARSON

Warmth surrounds me from the tip of my toes to the top of my chest. The welcome weight of pure naked woman is sprawled over my body. I run my hands up the inches of bare flesh. My fingers encounter a few pebbled areas where I hug her across her back, my hands landing on her ribs. As I open my eyes, I'm greeted by deep amber pools of hot lava. In the morning light, her normally caramel-brown gaze has turned to a fiery crimson color.

God, I've missed this. Missed her.

"Morning, Sweetcheeks," I grumble, my voice not quite awake.

She nuzzles her face right over my heart and kisses me there several times. My Kat was never a morning talker. More a doer. I can remember countless mornings when I'd wake with my girl's lips firmly wrapped around my cock in greeting. Best way to wake up. Though having a Kathleen blanket wrapped around me is a close second.

"Hmm." She sighs, her lashes fluttering closed as though she's soaking in the moment. I know I am. With every damned breath I take.

"Nothing like seeing the woman I love, naked and sated after a night of sensational fucking." I embrace her warmth, wrapping my arms and legs around all the lusciousness that is my woman.

Kat chuckles and lifts her head, resting her chin on my chest. "I'll concede to the great fucking," she murmurs, a pretty flush pinking her cheeks. The woman let me fuck her six ways from Sunday last night, and she can still flush like an innocent schoolgirl. So many layers to my Kat.

"I believe I said sensational." I grip her ass with both hands and rub my hardening length against her.

She groans. "No, stop it. You fiend!" She sits up, resting her bare flesh against my lower stomach instead of where I want her. "You broke my vagina last night. Poor thing needs a rest." Her bare chest rises and falls, her coral-pink tips puckered tight in the morning chill.

In this light, I can see all of her. Everything she's tried to hide since her injury. "Honey..." I whisper as I run my fingers over her right shoulder, down the side of her scarred ribcage and breast.

Instantly, she moves to cover it, but I grip her hands and bring them down. "Let me see. Let me love all of you." I choke down the grit coating my words. She's the only woman besides my mother I've ever loved. And now, more than ever, as she bites her lip, firms her chin, and drops her arms to her sides, I love her more than anything I can comprehend. Her strength, determination, and insecurities are glaring, but she's breathing through it. Allowing me to see this side of her. The side she doesn't want anyone to see.

Slowly, I lift my hands again, wanting—no, *needing*—to make her understand she is no different to me. Is her skin marred? Yes. Does it disgust me? Not even close.

"Kathleen...these scars"—I run just my fingertips over her shoulder and down her side, where I curl my hand around her small ribcage—"they prove you're alive." I lean up and push us both back so she's sitting in my lap and I'm leaning against the headboard. Moving with intent, I bring my face closer to her shoulder, the same one I used to lick, bite, and nibble during sex. Pulling her closer to me, I press my lips to the tortured flesh. She gasps and I close my eyes, allowing her the time she needs to get used to this touch.

With more purpose, I curl my left arm around her back and cup her nape, forcing her to look at me. Tears are dripping down her cheeks. I kiss them away as I take my right hand, place it on her shoulder, and with a firm grip run my hand down every inch of her scarred arm before I intertwine our fingers and bring her hand up between us. She opens her eyes. They are full of unshed tears and so filled with grief and sorrow I want to look away. But I can't. She needs me to be strong during her moment of weakness.

I bring her hand to my lips. Her eyes narrow on me as I kiss each fingertip, the top of her puckered flesh, and the center of her palm. "I love every fucking one of these scars, Kat, because they mean you're alive. You're here with me. Right here, and you're never fucking going anywhere."

Her voice cracks as she opens her mouth and the tears fall. My God, how they fall. "I love you," she says between sobs before kissing me. Both of her hands are in my hair, tugging me close. Her legs tighten against my sides as if she wants to burrow into me. "I'm sorry, Carson. I'm so sorry I pushed you away," she chokes out between deep presses of her mouth to mine.

I take every kiss and lick every tear away. They're mine now, just as she is.

"Kathleen"—I cup her face and lift her chin with my thumbs—"it's over. From here on out, it's me and you. Everything else we'll brave together."

She swallows and licks her kiss-swollen lips. "Together."

★ ★ ★

"Damn, woman, you can cook." I'm stuffing my mouth full of another huge bite of waffles smothered in peaches. I'm already on my second waffle and feel like I could hammer back two more.

Kat snickers, leaning against the counter on the other side of the kitchen, wearing nothing but a camisole and a pair of the tiniest sleep shorts known to man. I can't say that I'm bothered by them, because every time she turns around and bends over just a hair, I can see a sweet slice of cheek. And I've always been an ass man when it comes to my woman.

"Would you like more?" she asks over the rim of her coffee.

I suck in a big breath, lift my arms to the sky, and stretch. Her eyes watch every movement with such intensity I can almost imagine her tracing every inch of my bare chest with her tongue.

"Keep looking at me like that and you're gonna get yourself fucked on top of your kitchen counter."

She pouts, but one sexy eyebrow lifts as if she's thinking about it.

I rub my hand down my bare chest and slap my belly. "I think I could eat one more." I grin. "Even though I was supposed to be making you breakfast in bed. Guess I'll have to do that next weekend."

She laughs and shakes her head before putting down her coffee mug and sashaying over to the waffle iron. With the skill only years of practice can manage, she sprays the iron, pours more batter, flicks the lid down, and gets another carb-loaded batch of heaven ready for her man.

"So, what's your plan for the day?" she asks.

It's Sunday, and normally I'd plan to hole her up in her apartment and keep her naked all day, but I've already been away from home all night. Which reminds me, I turned my phone off when I got here. I wanted nothing between Kat and me last night. I'm so glad I did. We made a huge breakthrough when it came to her scars and our relationship. Now I just need to get over the hump of telling her about Cora.

Guilt whistles through my body like an ice-cold breeze on a hot day. I step off the stool and find my jacket, plucking out my phone.

"Uh, don't know my schedule just yet." I go the cryptic route, not wanting to cause any suspicion.

Fuck, I hate lying to her. A lie of omission is still a lie, and this one is a whopper.

I power up my phone. "Need to check some things. What's your plan?" My phone comes to life. And when I say it comes to life, I mean angry dings sound off as text message after text message assault my phone. Then come the dings of voicemails. Five to be exact. Five fucking voicemails and fifteen text messages. All from one number. Misty.

"Fuck!" I growl and scan the first set of messages.

Where are you? I have dinner warm in the oven waiting.

We're going to eat without you. ☹

I guess you're not coming home for dinner. Cora misses her daddy. Me too.

It's two in the morning. I'm worried. Cora isn't feeling well. Cora's been throwing up all night. Where are you?

"Jesus Christ!" I run my hand through my hair and start pacing as I see the next set.

Cora's really sick. We need you.

Come home. Please. I don't know what to do. She wants her daddy.

Carson. I'm scared.

Carson. Cora needs to go to the emergency room.

Carson! Where are you? Please, please, come home!

The once scrumptious waffles now lie like lead in my stomach. A set of hands falls against my bare back.

"Hey, hey, hey. Babe, what's wrong? What is it?"

I swallow. "She's sick. I gotta go. I gotta go right now," I say with more force, shaking off her touch and searching for my shirt. Once I find it, I tug it on, slip on my shoes sans socks. I don't have time to find my fucking socks.

"Who's sick? What's going on?" Kathleen's voice cracks as I clutch my keys with such force, the metal cuts into my palm.

"I'm sorry. I can't talk about this right now. I need to go!" My voice is practically a roar as I grip the handle for the door.

Kathleen grabs the door, pushes it shut, and slams her palm against my chest. "Carson, don't do this to me again. Fucking talk to me!" Her voice is as sharp as her gaze. She's pissed and hurt at the same time, but there's nothing I can do to fix it right now.

I tug her to me and kiss her hard. Once is all I can handle or I'll lose myself in her again. Instead, I grip the door and pull it open. "Baby, trust me. I'll call you later."

And I'm out the door.

"Carson! Carson!" she yells as the elevator doors close out the sound of her voice.

★ ★ ★

The tires of my car screech against the pavement as I jump out of my truck and take the stairs to my house two at a time. I open the door and instantly hear them. Cora's cries rip through the walls of my home. I follow the sound.

"It's okay, baby. It's okay. Daddy will be here soon. He will. He loves you," Misty says against Cora's temple.

I enter the room with heavy feet. "What's wrong with my daughter?" I reach for her. She's clad only in a diaper, but her little arms cling to me as I pull her against my chest. Her crying starts to settle down into a low whine of whimpers once she's against my chest.

"Where have you been?" Misty's voice is tinged with an anger I haven't heard from her before. "I've been up all night, taking care of our sick daughter. And where were you? Huh? Nowhere to be found!"

I ignore her rant and kiss my baby, focusing all my attention on her. Her little body is hot as Hades. "You don't feel good, baby girl?" I place kiss after kiss on her face. She stuffs her thumb into her mouth and nuzzles against my chest. "Why is she so hot?"

"Because she has a fever. I haven't been able to get it to break all night. Not that you care."

I grit my teeth and try to be calm. She's upset and unraveling because Cora's sick. "Have you given her any medicine? Gillian told me last week when she brought both medicines that we should alternate Tylenol and ibuprofen. It will take a fever down quicker. I'll call her."

"I gave her Tylenol every four hours. Alone. While you were out gallivanting around with God knows who and your daughter was at home sick!" Misty is positively seething. Her face is pinched and red, her lips a tight white line. Even her chest is heaving up and down as though she's a bull ready to charge.

"Why don't you go and take a shower. I've got this. We'll talk later."

She crosses her arms over one another, pushing her breasts up, baring more than I want to see of her tits. "Were you with another woman?"

Another woman? What the ever-loving fuck?

"Yeah, Misty. I was with a woman. *My woman.* Everything happened rather quickly and I didn't get a chance to mention Kathleen. I don't even know if you have a man in your life. If you haven't noticed, we've spent the last two weeks learning to live together and take care of our daughter."

Her eyes fill with unshed tears. Again... What the fuck?

"You...you...you have a girlfriend?" Her voice shakes and her bottom lip trembles.

I sigh. Kathleen is so much more than my girlfriend. She's my fucking soul mate. My everything. "Yeah, you could say that."

"I could. I just did." She purses her lips and firms her chin.

"Look, go take a shower. I'm going to call Gillian about Cora. She seems fine other than the fact that she's hot and you said she was vomiting. When was the last time she vomited?"

"A couple hours ago."

"And the Tylenol. When did you last give it to her?"

Her eyes narrow. "Just after that. After I cleaned her up for the hundredth time. *Alone.*" On that note, she spins around and stomps off toward the shower.

I take a few slow, deep breaths, reining in my frustration. She's just angry because she had to go it alone. But she's done that for almost two years without me. I shake my head, not letting myself think those thoughts. It will just send me into a bigger tailspin of guilt than I'm already in.

Cora mumbles something and I look down. My sweet girl is asleep on my chest, but her skin is startlingly hot. I pick up the house phone and dial my cousin's line.

"Good morning. Davis residence."

"Hi, Summer. It's Carson. I need to speak with Gigi. Is she available?"

"Yes, Mrs. Davis is in the family room with the kids. One moment."

With my precious bundle sleeping soundly, I take a seat in the living room on the sofa. Cora snuggles more deeply, her thumb falling out of her mouth, a little drop of saliva clinging to her lip. I run my knuckle against the spot and rub it on my pant leg, and then I resume caressing her back in soothing strokes, doing what feels most natural. Man, I wish Kathleen were here. She'd know what to do. She's very active in her nieces' and nephew's lives. Plus, she's a natural nurturer.

"Hello?" Gigi comes on the line, sounding more chipper than I could muster.

"Hey, Gigi, I need advice. Cora's sick."

"Oh no. What's the matter with my sweet niece?"

"She's hot. Really hot. Misty gave her Tylenol two hours ago, but she said she's been throwing up all night."

"How many times?" she asks.

I lick my suddenly dry lips and breathe out. "I don't know. I, uh, wasn't here. I was with Kat last night."

A dead silence greets me.

"Gillian, don't. Please. I need your help with Cora."

She makes a sound like she's letting all the air out of a tire. "You haven't told her, have you?"

"No. But I'm going to. I swear it. Just, please, help me with Cora."

"Well, first you need to take her temperature. Did Misty do that?"

"I don't know. She's in the shower, but I saw the thermometer on the counter. Just walk me through it."

Gillian tells me how to set the thermometer and run it across my daughter's forehead in one swoop. I feel like a hero when I'm able to do it without waking her up.

"It's says one oh three point one. That's bad, right?" Isn't the normal human temperature ninety-eight point six? That means my daughter is over four degrees hotter than that. "Gigi, tell me my baby is going to be okay?" Now I sound desperate.

Fuck. I should have been here.

"No, no, no. It's okay. Is she teething?"

I remember Misty telling me yesterday she could feel some new teeth coming in. "Yeah. Yeah, she is."

"Okay, it's probably that. What you need to do is give her some ibuprofen, and then you need to cool her body down."

"How do I do that?"

"She needs to be submerged in lukewarm water for a while."

"What if she starts screaming again?" I sound like such a useless asshole.

Thank God Gillian takes pity on me. "Then get in with her. Chase normally gets in the shower with the twins if one of them is feverish. They want to be in their daddy's arms. Makes them feel safe and loved."

Shower. Okay. Got it.

"Thank you, Gillian. I owe you."

"Just take care of my niece. I'll call later to check on you guys."

I hang up the phone without even saying goodbye. With one hand, I fill the dropper with ibuprofen and then rouse Cora just enough to get her to swallow the medicine. She takes it like a champ. The poor thing is exhausted, lolling her little head against my chest. Misty still hasn't gotten out of the guest shower, so I'm on my own.

Once I get to my room, I ease Cora onto my bed and strip off my clothes, leaving my boxers on. Then I rush to the bathroom and set the shower. I remove her diaper and pull her against my bare chest. Once I've got her situated, I bring her into the shower. She wakes instantly and starts crying.

"Shh, shh, shh. It's okay, baby. I've got you. Daddy's here. We need to get you cool, honey."

Her tears subside and she flattens her cheek against my chest. There is no feeling like this. Being someone's entire universe. Having them trust you to care for them completely. It's humbling and makes me fall even more in love with my daughter.

"What are you doing?" Misty opens the shower door, and

Cora startles momentarily but nestles her head back down, allowing the barely warm water to cool her hot skin.

"I'm cooling her off. Gigi says we need to get her temp down. I gave her some ibuprofen too."

Misty's eyes widen. "You did? By yourself?"

"Yeah, by myself. She's my daughter. I can handle this. Now can you please shut the door? It's making her shiver. Good news is, I can feel it working. She's cooling down."

Misty blinks a few times, tilts her head, and looks at me from head to toe...slowly. For a moment, her eyes darken. I know that look. I made sure to see it as many times as I could last night when I had Kathleen under me. Lust. Pure, unbridled desire.

"Misty. The door. She's cold."

She shakes her head and closes the door without a word.

I cup my daughter's head, making sure water runs over her crown but not her face. After about ten minutes, I can feel the heat seeping out of her limbs. She doesn't seem as warm. Thank God.

Trying not to jostle her too much, I turn off the water and open the shower door. Misty is standing there with a towel, ready to grab Cora.

"I'll take her and put a onesie on her."

"Thanks. I want to lie down with her," I say, needing to be near her right now. The instinct to hold and protect is fierce. Nearly uncontrollable.

Misty nods and leaves the bathroom. I put on a pair of pajama pants without a shirt. Cora likes to rest on my bare chest. I pull back my covers and get in. Misty brings Cora in with a sippy cup of pink-colored liquid.

"What's in the cup?"

"Pedialyte. She needs fluids." She sets Cora on my chest, and I wrap my arms around her and take the cup from Misty.

I nod. "Okay, I'll make sure she gets it. Can you give us some time alone?"

Her lips tighten and her shoulders seem to rise before falling with what I can only assume is defeat. "Yeah. I'll be in the other room resting. I didn't get any sleep last night." She turns around briskly, and I feel like such a shit.

"Hey, Misty," I call out.

She stops at the threshold to my door. "What?"

"I'm sorry I wasn't here. We're going to have to talk about Kathleen and how she fits into all of this." I gesture to the bed and my girl grabbing for her cup, now awake and thirsty as the dickens.

She huffs. "Her name is Kathleen, huh? Honestly, Carson, the simple answer... She doesn't fit in."

That's the last thing she says before shutting my door and leaving me alone with Cora.

I sigh and get Cora situated so she can lean against me and drink her juice. Her fever seems to have gone down, but she's not perfectly cool just yet. Once her juice is half gone, her blue eyes start to droop and she only sucks from her cup every few seconds until she doesn't at all.

Making sure not to disturb her, I gently pull the cup out of her mouth and set it on the nightstand. Then I prop my little girl over my chest the same way I had Kathleen just this morning. Two totally different scenarios, both equally precious.

I rub a hand down her hair and back. "How am I going to tell Kathleen about you? Huh, Cora? I know she'll just love you to pieces, but getting over the shock of you is going to be a battle. One I'm not ready to handle. You see, I want her to be so far gone for me that she can't push me away again. Us. So she can't push us away."

Cora's eyelids move back and forth as she enters a deep sleep. Her hand is splayed out over my chest, her head on my heart. Just where I want her.

With my little one wrapped in my arms, I close my eyes and dream of beach dates with Cora and Kathleen, dinners on the patio, waffles and peaches, and the most beautiful life. Together.

Until I'm rudely awakened two hours later by the doorbell ringing.

It dawns on me in my sleep-deprived brain that there are only a handful of people who have the PIN code to the gate out front. Mostly all members of the family. It could be Chloe, Cooper, or worse, my father. None of them have met Misty or Cora, but I did tell my dad what happened, especially since he's going to hire Misty to be his personal assistant. He promised to give me time to connect with Cora and settle in before he intruded. That leaves my siblings. Or... No. Fucking no. She wouldn't come here. Would she?

A sliver of fear trickles up my spine and wraps around my chest. It's exactly what she'd do to try to get to the bottom of why I left so abruptly. Not once but twice. Fuck!

Please God, don't let it be Kathleen.

CHAPTER THIRTEEN

KATHLEEN

Sometimes in life, people have out-of-body moments that shock them straight down to their core. The ability to move is gone. Each breath is harder to drag in than the last. Stars blink and fizzle like a halo of Christmas lights in their peripheral vision. Then, slowly, the ability to function comes back, yet speech is practically impossible.

"Who are you?" A petite blonde with messed-up, just-fucked hair, sharp dark-brown eyes, and tits the size of cantaloupes greets me at Carson's door. I know their size because they are on full display under a miniscule cotton teddy with a matching robe that's hanging wide open.

I blink a few times, take a few steps back, and look up at the house. Carson's house. Yep, still his house.

"I'm, uh, here to see Carson." My voice doesn't even sound like my own as the air pushes past my lips.

The woman narrows her eyebrows and purses her lips. She nonchalantly quirks her head over her shoulder. "He's in bed. Had a long night." Her voice lowers in timbre, echoing a deep, more sultry sound.

What in the world is this woman suggesting? That he's

been with her all night when I know for a fact he was with me? And yet, here she stands, scantily dressed in the entryway to Carson's home, making no effort to invite me in.

"Yeah, I know. He was with me," I spit out, venom coating every word, ire rising heavy in my chest.

She sets a hand on her hip and juts her tits out like a shield, putting those fake melons on display like a stripper standing in front of man holding up a handful of twenties.

"So, you're the homewrecker."

Homewrecker.

Homewrecker?

Home. Wrecker?

I open my mouth but no words come out. The woman sizes me up from my loose flowy skirt to the tank and cardigan I'm wearing. She notices my scarred hand and her eyes squint enough to punch me out of my funk.

"Who the hell are you?" I demand.

She crosses her arms, pushing her tits up to maximum height, and leans into the doorjamb. "I'm Misty. The lady of the house and the mother of his child."

Lady of the house.

Mother of his...

Just as the words hit me like a sledgehammer to the face, Carson comes around the corner from the hallway that leads to his bedroom. He's wearing a pair of pajama pants and nothing else. His hair is also mussed, but that's not what freezes me to the concrete where I'm standing. No, it's the blond-haired, blue-eyed toddler cuddled against my man's chest that makes ice coat my heart and soul.

"Carson..." I whisper, my eyes glued to the child with the most startlingly familiar baby blues. I'd know those eyes anywhere. I've looked into them countless times and confessed my love. Did so again just this morning as I bared my body and soul to him.

"Misty, hold her." He hands the toddler over to Misty as if he's a professional at caring for a child.

Carson, with a baby.

His baby.

Her baby.

Not mine.

I step back and stumble down the stairs, shaking my head. "No, no, no. This can't be. What is happening?" I put both hands into my hair and turn around, not capable of looking at the visual of the three of them together, one happy family.

Carson's arms come around me from behind. "Kathleen, it's not what it looks like." His voice is desperate against my ear.

The words rip through my consciousness, bringing out the lioness ready to kill.

I spin around in his arms and back up so he can't touch me. "Then what is it, Carson?" I point to the entryway, where, thankfully, the door is shut and Misty and their baby are no longer visible. "You have a family! A fucking *family*. My God...I can't even..." My footing falters as I head toward my car, but I catch myself. No fucking way am I staying here.

Carson is one step ahead, even in his bare feet. "They are not my family... Well, technically Cora is. But you don't understand. I need to explain." He holds on to my biceps, keeping me in place.

"No, you need to let me go!" I yell directly in his face.

He overpowers me in a few steps, pushing me back against my car, towering over me and caging me in. "I'll never let you go again. Didn't we decide that just this morning? It's us. Together. Facing all odds."

I swallow and my eyes fill with tears. "That was before... before I found out your fucking secret. How long have you been cheating on her? And my God. Blond hair, brown eyes? You've definitely got a type!" I sob and push against him.

"Yeah, I do have a type. You. Only you. I'm not with Misty."

I lean harder against the car behind me, not wanting any part of him touching me. It's too much. Too everything. "Really? She's wearing a nightie in your house and holding your daughter. My God, Carson. You have a daughter. Not *our* daughter. *Your* daughter!" The emotions come barreling out in a heap of sadness and loss. "You. Have. A. Child!" I choke on the words, each one of them shredding my very soul to pieces.

Carson cups my head and holds my chin so I can't move away. I'm forced to watch his beautiful blue eyes swirl with regret. "Yes. I do. And I just found out about it less than a month ago."

I sniff and wipe at my nose, not understanding what he's saying. "What?"

"Will you talk to me? Let me get some clothes on. Come in and talk? Please."

I jerk my head back. "With that woman here? Prancing around like your wife? I don't think so."

He sighs and leans his forehead against mine. "She's not my wife. She's not anything other than the mother of my child. I swear it. I'll explain everything, if you'll just come in."

I shake my head, my heart breaking with every breath.

"Please. Please. Don't push me away. Not after this morning. Last night. Last week. Kat, baby, I'm begging you to hear me. See me. Trust me."

Trust me.

That's what he said when he left my apartment this morning and ran home to this woman and his daughter.

I close my eyes, a traitorous tear slipping down. Carson's lip covers my cheek and kisses it away. I moan in agony at his touch, the simple press of his lips to my flesh. I want nothing more than to drown in him. Hug him and make it all go away... but I can't.

"I'll take all your tears. Happy or sad. They're mine. You're mine. And I'm yours. Don't throw us away before I've had a chance to explain."

"Carson."

"No, Kathleen. I'm not letting you leave here, leave *me*, until you've heard every word of what I have to say. You owe me that. Please."

And I do owe him that. I pushed him away two years ago with everything I had in me. If anything, I deserve to sit through what I can only imagine is going to be a horrifying tale of him falling in and out of love with another woman before coming back to me.

I can't control my lip trembling or the tears from falling at the sheer visual that image presents. My worst nightmare come to life...and I've seen a lot of shit. Went through more with my soul sisters. But this? This has the power to destroy me forever.

"Trust me." He whispers the words against my lips. "Just trust me." He presses his lips to mine, and I can't help but kiss him back. I'm incapable of not reacting to his touch, and with this kiss, he pours himself into it unlike any other. His lips, teeth, and tongue are ravenous, desperate. I'm no better. Kissing him as though it's our last, like we might never see one another again, and depending on what he has to say, that could very well be the truth.

When we both can't breathe, he pulls away, sucking in air, his bare chest moving rapidly against my palm where I've laid it over his heart. His skin is cold to the touch, and I realize he must be freezing, standing out in the chilly midmorning air with no shoes, socks, or shirt to ward off the cold.

"You need to go inside. You're freezing."

"I'd stand in a fucking ice storm in Alaska if it meant I'd come out of it with you by my side."

"Carson." I lean forward and wrap my arms around his bulk.

He burrows his face into my neck. "Will you come inside? Let me explain?"

I can't deny him this one request. He needs it. Hell, I need it, or I won't be able to move on one way or the other. I nod against his chest.

"Okay. Come on. We'll talk."

He leads me into the house and walks me directly into his room. He grabs a T-shirt out of his drawer and tugs it over his head. "Can you wait here a moment?" His eyes are pleading, one hand holding onto the doorknob as he waits for my acquiescence.

I nod, standing in the center of a room I haven't been in for over two years. It looks exactly the same. Except there are subtle differences. On the nightstand I see a pink sippy cup and a pacifier. A baby towel is haphazardly tossed on the bed.

Needing to see the truth for myself, I walk into his open closet. Not one stitch of women's clothing hangs there. No petite shoes line the rack next to his. I scrunch up my nose in surprise. The bathroom is my next destination.

I enter the bathroom and open the shower door. The only thing different in the shower than his shampoo, conditioner, and men's soap is a big yellow bottle of baby wash. No frilly, girly-smelling shower gels anywhere in sight. I go over to the sink and notice the second sink is bare. There is one extra toothbrush in his holder, but it's tiny and glittery purple with itty bitty bristles. It's his daughter's.

Leaving the bathroom, I set about making his bed, satisfaction filling my heart when I notice only one side of the bed is disheveled. I fold the baby towel and set it on the counter in the bathroom when Carson returns.

"Okay, we won't be interrupted. Cora's temperature broke and Misty has her in her room."

"So, she does live here?"

He sighs and pushes a hand through his wheat-colored hair, the layers falling in perfect formation along the sides of his sculpted handsome face. It would be a lot easier to hate him if he weren't so damn good-looking.

Carson takes a seat in the chair opposite the bed, opening his knees wide and leaning his elbows on them. He clasps his hands in front of his chest. "Yeah, she does. For now. Her place burned down to the ground a couple weeks ago."

Fire. Fucking fire. The root of all evil. A chill ripples down my arms and the ghost ache throbs against my nerve endings. I rub my arm but stay silent.

"Let me go back to the beginning. That last night when you pushed me away just over two years ago, I couldn't take it. I was drowning in my grief. I didn't want things to end between us, but you were unreachable. I'd begged you, and you still pushed me away. For the last time." He swallows, his Adam's apple moving up and down slowly, mesmerizing me from my seat across from him. "Do you remember that, Kat? You tore my fucking heart out, stepped on it, and tossed our love in the trash."

And the pesky tears come back. With him, I'm a ball of tears and emotion. Usually I'm able to be strong, but the past two weeks? Not so much. He's consumed everything in me, including my emotions. "I remember," I return quietly, clasping my fingers in my lap and twisting them around and around one another.

"Well, that night, I lost all reason. I went to a shithole bar and drank my weight in whiskey. Misty was the waitress there. In my drunken haze, she looked so much like you. I don't know... Fuck. I just wanted you so bad. Wanted to be with you more than anything. I lost control." He looks up and his blue eyes are dark, filled with remorse.

The tears fall, and I let them. "Continue." I need to hear it. What I did to this beautiful man. How I broke him.

"The next morning, I woke up and she was gone. I was so far gone I didn't even care that I'd had a one-night stand and couldn't even remember the woman's name. I called Chase. He picked me up, took me home, nursed me back to myself, and that was it. Until a month ago, when I walked into that same bar for a beer. A simple fucking drink, and my life changed again."

I close my eyes and imagine how that must have hit him. To find out he had a daughter he never knew about. My God.

"Misty approached me and told me about Cora."

"And you believed her?" I can't imagine he'd take something so life-altering at face value.

He shook his head. "No. Not even close. I chewed on the info for a week. Then had a friend of mine do a paternity test.

The test proved my paternity. But that was before I'd seen her. She looks exactly like Chloe as a baby. I mean, spitting image."

"And she has your eyes."

He closes said eyes and nods. "Yeah. She does."

"Why didn't you tell me?" I choke down the dry lump forming in my throat.

Carson stands up and paces the room. "Kat, I'd just met my daughter for the first time a few days after I saw you at Chase and Gillian's for breakfast. Then, when we had our night after the pub, shit, I was so confused. I still am. That morning was the morning the fire burned down Misty's apartment and I truly met Cora face-to-face. They had nowhere else to go. And I haven't been there. My daughter is eighteen months old, Kat, and I wasn't there."

I stand up and go to him, wrapping my arms around his tension-filled form. He embraces me and holds me close, holds me like he's never going to let me go. "I can't be a shit father. I'm so scared of fucking this up. Her...and you. I just want to find a way to make this all work. I love you, Kathleen, but I love Cora too."

"Of course you do." I cup both his cheeks. "Hey, I'd never make you choose between me and your daughter. Me and Misty? Yes..."

He tugs me against his chest and curls a hand into my hair. "There is no you or Misty. Never has been. That night was a mistake. A fucking drunken, emotional mistake. But it doesn't change the fact I got Cora out of the mistake, and I'm not sorry about her. She's perfect, Kat. You'll see. I just know you'll fall in love with her if you give her a chance. Give us a chance."

Tears slip down my cheeks at the sheer anguish in his tone. This big, strong man in front of me is broken. Confused.

Afraid. Hurt. Like me, he doesn't know what to do or how to hold on to what he wants. Which is me. I can see it in every fleck of aqua in his eyes, in every breath he takes, and in the way he's holding me as though I'll disappear at any moment.

"I'd like to get to know Cora. But I don't know how we move forward. You have a daughter who needs you. Apparently a woman who needs you too. Where do I fit in?" I swallow my own desperation and personal desires.

He leans his head against mine. "We're going to figure it out. People have mixed families all the time. Look at you and your soul sisters. You're not related by blood but by choice. And they are just as important to you as any true family. More so because you chose them. Right?"

I think about Maria, Gigi, and Bree and know with my whole heart he's right. They are my family, my sisters. I'd never forsake them or their children because we didn't share a blood bond.

"No, you're right."

His eyes lighten, and he smiles. "See? It can be done. I just need to work through this situation with Misty. Get her set up with a new job and a place of her own. Then, of course, I'll have to work out custody. I need you with me, Kat. I need your love and support. Can you do that? I know it's asking a lot. It's asking for the world, but I don't know any other way. I love you. I love you so goddamned much, and the only other woman I've ever said those words to died when I was a child. Don't leave me like she did. I couldn't survive it."

The truth in his statement rips into my gut, leaving a gaping wound in its wake. "Baby..." I whisper, cupping his cheek. "Is that why you never told me you loved me before? Because you thought I'd leave?" My heart beats so hard I fear it will break a rib.

"You did leave, Kat. I showed you I loved you in every way that mattered, and you still pushed me away."

I let all the air leave my lungs and close my eyes. Everything he's admitting is true. All the times he doted on me, made love to me as though I was his universe, tried to take care of me after the fire. All of it was him showing his love in countless ways, and all I did was set it aside like it meant nothing.

"I'm sorry. Carson, I don't know how to make it right. I wasn't in my right mind. I didn't know how to be me anymore. It's taken me years to get back to this place."

He breathes heavily against my body, holding me close. "Then you understand what it's like to have your entire existence flipped upside down. That's where I'm at right now. I have a daughter, Kat. A fucking kid who needs me and loves me. Jesus Christ. I love her. Ever since I took her into my arms, I've loved her. The only problem is she's not *our* child. I'd always believed it would be me and you."

"Me too," I admit shakily.

"She has a lot of love in her. I can see it in her eyes. She's a Davis. Do you think you could let her into your heart? Share in this experience with me? Stumble through it together?"

"Together?" I look up at him using the same words we'd promised one another just this morning.

"I need you. I need you so fucking much. I don't want to do this alone. I don't know if I can." He lays himself wide open, spilling out his insecurities.

The answer within me fills me up to bursting. I don't want to live my life without him anymore. I'm not sure, after having him the last two weeks, I could go back to being without him. So, he has a daughter. A perfect little bundle of love he's obviously smitten with. I love children. Love my nieces and nephew, and they love me. I could love Cora. She's half Carson. It will be easy. However, I do not feel the same will occur with her mother.

Misty.

That's a person who needs to be set straight.

Firming up my spine and wiping away my tears, I consider Carson's soulful eyes. "I'm with you. I'm not going anywhere. We're in this together."

"Really? You're not going to disappear on me?" He smiles softly.

I shake my head. "No, I'm not. I want to be with you. I never stopped loving you, Carson, and I don't know that I ever could. Cora is a part of you, which is enough for me. I already love her because I love you."

Carson closes his eyes. His shoulders slump, and he curls both hands around my hips and smashes me against him. "I love you. Jesus Christ, thank you. Thank you for giving us a chance. A real chance."

For a few minutes, we lightly kiss and touch one another tenderly, reminding ourselves of our commitment.

I scratch my nails down Carson's scalp the way I know he loves. He groans and pushes his hips against me automatically, his length hardening by the second. I allow myself a minute of feminine pride at his response to my nearness and touch before I back away.

He pouts.

"We have to figure out how to handle Misty. She called me a homewrecker when she answered the door."

He growls and fists his hands at his side. "Not acceptable. She's not allowed to talk to you like that. Not to mention the inaccuracy of her accusation."

"Be that as it may, Carson, she wants you. Thinks she has some kind of claim on you because you're the father of her child. I kind of get it in a way. I'd be possessive as hell if you were the father of my child."

"I am the father of your future children, Kat. This situation doesn't change where our lives are headed. Don't for a minute think I don't want to see you swollen with our child. That baby will have Cora for a big sister."

I let out a big, frustrated breath. "You can't talk like that right now. We need to deal with today. Right now. And the simple fact is you have a woman, the mother of your daughter, living in your home, and she thinks you belong to her. How are you going to handle the situation?"

He huffs. "I know exactly how I'm going to handle it." He grabs my hand and pulls me toward his bedroom door. Before I can ask what's going on, he drags me down the hallway and into the kitchen, where we can hear Misty cooing to Cora.

"That's a good girl. Eat your Cheerios. Get something in that little belly of yours and make Mommy happy," she says while pouring another handful of the wheat circles on the baby's tray.

"How's my baby girl?" Carson addresses Misty firmly but without malice, though I know he has a few things he wants to say to her.

"Fever broke. Looks like you showering with her and taking a nap with her helped. You're so perfect with her. Isn't Daddy the best, Cora?" she coos sappily to the pretty little girl, her blond ringlets bouncing as if she wasn't just sick. Babies sure bounce back quickly.

"So, she's feeling better?" He walks over to his daughter

while still holding my hand in his firm grip and leans his head down to run his lips against her forehead. I've seen Gillian and Bree use the same move with their babies to check their temperature before. "Nice and even." He kisses her on the top of her head.

Carson leads me to a stool and practically puts me on it. "Coffee, Sweetcheeks?" he says to me, but Misty answers.

"Oh, no thanks, I've had enough."

"Now, Misty, you know I've never called you that name once in the two weeks you've lived here. I was talking to Kathleen. My girlfriend. Speaking of, we need to talk."

Misty leans against the counter on the opposite side of the kitchen. Her gaze from this distance is lethal. "Do you really think that's a good idea in front of our daughter? She's liable to get confused. I mean, she knows I'm Mommy and you're Daddy. This woman is a stranger."

Carson visibly bristles. "No, she's not. She's the woman I'm in love with, and it's time I introduce her to you and my daughter. You're going to start seeing a lot more of her from here on out. Isn't that right, Kathleen?"

"Yep." And on that note I get up from my spot and hold out my left hand toward Misty. She narrows her eyes at the oddity. "Kathleen Bennett."

She doesn't take my hand, so I drop it to my side, feeling the discomfort pumping off her in waves of negative energy. Carson wraps an arm over my shoulders, providing me the extra boost of strength I need.

"I understand this is a difficult situation and time for you, Carson, and Cora. I'm happy to help this transition in any way I can."

Misty snorts. "Help? The only thing you're doing by being

here is breaking up my family."

Carson lets me go and stands in front of me, thankfully breaking the dagger-like stare she had going. If looks could kill, I'd already be dead by now. The woman absolutely hates me. Then again, if she wants Carson and I stand in the way, she has good reason to.

I remind myself it's going to take time for all of this to sink in for everyone, and more time to get things on an even keel.

"Misty, that's uncalled for. Kathleen is my family. Cora is my family. You are the mother of my daughter."

"But you said you were going to change Cora's name and make us a real family. You said that, and now that she's here, you're taking it back!" Her voice breaks and she runs out of the kitchen in tears.

Well, that didn't go very well.

Carson presses thumb and forefinger into his temples. I can't imagine the weight he's feeling on his shoulders. I rub a hand down his back. "Carson, baby, how about I leave?"

"No! This is just a misunderstanding. I can fix this." Misery coats his tone.

I bring him around to face me. "I believe you can and you will. But having me here is not helping. She needs time to get used to this idea. I think we all do. You've leveled me with a blow I need some time to come to terms with too."

He grips my shoulders. "I don't want you to overthink this and decide you can't handle it. I want to work through this with you."

I shake my head and pat his cheek. "Honey, you can't. We all need this. I'm not going anywhere. I'm going to go to one of the girl's houses, hash it out with copious amounts of wine, and then go home to bed. You deal with Misty and make sure Cora is taken care of. Then call me tomorrow. Okay?"

He pushes me against the counter and kisses me soundly. His tongue dips in, swallowing me whole. I love every second. Until we're broken apart by a giggling squeal coming from a few feet away.

"Someone wants her daddy's attention." I smile against his lips.

"Yeah," he says softly, kissing me once more. "Will you meet my daughter before you go?" He sounds needy and wistful at the same time.

"I'd like nothing more. Lead the way, Daddio."

He chuckles and pulls the squirming toddler out of her chair. He grabs a towel, wipes her mouth, and then tosses the towel back on the counter.

"Cora Duncan, soon to be Davis, meet Kathleen Bennett, soon to be Davis."

I try not to allow the shock of his words and intention hit me too hard. Carson was never shy about his desire to marry me. He mentioned it often when we were together. It was always me holding back. I should have jumped in before the fire. Had I done so, we'd be in an entirely different place. Then again, sometimes fate has other plans. Maybe we were meant to do things differently.

Considering the crystal-blue eyes of Carson's daughter makes one thing very clear to me. If we had not gone through what we had, this perfect angel would never be here.

"Hi, angel baby. I'm Kat, and we're going to be great friends." I wrap a finger around her chubby one, lean forward, and kiss the top of her head.

She giggles, and my heart melts. It is definitely not going to be hard to fall in love with this little girl. I'm half in love already.

CHAPTER FOURTEEN

KATHLEEN

"A child. As in, a real-life human being made of bone and flesh?" Bree beams.

"Sugar and spice and everything nice?" I quip, trying to soften the blow a little.

She gets a faraway look in her eyes, glancing off into the distance. "Like a real boy? Not like Pinocchio?" Her glossy pink lips curve around the salted edge of her melon margarita.

"Girl. A real girl. An eighteen-month-old daughter to be exact," I correct.

Bree blinks as if she cannot comprehend any of what I've just shared.

"Jesus, Bree, you need to lay off the Disney flicks." Gigi shakes her head and plucks at her napkin, head down and surprisingly quiet. She hasn't so much as said a word about the elephant-sized bomb I just dropped.

Maria dunks her tortilla chip into the salsa bowl, loading far more salsa on the chip than should be humanly possible, before lifting her icy gaze. "No *problemo*. I'll chop off his *cojones* and mail them in a jar to his father, so he knows where to bury them along with the body I'll have Eli beat to a pulp."

Dead silence settles among the four of us. They're not sure how to respond because I haven't given them a vibe either way of how I'm feeling about this new information. Soul sisters are like that. We can be opinionated, straightforward, but we can't do it until we know exactly what kind of emotional fallout we're dealing with. Time to lay it all out on the table.

"Okay, girls. I'm going to say everything all at once. You're going to let me without interrupting. Then we'll address this one at a time. Soul sister solidarity. All right?" I narrow my eyes and meet three gazes. One Caribbean-blue, one emerald-green, and the last icy-blue.

Slowly they each nod but don't say a word.

I lick my lips and suck in a breath. Here goes nothin'.

"One. Carson and I are officially back together. Long-term. Future, marriage on the horizon possibly, all of it."

Three sets of gasps in varying lengths and volume blast the air around me. I wish I could dive into the monster-sized blended margarita sitting in front of me, but I carry on with valor.

"Two. He met Misty, the baby mama, during a one-night stand the same night I pushed him away for good."

I stop to make sure all three of them are breathing. Maria looks ready to pounce or cut someone. Bree looks shocked beyond compare. And Gigi looks straight-up guilty as shit. I'll have to address that later. Though I worry why Gillian's showing guilt and not concern. That's unlike the peacekeeper.

"Three. We're head over heels in love with one another and in a fucked-up situation because Baby Mama does not like me and wants Carson for herself."

Maria's mouth opens, but I hold up a finger. "You promised."

She closes her mouth, her lips firming into a tight line of repressed anger.

"Four. Misty and Cora—that's his daughter's name..."

Three sets of "aw" slip out of their mouths. I allow it because Cora is a lovely name and sticks with the tradition of C names in the Davis family. Something I know Carson is very proud of.

"They both live with Carson at his beach-house ranch," I finish, letting out all of my remaining breath like a balloon going flat.

"¿Qué mierda?" Maria hisses. Loosely translated—*What's this shit?*

"My God!" Bree gasps.

Gigi stays completely silent, which can mean only one thing. This news did not surprise her. She knew about the baby, and she knew about them living at Carson's house.

"Cat got your tongue, Gigi?" I narrow my gaze.

She blinks rapidly. "Uh, no. You said not to say anything until you were done."

"You don't seem surprised by this news. Not at all, actually."

"Um, yeah, I kind of..."

"You knew about Cora. You knew about them living in his house. You knew, and you didn't fucking tell me? What the fuck? What happened to the sister code?" I grate through clenched teeth, loud enough that only the girls can hear me, not the patrons happily eating lunch around us.

Gillian's face pales even more, which is shocking because the girl glows in the dark.

"It's all Chase's fault!" She throws her husband right under the bus and rubs at her swollen belly. "He made me promise not to say anything. Literally told me he'd take away sex if I didn't give Carson two weeks to speak the truth. I'm horny as all get-out with this pregnancy. Do you know what no sex would be like?"

"No. I don't. Probably because I spent almost three years not getting laid!" I fire back.

Ria shakes her head. "*Tres años.* We should be giving your va-jay-jay a party now that the three-year dry spell is broken. *¡Jesucristo! Tres años.* I can't even go three days!" Not that we didn't already know Maria is our resident nympho.

"If I didn't need you so bad, Gigi, I'd be so pissed at you! You owe me. Big-time. Huge! You might have to name your baby after me!"

"Can't. She's having *un niño,*" Ria chimes in directly, but I ignore her.

Unshed tears fill Gillian's eyes, and she nods emphatically. "I'm sorry. I didn't know what to do. Choose between my husband and my sister? Besides. It was Carson's truth to share. Not mine. You wouldn't have wanted to hear that from me. Would you?" Her voice cracks with overwhelming emotion and a truckload of pregnancy hormones.

Now I feel like a hateful bitch.

I slump in my chair. "No. I wouldn't have. As much as this was a shocker, I'm glad Carson told me and we had time to reconnect. To firm our commitment to one another before I found out. Otherwise, I'm not sure I'd be sitting here talking to you three about how I'm going to get through all of this instead of just running from it."

"So, you're in it to win it?" Bree asks.

"Yeah, I am. Do you think it's stupid?" I ask all three but start with them one at a time. "Ria?"

She shoves another loaded chip in her mouth, chews thoughtfully, swallows, and crosses her arms over her chest. "Obviously, we're going to support you, but honestly, *gatita*, I've never seen anyone lose himself in sorrow the way he did when you pushed him away after the fire. That man loves you. Always has." She shrugs. "Seems pretty simple to me. If you love him, there's nothing else that matters. I learned that lesson the hard way between Tommy's death and falling for his twin brother Eli. Love isn't easy. It definitely bitch-slaps you upside the head when you least expect it."

Gillian and Bree both nod, and I take a brain-freezing gulp of my margarita to let her words settle.

"Bree? What do you think?"

She pushes her long waterfall of blond hair over one shoulder and leans forward to clasp my hands in both of hers. As usual, I have to force myself not to flinch at the touch on my scarred flesh. It doesn't ever seem to faze the girls in the least, and I've been working on it not fazing me, especially around them.

"Kathleen, we love and adore you. We're your sisters and we're here for you, whatever that means. You've always got us. But I'm going to throw myself out on a ledge and say that no man will ever love you the way Carson does. He's your soul mate, babe. Do you feel that with him?" Her ocean-blue eyes swirl with love and friendship as I watch her lips quiver, a deep emotion filling the air around us.

It's always been this way with my soul sisters. We feel each other's pain. When needed, like now, we take some of the burden and help relieve one another. It's our way.

I close my eyes and squeeze her fingers. "I do. Lord knows I do."

"Then you have your answer." She leans back and wipes at a tear that has fallen down her pretty cheek. Always our softie.

"Gigi? What would you do?"

Gillian leans back and lays one hand over her bump and the other on the table, one finger making the rim of her virgin margarita glass sing. "I'd hold on to him with everything I have. We all know how hard it is to hold on to true love. It has gossamer wings and can fly away at any moment. It's up to us to capture love and cherish it every day. What does your heart say?"

"That being with Carson, getting back together, is what it is."

"And what's that?" She tips her head, her fiery red hair tumbling over the side of her shoulder.

"Fate."

★ ★ ★

To: Kathleen Bennett
From: Carson Davis
What's cooking, hot stuff?

I chuckle at the text Carson sent me. We've been seeing one another twice a week for the past two months and talking nightly as well as texting regularly. On Wednesdays, when we both have a light day, I meet up with him and Cora for what he dubs "family time." We usually take Cora to the park, or to Gillian's to play with the twins, or to Bree's to play with Dannica. We have dinner, spend quality time with one another, and then I retreat back to my apartment. Alone.

Carson has what he thinks is a "stellar plan" for solving

the problem. He wants me to just sleep over at his house. But I can't. Not with Misty there. It feels wrong somehow. As if we're having some type of tawdry affair under her nose. I don't want to feel that way when I lay my head down in Carson's bed. I want to feel as if I belong there, with him and Cora. The three of us. Until Misty has her own place, I'm firm on my stance. It's driving Carson crazy, but I think moving through this scenario slowly is working for us. For all of us, including his daughter.

Of course, on Saturday nights, all bets are off. Saturday nights...those are mine. All six-foot three-inches of hotness wrapped around me from the second he enters my apartment until after breakfast on Sunday.

I hate Sundays. Not only does he leave to go back to *her,* but it's their combined family day. Not like he doesn't have Monday, Tuesday, Thursday, and Friday. Alas, I'm trying very, very hard to accept the things I cannot change. At least right now. I can see that Carson is trying to make the best of a very trying situation, and he doesn't need me adding to the problems, but damn, I'm tired of seeing him based on scheduled dates.

To: Carson Davis
From: Kathleen Bennett
Wouldn't you like to know? Let's just say something saucy, spicy, and mouthwatering.

I respond to his text, proud of my charming wit.

His response is the emoji with the big heart eyes. Then my phone rings.

"Hello, hot stuff speaking," I joke.

Carson's throaty laugh rumbles through my body, settling hotly between my thighs. Damn. He can take me from zero to wet with a simple laugh. I stir the marsala sauce I'm making for dinner. It will last me three days. I can't eat out every night. I'd be as big as a cow. How would I compare standing next to petite, fake-titty Barbie?

"Hey, I have news!" His jovial timbre sets my heart abuzz.

"What kind of news?" I smile, knowing it must be good by the tone of his voice.

"The best."

"Really? Well, don't keep a girl waiting."

"I've found the perfect place for Misty and Cora. And you're never going to believe where."

Just the fact he's found a place for his house guest—aka Baby Mama Drama, according to my girl Bree—is amazing news on its own. A prickle of excitement skitters along my skin. I turn the sauce down and lean against the counter, pressing the phone closer to my ear. I do not want to miss this.

"Where? Better yet, when is it available?" I ask in a rush. The excitement of getting my boyfriend back all to myself is nudging my exuberance.

"In your building! Chase has an opening. A couple on your floor is growing their family, and they need more than two bedrooms. It's perfect! And you'll be right there. Then I can stay over more and not feel like I'm too far away. It's a win-win."

In my building.

On the same floor as me.

I clench my jaw and try to sound happy. "That's...uh...great news, babe. When is all this happening?" I try and fail to sound impressed. I cringe when silence greets me on the line.

"You're not happy about this?" The question is breathy and filled with concern.

I slump against the counter and let out a tired burst of air. "It's not that I'm not happy she's leaving your house. I'd scream it from the rooftops if you'd let me. But moving into my building? On the very floor I live on?" I groan, unable to hold it back. "That's kind of weird, isn't it?"

Carson sighs. "Sweetcheeks, I gotta say, sounds like you're being a little unreasonable, don't you think? Do you have any idea how happy it makes me to know the woman I love is right down the hall in case Cora needs anything?"

"You mean Misty," I deadpan.

"Honey. I'm surprised at you. I thought you'd be happy..."

Mentally I chastise myself for being so obstinate. "Ugh. I am happy. I'd just be happier if she was in another building," I admit rather stubbornly, bordering on bratty.

"You're just going to have to get over it. You'll see. Have a good night's sleep and think it over. This is the best possible outcome we could have hoped for. Really, it is. And besides, before long, you'll be moving in here, so it won't matter where she lives in the long run, now will it?"

And there he goes again with the moving in and marriage angle. He hasn't let it go, but he's yet to make an official proposal. I think it's because he knows I'll decline. We need more time. More time to adjust to this new us. Not just Carson and me, but Carson, Cora, me, and even Baby Mama Drama.

"Can you promise me you'll think it over? I have to tell Chase tomorrow. Three other couples are on the waiting list for the building, and Chase is doing me a solid by letting Misty skate to the top. I really don't want to turn him down, and I want to tell Misty what the plan is. If this works out, she could be out of my house by month's end. Don't you want that?"

I grind my teeth and rub my temples. He's right, and I

hate it. How did I become the adolescent in this relationship? Perhaps it happened when I found out my boyfriend had a child and became someone's daddy.

"No, Carson. You're right. You are. I'm being childish. It would be wonderful to have privacy with you again. And to have more one-on-one time with Cora would be a delight. I love my angel baby."

"And she loves you. I can feel it deep in my bones, babe. This is the answer. The start of our new harmonious future."

I giggle, momentarily taken by his joy. He's such a free spirit sometimes. It's refreshing to know he hasn't lost that side of him. Then a thought hits me. "Oh, you didn't tell me how Misty was doing with Charles." I fire up the sauce again and take the time to get it back to temperature before adding the chicken I'd already cooked.

"Actually, really well. Dad says she's a quick learner and smart. He's enjoying her company."

Huh. Enjoying her company. Shocking. Then again, that's probably just my pettiness rearing its ugly head. I curb that bit of enthusiasm to keep the peace. "Wow. Great. Good to hear. So, she's got a solid job and a potential new place on the horizon. One I assume you're paying for..." I filter the irritation from my tone. I know Carson too well to believe he'd ever let the mother of his child pay her own rent.

As expected, his response is warning yet kind. "Kat, you know my daughter having a roof over her head, food in her belly, and a happy family is paramount to my sanity. I'm a new father. I don't care if Misty ever pays her own rent. As long as she has my daughter living under her roof, I'm happy to foot the bill. You know it's a drop in the bucket. Hell, I'd pay your rent if I could get away with it."

"Don't you dare, Carson Davis! Take the thought right out of your head. I've got plenty of money on my own. I don't need or want you paying my way, thank you very much. I know you're old-fashioned, and I appreciate the offer, baby." I finish my diatribe with as much grace as I can muster.

"Won't matter in the long run. You'll be living here soon enough." He prods the beast once more for good measure.

I chuckle, pour the uncooked linguini into the boiling water, and set the timer on the microwave. Again, I turn down the marsala and chicken so it can simmer together while I finish the noodles.

"Keep it up, he-man. Keep it up and you're liable to never get me to move in."

"Oh, I have my ways." His tone carries a sultry note, and I feel my nipples tighten with the erotic suggestion of what he might do to me.

"Not if you can't nail me down."

"Oh, Sweetcheeks...I have absolutely no problem nailing you. Monday, Tuesday, Wednesday, Thursday, Fri—"

"Shut up! Crazy man."

"Crazy in love with you."

I roll my eyes. "Go ahead and tell Chase you'll take the place. I can put my big-girl panties on and take one for the team."

"Team Davis?"

"Yeah, Team Davis." I hum, knowing it sounds good to say that I'm part of a team again.

"I'm excited about this. I really believe it's the answer we were looking for. I get my home back, Misty gets a place, and my daughter has two loving, safe homes to go to."

I grunt. "Except the hard part will be getting her to A,

leave without a fight. And B, divide custody."

"It shouldn't be an issue. Misty's reasonable, babe. She is."

My eyebrows rise as if of their own accord, but thankfully, he can't see me. That woman is not quite right. Definitely has a few screws loose. "If you say so. I'll have faith."

"I'm sure sharing custody will be hard at first. She's not been without Cora even one full night, and I want a fifty-fifty split."

Trying not to let my Negative Nancy come out, I suck in a long, slow breath before speaking. "That might be difficult at first. Perhaps you should start with one or two nights a week and then gradually over a period of several weeks, possibly even months, increase the number to three and four nights."

"I just don't see why this would be a problem. Do you really think she'll try to keep me from my daughter?" A hint of fear enters his voice.

Quickly I dump the cooked noodles in the strainer and turn off the sauce. "It's not that I think she'll try to keep her from you, but it's a huge change for her. To go from having her daughter every single night under the same roof where she can keep a watchful eye... I don't know. My Spidey-sense, as Ria would say, is telling me this isn't going to be an easy transition."

He sighs heavily, and it sounds like the weight of the world just crushed his happy, unicorn-revealing, rose-colored glasses.

"Honey, I don't know what she's going to say or do. Just tread lightly. Think about how this is going to affect her and you right now, not just a year from now. By then it will all be a moot point. So go slow."

"Yeah, you're probably right. Maybe I'll discuss it with Chase. See what he thinks."

I snort. "Chase is going to say sue her ass and get full custody. Um, hello, Chase is a happy family man, but he's a right bastard when it comes to what he perceives as his property. Children are everything in his mind. You'd be better off talking to your dad."

He chuckles, and some of the lightness he had when he first called returns to his words. "You're right again. Good idea. Hey, have I told you lately that I love you?"

"Isn't that a song? Plagiarist." I laugh.

"Doesn't mean it isn't true. I'm looking forward to tomorrow night with my two best girls."

Tomorrow is Wednesday.

"Me too, babe. I'm going to let you go so I can eat my chicken marsala for one."

Carson groans. "Argh! I love your chicken marsala. Save me some?"

I snicker. "For when?"

"Tomorrow, when I see you."

"We're going to dinner with your family, remember?"

"Fuck. You're right. Well, promise to make it for me soon?"

I smile and shake my head. "I promise. And hey, I love you too."

"Plagiarist. I said it first," he goads.

"Kiss my angel baby for me."

"You know I will. Tomorrow?" His voice takes on that sexy, sultry timbre I adore.

"Tomorrow."

CHAPTER FIFTEEN

CARSON

I squeeze Kathleen's left hand as I hold Cora against my side, anchoring her diapered butt on my hip. Her little legs are flapping against my gut and back excitedly. When she's awake she's always happy. I love that about her. Her personality is going to be fun-filled and loving. Still, a tingle of dread is nagging at my subconscious while we stand at the entrance to my childhood home.

Will the family like her?

Will they treat her like one of us?

What are they going to say about Kathleen?

What about Misty?

The questions that have plagued me since this whole debacle started are running rampant through my mind and stressing me the fuck out.

Kathleen runs her hand down my chest. "Relax. If I'm not nervous, you shouldn't be either."

I huff. "You have nothing to be nervous about. My family loves you." I level her with my no-bullshit stare.

She smirks. "And they love you too. They're going to lavish Cora with love and attention. You'll see." Her soft, secretive smile reminds me I have her no matter what happens.

Before I open the door, I turn to her. "You know, I couldn't do any of this without you."

Kat beams and tilts her head. "Yes, you could. You're stronger than you think. But you'll never have to worry about being alone, because I'm here now."

"Thank Christ!" I sigh and press my forehead to hers. I lean in and lay my lips against hers.

Cora takes that moment to participate, pushing her little face in between ours and giving us both an openmouthed slimy cheek kiss.

Kat and I crack up. Leave it to Cora to lighten the situation.

"All right, let's do this." I open the door and lead my girls inside.

Cora's eyes widen at all the lights. Most specifically, the chandelier hanging over the entryway. She points her chubby finger at it and says, "Ooooo."

"Yes, baby girl. This is where Daddy grew up."

I snuggle her closer, taking as much comfort as I can before we enter the sitting room off the entry, where I can already hear voices, laughter, and soft music playing. Dad must have put on the record player, because easy, jazzy blues crackles through the door.

Once we enter, I feel the stares as they travel from me to Kat and zero right in on Cora. Chloe is standing near the bar, pouring amaretto into a tumbler. Cooper is leaning against the fireplace with his phone at his ear. Chase is sitting on the couch, his arm around Gillian. Their twins are nowhere in sight. My father is sitting opposite them in a single chair. The only people missing are my brother Craig and his wife and kids, but they're in New York. We have a promise to Skype in the near future so they can virtually meet Cora.

When I make my way farther into the room, my father stands up. He smiles widely and opens his arms.

"You are a vision, Kathleen. I'm thrilled you came tonight."

Kat willingly embraces him. "Charles, it's been too long."

"Hopefully that time span is but a memory?" He cocks an eyebrow coyly.

She grins. "That's the plan."

He pats her hand. "Good."

Then he turns to me. I haven't moved an inch. Never in my life have I felt fear when approaching my father, but I've never been in this type of quandary either. Charles Davis is a man who has earned the love and respect of his children, high-powered businessmen, and leaders all over the world. And right now, I'm afraid this situation provides the potential for either his disdain or disappointment.

However, as is his way, he walks over to me, puts a hand to my shoulder, and squeezes. "Son. You look well."

I swallow the cotton ball in my throat. "I am, sir."

"Are you happy?" He squints as if he's assessing me straight through to my soul. Fathers have that ability. I hope to have it with Cora one day too.

"Yes, sir."

"Then I'm happy for you." He returns just a hint of a smile before his eyes turn to my daughter.

"And you must be my granddaughter, Cora." His blue eyes soften instantly when he pets her soft blond hair.

Cora perks up when she hears her name. "Da-da," she says proudly.

I'm stunned stupid as my daughter lifts her arms out toward my father. He reaches for her and expertly pulls her into his arms and against his chest. Even dressed in a suit and tie, my father manages to be approachable to a toddler he's never met. My heart melts instantly.

"That's my little love," he coos to her. "Come visit with your granddad, eh?"

Kathleen comes back over to me, loops an arm around my waist, and leans into my side. I wrap an arm around her and watch while each member of my family introduces themselves to my daughter. It's a moment I'd never imagined in a million years but one I'll remember for a lifetime.

"See, babe, they love her already." Kat rubs her hand down my chest warmly, and I hold it over my heart, just where I want her.

"She's a Davis. What's not to love?" I quip, making her giggle.

★ ★ ★

The dining room is bustling with activity, laughter, and people talking over one another. Cora is sitting in a high chair next to Chase's twins, who are both in booster seats, at the table set for ten. My father should be sitting at the head of the table, but he isn't present yet. Chloe is already sitting to the right of his chair. Ever since Mom died, Chloe has stepped in as the matriarch of our family. Cooper, the second oldest, is at the opposite end of the table. Chase and Gillian of course are as far away from Coop as possible. Even though they've mended fences considerably, they will never have great fondness for one another, but they've become civil over the years. Mostly after Chase lost Aunt Colleen to the same madman who hurt my girl and her soul sisters. I think that time gave us all a cold, hard look at our mortality and made past transgressions seem more trivial.

The staff brings in the children's plates first. All perfectly cut up with a mixture of healthy and kid-friendly options and three bright sippy cups.

"I want a weal cup, Mommy," Claire demands loud enough for the server to hear.

"Mrs. Davis, I didn't know. I can bring her one."

Gillian purses her lips. "No, she's fine. Claire, next time we have dinner here, we will tell the staff in advance. Not after. You get what you get, and you don't throw a fit. Remember?"

Claire glares at the sippy cup and crosses her arms. "But it's for babies!"

Gillian closes her eyes and takes a breath.

Chase leans forward. "Claire, use the cup and there will be dessert in it for you. I'm pretty sure I saw some home-baked cookies in the kitchen."

On that note, Claire picks up her cup, sucks down the drink, and tucks into eating her dinner quietly.

Gillian shakes her head. "Must you always bribe her?"

"It worked, didn't it?" He grins.

She nudges his shoulder playfully.

The server sets plates in front of each of us and then sets another one down in front of the empty seat next to me. Just when I'm about to ask who's missing, my father enters the room, escorting Misty, her hand resting daintily in the crook of his arm. I squeeze the hand I have casually resting on Kathleen's thigh so tight she yelps and looks up.

What. The. Fuck.

I narrow my eyes at my father as he approaches my seat. "I found this little thing working away in my office. I figured since we were having a family dinner, she should come and eat with us. Don't you agree, Carson?" Father directs her toward the empty seat.

"Uh..." There just aren't words.

He pulls back the chair to seat her. She's wearing a black pencil skirt and a blue silk blouse showing more cleavage than would ever be necessary or even appropriate at work—let alone a private dinner.

Misty pushes a lock of her blond hair behind her ear. I notice belatedly that her hair is in beach waves, flowing just to her shoulders. It looks identical to Kathleen's hair. Which is shocking because just this morning, Misty's hair was perfectly straight and hung down past the middle of her back.

I squeeze Kathleen's leg again, still not able to utter a word.

"See, now the entire family is here," Charles says in a "more the merrier"-type way.

Heat fills every pore, and I have to remind myself my father knows not what he's done. He has no clue what the situation is between Misty, Kathleen, and me.

Without even looking at Kat, I know she's pissed. The fire scorching my palm is enough to show she's seething on the inside, regardless of how she appears on the outside.

"Isn't this awesome!" Misty says to me, loud enough for most of the table to hear. "Now Cora will feel right at home with her mommy and daddy and the entire family together." She puts her hand on my shoulder and then caresses it down to my elbow, as if she has the right to such an intimate touch.

"We're going to have to have a serious discussion about this," I say in a low growl.

She blinks innocently and places her napkin in her lap.

"Are you not happy I'm here?" She speaks so loudly the entire table stops eating and looks at me.

Chase's jaw locks down and a muscle ticks away in his cheek. Gigi has eyes only for Kathleen, probably doing the secret girl-talk thing where there are no actual words exchanged, just subtle body language only the best of friends would pick up. The kids are eating away and talking nonstop. Cooper is smiling like a loon, happily picking up a forkful of food and shoveling it in his mouth, obviously completely entertained by my horror.

"Honey, would you fill my wine?" Kathleen's request breaks the tension, allowing me to ignore the question.

"Oh yes, for me too. I'll have whatever you're having, Carson. We seem to like *all* of the same things," Misty says, embellishing. "Makes living together so easy. Wouldn't you agree, sweetheart?" she coos, handing me her glass.

Sweetheart. Fucking fuck.

The muscle in Kathleen's leg tightens so much it lifts my hand. I squeeze back, letting her know I'm with her, right here, just as horrified as she is, but trying to push through. Honestly though, I'm in hell. Actual. Living. Hell.

Kathleen, the woman I love, the person I want to be with for the rest of my life, is sitting on my left. The woman I will never be able to escape, because we have a daughter together, and she's pushing her way into my life, is sitting on my right. Sandwiched between heaven and hell. Lord help me.

Conversation between my family and Misty moves throughout dinner. Kathleen and I stay quiet, both of us feeling the same things for different reasons. I know Kat's angry. Who wouldn't be, when faced with your first dinner with a family you've missed for years and then being forced to share the moment with the mother of your man's child? It's not right. It's twisted as fuck. I'm going to have to talk to my father about not allowing this to happen in the future. Kathleen's and Cora's comfort is my first priority.

Chloe seems to save the day, talking about work and what she and Kathleen have been working on for Paris Fashion Week. Which, I'm reminded, is in another month. My Kathleen will be heading to Paris without me. Then an idea hits. Perhaps I can go visit her after her week is done and spend a few days just with her, motoring around the most romantic city in the world. Right then, I plan on enlisting Chloe and their receptionist to block off the time in Kat's calendar.

Just the thought of having a few uninterrupted days with my woman is exactly what I need. Hell, what we both need right now.

★ ★ ★

As the night wears on, Kathleen spends time chatting it up with Gillian and the kids, playing on the floor. It's as if time paused for almost three years until she re-entered my life. I feel as sappy as shit and think all is right with the world again.

Unfortunately, Misty, who I thought would leave immediately after dinner, follows us into the living room for family time and a nightcap like she owns the place. She chats up Cooper, touching him in a way that could only be construed as flirting. I clench my teeth and try to breathe through my anger. Coop is a douche. Has always been one. Especially when he fucked Chase's fiancée Meghan on their wedding night over a decade ago. To this day, he's not exactly sorry. Claims he was saving our cousin from a mistake. I could just see him taking

Misty to bed to spite me.

Misty looks my way and smiles shyly, tilting her chin down while running her finger along the edge of her blouse near her almost bursting cleavage.

What the hell is her game? Does she seriously think flirting with Coop is going to make me jealous? I groan and head toward Kat and the kids. Kat pulls herself up and into the chair and slumps back, putting her hand to her forehead.

"My goodness, I'd forgotten what a bundle of energy kids can be when they are all together like this. So much fun though."

Kathleen's smile is huge and brightens even more when Cora rushes into her, hugs her around the middle, and then climbs up onto her lap. My heart fills with pride and joy, and I pull out my cell phone and snap a couple pics of the smiling beauties. My girl loves my woman. There is nothing in the world better than that.

Out of nowhere, Misty screeches, "Be careful with her!" She scares me, Kathleen, and most of all, Cora, who jolts back with her entire body. Kathleen tries to grab her with her injured arm, a flash of pain crossing her brow when she does, but Cora still slides right through her hold.

I swear the entire thing happens in slow motion but is probably only a second flat.

Cora's little body flies backward over the arm of the chair.

Her head hits the carpet before her neck, shoulders, and body.

Misty rushes over and falls to her knees.

Kat's eyes are huge and round.

My baby girl screaming.

I pick up my daughter so fast you'd have thought snakes

were attacking her. She is crying so hard my shirt is soaked through.

Kat stands up and lifts a hand toward the back of Cora's head, where I have it clutched to my chest. My heart is pounding a mile a minute. Misty slaps Kat's hand away before she can even so much as touch a hair on the child's head.

"Don't you touch my daughter. You did this! You're not strong enough to hold a baby! I've seen how you can't even lift a full glass of wine with that mangled thing, and you tried to hold my daughter. My baby! How dare you put Cora in danger. Do you hate me that much you want to hurt my only child?" she screams at the top of her lungs.

Tears fall down Kat's cheeks as I neglect to say a single word. I should defuse the situation, but my baby is screaming, a goose egg the size of a softball is forming on her sweet baby head, and I'm currently doing everything I can to calm her down.

"I...I...I'm sor-ry," Kat whispers brokenly.

"You're sorry? First you wiggle your way back into Carson's life. Now my daughter's. Can't you see Cora needs a mother and a father?"

That's when my brain starts working again. "She has one. And a lot of women and men in her extended family. Kathleen included."

"I'm. Her. Mother." Misty points at herself, emphasizing each word with a tap to her chest.

I shake my head. "No one is trying to take that away from you. But when you move out, and Kathleen moves in..." I start but stop the minute I feel an ice blast of energy slam into me.

The timing could not have been more wrong for this conversation.

Insert foot into mouth.

"What!" Misty cries out, clutching at her heart. "You're kicking out your own flesh and blood for her!" She flings a shaky hand at Kathleen.

I pass a now resting Cora off to Chase. She goes willingly. Chase has some type of voodoo magic with kids. To everyone else, he puts off the asshole-scary-business-man vibe, but with kids, he's putty.

"I'm not kicking out my daughter." I lift my hands in a placating gesture. "But I have found a new apartment for you and her to live in. When Cora is not with me, that is."

"So, you're kicking me out?" Her tone is so cold it could freeze hot water in an instant. "I can't believe this. You said... you said we'd be a family." She shakes her head back and forth wildly. "You said I was going to be safe and sound with you and our daughter. Now because of *her*, you're kicking me out." She chokes down a sob, her eyes widening. "Oh my God. You're going to take my daughter away! And leave her with someone who will hurt her!"

I shake my head. "I would never take Cora away from you, and Kathleen loves Cora. She'd never hurt her!" I take a huge breath and try to figure out what my next steps are.

Misty's hands fly into her hair and tug. "She just did! Look at my daughter. She can't even keep her eyes open. She probably has a concussion. We should take her to the emergency room!"

I sigh and glance at Gigi. With all her motherly wisdom, I figure she'd know.

She shrugs. "It's an option, but kids are made to be bouncy. Mine fall all the time. Chase, do you think she needs to go?"

He looks down at Cora, runs long fingers over the back of her skull, and nods. "I think a checkup by our house doctor is

in order. Just to be safe. Seems fine though."

Finally, with a task at hand, my father enters the fray. "I'll call him. He'll be here momentarily. The good doctor lives just down the road from us." My father leaves the room at a clip.

I glance around. Chloe is leaning against Coop, steely daggers leaving her gaze resulting in a direct hit for Misty. Coop is all smiles. He thinks my cock-up is funny. Asshole. I can't wait until one day he's in a situation. Instead of helping, I'll be poking the beast and laughing my ass off. Fucker.

Misty's shoulders slump, and she crosses her arms in what I can tell is a protective gesture.

I really need to get this back on even ground. "See, that's settled. Cora will be seen by our family doctor. He can be here before we could see a doctor at the emergency center anyway. Now listen, we have got to get past this. Let's sit and talk it through, okay?" I'm hoping she'll relax for a solid minute and see that she's overreacting.

I was wrong. Dead wrong.

Misty walks right up to Kat, pulls her arm back, and slaps my woman with all her might, her body moving forward with the effort.

"Jesus fucking Christ! Misty!" I roar, but it doesn't stop her from running her mouth and digging a hole she can never get out of.

"You're a disgrace," she sneers at Kathleen. "A homewrecker. And a horrible example of a mother. A mother *protects*, not *harms*. You remember that the next time you think about laying a finger on my baby."

Kat's eyes fill with tears once more, and she turns and runs out of the room.

Gigi follows after her. "Kat, honey, wait! It's not your

fault."

Misty turns so fast she reminds me of the Tasmanian Devil in the Looney Tunes cartoons I used to watch as a kid.

"She had no right. No right to hold our daughter, Carson." Her normally brown eyes are black as coal. Her lips are set in a menacing snarl.

I've had enough.

"Shut up," I growl between my teeth. "Just shut up. You're making it worse. Kathleen already feels bad enough."

Misty's head jerks as she strides over to Chase and pats Cora's back. "You saw what she did." Her voice lowers into a lethal timbre. "She hurt our daughter. I can't allow someone so completely clueless of her own disability to be responsible for Cora's well-being. Absolutely not. Over my dead body," she warns. "I can't believe you'd do this."

"Me? Misty, you're acting like I promised you marriage and more children."

She turns on a spiked heel. "Didn't you?"

"No! Not even close! I promised you safety and security. That's what I'm giving you."

"How can we possibly have that when you are all the way across town in your home and Cora and I are in some stuffy apartment? Cora, away from her daddy. The only man who will always protect her!" Her voice shakes and the tears fall. Her shoulders tremble with the effort.

Fuck. Two women crying now.

"Misty, I'm going to take care of you and Cora. I said I would and I will. But this thing you think there is between us, you're mistaken. We had one night over two years ago. I don't even remember much of it!"

Her crying turns into a full-blown sob.

I make my way over to her and lay my hand on her shoulder. "Listen, it's going to be okay. We're going to work through this for the sake of our daughter. She's what matters."

Instead of nodding and accepting her fate, she flings her body into my arms and locks on to me in a vise-like embrace. I have no choice but to pat her back and try to calm her down. It's not good for Cora to see her mother and father fighting.

Of course, that's when Kathleen walks back into the room, Gigi holding her at the waist in what I assume is sisterly support. Gillian clocks my position with Misty and glares, her green eyes turning a fiery emerald. Kathleen, on the other hand, is worse. Her entire face goes completely blank, devoid of all emotion.

With self-preservation in mind, I push Misty back and go to Kathleen right as she's about to leave. I know when my girl looks like she's about to run, and there was fire licking at her heels a moment ago.

"Sweetcheeks." I open my arms, and she face-plants right into my chest.

"I'm sorry. I tried, Carson. I tried to catch her, but I just..." Her voice catches. "I just couldn't."

"I know, honey. I know. Cora's fine. She's going to be just fine. We'll wait and see what the doctor says. Okay? Then we'll take her home."

She nods against my chest before firming her spine, wiping at her tears, and looking up at me as though the entire world has just crumbled at her feet.

"I know you love her."

She nods. Another set of tears falling down her cheeks. "So much. I'd never hurt her on purpose. Never."

"She's going to be okay," I say to her as much as to myself.

I put my arm around my woman and bring her into the room.

The doctor is right behind Kathleen and me, my father quick at his heels.

"Where's the patient?" he says, all business.

The doctor looks over my daughter, with Misty and me and everyone else in the room watching closely.

"She's fine. Just a nasty bump on the head. She'll want to sleep on her belly. Give her some ibuprofen for the pain and keep an eye on her. If she starts to vomit for any reason or cry uncontrollably, or in reverse, act too lethargic or be hard to wake, take her to the emergency room."

Father and I thank the doctor and send him on his way.

Now I have to get Kathleen, my daughter, and Misty back to my house so the three of us can watch Cora and get through the evening. Yippee. Not.

CHAPTER SIXTEEN

KATHLEEN

I adamantly refuse to go home with Carson, Misty, and Cora. Even though my heart is breaking into a million tiny pieces and I want so badly to hold Cora close, watch her sleep, and make sure she is okay, I have to let her mom and dad take care of her. Alone. It is the hardest decision I've made in a long time. Carson is totally mad. Mad is not the right word. He is straight-up angry. The stunt Misty pulled by coming to dinner, the after-dinner family time botched, and then laying into me for an accident I have a sneaking suspicion she caused, all sent Carson over the deep end.

Right after the blowup, I ask Chase if he and Gigi could take me home. Of course, they agree. Carson comes after me like hell on wheels when I make it outside before him. The first thing he does is press me into the side of the shiny black limo with his body and gets into my space. Way into my personal space. Leaving zero space, in fact, and nothing but his delectable hips, abdomen, and chest plastered against mine. This is where he cages me in and dips his face down low.

"You running?" he growls, his warm breath feathering across my cheek.

I shake my head.

"Words. I need the words." His voice rumbles like an approaching storm.

With a strength I've never experienced before, I wrap my arms around his waist, tilt my head up, and look right into his eyes. I'm letting him see my sadness over the night not going well, my devastation over failing Cora, and most of all, my weakness and hurt over seeing him comfort Misty. It's all there in one look.

"Baby..." He rubs his nose against mine. "Please."

I swallow down the emotion, even though I want to crumble in his arms and let him make the hurt go away. This time though, I'm going to be strong for him. "Carson, I'm not running, but you need to be with your daughter."

"Yes, I do. I'd like to have my woman by my side to help me through it." His words hit my heart like a sledgehammer.

I groan. "You have Misty. You two need to talk. Deal with this scare but also set some things straight."

"What I need is to get her in her own place so I can have my fucking woman in my bed again." His tone is harsh and grating.

A flutter of excitement ripples through me at the possessiveness and need he's openly displaying. My body betrays me and shivers under his hold.

"I can feel you like that idea too." He smiles against my cheek and I close my eyes.

"I do. Very much," I admit.

"Come home with me." His plea is like a healing balm over my battered soul. Just knowing he wants me there is enough to get me through this and let him go.

"No. We'll be together this weekend. Maybe by then you'll

have some good news for me."

An animal-like sound leaves his throat. "By this weekend, you'll be sleeping in my bed, head on my chest, legs wrapped around my body, and my daughter will be in her fucking crib. The next morning we'll be eating your world-famous waffles. You got me?"

I smile and nuzzle against his neck, allowing his warmth to seep into my lips. "I got you, honey."

He curls his hand around my neck and slants his lips over mine. The kiss is long, deep, and so good, I lift a leg up to his waist and he grinds against me, his intent very clear.

Someone behind us clears their throat.

"Kids are coming," Chase says, bringing us back to the moment.

"I'll call you tomorrow." He kisses me once, twice, and a third time. "For luck."

I grin. "For luck." Then I get in the car with Gigi, Chase, and the kids. Claire crawls right up onto my lap and straddles my thighs.

"Why you crying, Auntie Kitty?" Claire purses her lips into a cherub's pout.

I didn't realize I was.

With the back of my hand I wipe the tears away. "No reason. But you should probably get down, I wouldn't want you to fall like Cora did." The memory has me wincing and locking my good arm around her little waist just in case there is a shift in the car or we stop fast.

"Kat..." Gigi whispers a warning, her voice soft and unhappy.

Chase, however, has far less tact. "Kathleen, don't push your niece away. Ever." He twines his fingers with Gillian's and hooks an arm around his son, Carter, who's already falling asleep against his dad's side.

Claire smiles, leans her body forward, and lies against my chest. She puts her thumb into her mouth and nuzzles in close, making herself comfy. With an audible wet plop, she suddenly removes her thumb so she can speak.

"Mommy says when you're sad, you just need more love and it's all better. I love you, Auntie Kitty. Like...a whole lot." Then she puts her thumb back into her mouth and closes her eyes.

"I love you too, Claire. So much, pretty girl." I kiss the crown of her head. She sighs heavily around her thumb. For good measure, I lock my arms around her and just let her love me. Turns out my three-year-old niece is right. Remembering I'm loved does take away all the sadness.

★ ★ ★

"Honestly, Kat, I wanted to wring that bitch's skinny neck!" Chloe tears a piece of fabric, her arm stretching out as far as it will go before she gathers it and does it again. It rips all the way down to the end, leaving flowing blue fabric to fall to the ground.

We are in our workroom, where we fiddle with fabric, embellishments, and other design paraphernalia during the crafting phase. This is where Chloe and I generally come to vent, bitch, moan, and groan about anything—men, work, vendors, staff, friends, whatever it is plaguing our creative sides. We work it out of our systems, surrounded by the one thing that brings us peace all the time. Our creations.

I hold up a broach to a pinned tangerine-colored bodice.

"Believe me. I know the feeling. I'm just not sure how it's all going to work out."

Chloe rips another shred of the blue fabric, making sure it tears along the grain. "He just needs to kick her ass to the curb, get custody of Cora, and all will be well with the world."

"Now you sound like Chase." I frown.

"Well, my cousin isn't a multi-billionaire mogul because he's a dimwit. The woman is not stable, Kat. Mark my words. She's fuming."

I furrow my brow and focus on finding the right pendant for the tangerine dress...and fail. "I don't think she's unstable. A little out in left field, sure. But unstable? I mean, she did raise Cora alone all this time, and the baby is in perfect health."

Chloe presses her hand to her chin and sits on the edge of the big rectangular craft table. She sets one red suede stiletto on the edge of a nearby chair. Damn, those are some sexy-as-sin shoes.

"I'm not saying she doesn't love her daughter. That's obvious. She's easy to love. Plus, she looks exactly like me."

I roll my eyes. "Yes, Auntie Chloe. She's your spitting image. Enough about it."

She laughs and rips another swath, this time of dark-purple fabric stained with pink swirls. I have no idea what she's doing with the mix of colors, but when she throws them on the table against one another, they somehow work together.

"I don't know, Kat. The way she acted as if you'd stolen her man and calling you a homewrecker? What's up with that? Did my brother promise something he shouldn't have?"

I shrug. "I doubt it. Carson is pretty straightforward when he wants something." I glance over at her to find her grinning like a loon. "Not a word." I smile, and she plays like she's zipping up her lips and tossing the key.

We work silently for a few more minutes, content within our own projects, until my phone buzzes on the table.

I grab for it and look at the display. It's a text identified as an unknown number. I click on it to see the message.

To: Kathleen Bennett
From: Unknown Number
Kathleen it's Misty. Can we meet. Clear the air?

"What's up?" Chloe asks, coming over to my side. I dip the phone to her so she can read it. "Huh. You should go. Maybe the whack-a-doo will apologize and the two of you can somehow be friends. For Cora?"

I cringe. "Friends? I'm not sure that's in our future, but being civil would be good. Especially for Carson and Cora. I know the divide is killing him."

Chloe pats my arm. "Well, then go. What's the harm?"

"Should I tell your brother?"

"Hell, no! Are you insane? Not until after, and only if it goes well. Haven't you learned it's better to ask for forgiveness than permission?" She shakes her head like I'm dumber than dirt.

I pinch my lips together and think about it. It could be an opportunity for the two of us to air our grievances and find a way to work together. Cora is going to need her mommy and stepmommy to be friendly in order to grow up well adjusted.

Then it dawns on me what I just said. Stepmommy. As if I'd already added the title to my résumé. Shit. I need to keep that to myself, or at the very least, talk to Dr. Madison about it. Definitely not Carson. He'd have us on the first flight to Vegas by morning.

I add her contact into my phone and type out my message to her.

To: Misty Duncan
From: Kathleen Bennett
Sure. When and where?

Her response is immediate.

To: Kathleen Bennett
From: Misty Duncan
Friday evening. Bubba's Bar on Colfax. 8 pm?

Colfax. A rough neighborhood. And eight at night. She has a daughter to take care of. Then again, she still has Carson at night. Last I heard, he's still working out how to get her comfortable with the idea of the new apartment. The hairs on the back of my neck stand up, and then I remember Carson loves me. He wants me. That doesn't change the fact they have a child together and I am never going to get rid of this woman. Ever. I have to find a way to get along for Cora's and Carson's sake.

I type back one word.

To: Misty Duncan
From: Kathleen Bennett
Fine.

There really isn't anything more to say. Whatever is going

to happen, we'll hash it out on Friday night.

★ ★ ★

The bar is dark as I push through the wooden door. The stale stink of cigarettes, grease, and sawdust hits my nose, and I cringe. There are a few Harleys out front sitting under the one functioning parking-lot light. The building from the outside is old and looks as though it could fall down at any moment. The inside isn't much better, though I can see the support beams doing their job from this angle. A ratty bar sits at the back wall with a bulky, sweaty man wearing a bandanna and a wifebeater behind it. He gives me a chin lift.

I approach him slowly, evaluating my surroundings to determine if I need to beat feet out of there. The vibe of the place is off-the-charts creepy and not a place my friends or I would naturally frequent. Still, I promised I'd be here to meet Misty, and here I am, ten minutes early. I should have waited in my car.

"What'll it be?"

I blink at the scary bartender and he grins a crooked, yellow-teethed version of what I think is a smile. Or maybe it's a snarl.

"Uh, I'm waiting for someone," I mutter and pull out a stool. It has flecks of peanut shells on the torn black leather. I pull a hankie out of my coat pocket, wipe off the shells and muck, and then sit my ass in the chair.

"You can drink while you wait." He leans both hands on the bar opposite me and glares. If I didn't know any better, I'd think we were entering a stare off.

"Sure. Ah...how about a rum and Coke."

His nostrils flare. "Does this look like a fucking Burger King to you?" He waves the filthy bar cloth he's holding around the general vicinity.

I glance around, noticing wooden chairs, a smattering of tables that have seen better days, a pool table where a couple of bikers are shooting pool, and not much else.

"No," I hedge.

"No. We've got Jack, Johnny, and José. And beer. Cold from the tap."

"I'll take a Jack and Coke."

He squints and snarls while making my drink, filling it mostly full of Jack with a splash of something that looks more clear than brown. Guess it's Jack and water. He sets the drink on top of the bar. It sloshes over the edge, but I don't say anything.

Right then, Misty bustles in, her blond hair pulled back into a demure ponytail. Her entire body from head to toe is covered in black. Black jeans, black belt, shoes, and a long-sleeved shirt. She looks like a bandit, but I keep that to myself too.

"Bubba, I'll have a shot of José and a chaser," she says cheerily to the creepy man as she sits next to me. Then she glances my way and sets her purse down in front of her. "Thank you for coming."

"'Course. You wanted to talk. I want us to be able to talk. Carson's and Cora's happiness is all that matters to me." I lay my cards on the table right away, hoping she'll do the same.

Something dark slides over her brown eyes but then disappears just as quickly. Bubba places the shot and a beer in front of her.

"Girl. You look good. Better than before. Your man

treating you right?" he says on a snarl.

Her eyes go straight to me and back to the surly man. "Absolutely. Best man in the whole world. Greatest father my Cora could ever have." She preens, and I know her words are genuine. That doesn't change the fact they are about my man. Fuck. This woman not only wants Carson, she's half in love with him or nearly a step away from completely in love with him already.

"Now"—she turns to me, sucks back the shot, chases it with the beer, and then slams the empty on the counter— "what's it going to take to get you to go away?"

Her words hit me like a Mack truck.

"Excuse me?" I cock my head back, not sure of what I've just heard.

"You heard me. I need you gone. Carson and I have a child. I'm living in his house. He's fucking me, and he's fucking you. I want him to stop fucking you and for you to disappear. So, what is it going to take?" She blinks slowly, waiting for me to catch up.

I bring my hands up and flail them in front of me like I'm swatting away a horde of angry bees. "Wait a good goddamn minute. Carson is not fucking you. Don't even try to lie to me. He'd never cheat." I know this simple fact like I know I don't need another hole in my head.

A sly grin crosses her lips. "It's cute you really believe that."

"With my entire being," I deadpan.

She laughs and knocks her beer over. It lands in my lap. I jump up and away, but it's too late. I'm tagged by most of a pint. "Fuck!"

Misty stands, grabs the ratty towel on the bar, and tries

to wipe it off. "My goodness me. I'm so sorry. Let me get that." She pats at my wet clothes, the dress I'd worn to work today completely ruined. I'd never get the beer stink off one hundred percent silk.

"Go on to the bathroom. There's some towels. I'll wait here," she says, and I go, mostly to get away from her and get my bearings.

He's fucking me, and he's fucking you. I want him to stop fucking you.

Those were her exact words.

Carson would not cheat.

It's cute you believe that.

I grab a handful of towels, run them under the cold water, and blot at my dress. It's no use. Definitely ruined. Doesn't matter. I need to get to the bottom of what she'd said. I pat away most the moisture and take a look at myself in the hazy mirror above the dirty sink.

"She's playing you. Don't believe her lies," I tell my reflection in the mirror.

Don't believe her lies.

Don't believe her lies.

Don't believe her lies.

I chant the phrase in my head over and over until I make it back and sit down next to her. I pick up my Jack and water and chug it until it's gone. She smiles and her eyes light up like Christmas Day at Disneyland. The burn of the whiskey hits my belly hard. That's when I turn to her.

"Prove it," I sneer, leaning against the bar.

"Prove what?"

"That Carson is cheating on me." The words come out smooth, but my insides are churning.

She snickers, pulls the cowl neck of her shirt aside, and shows me a couple hickeys on the valleys of her breasts. "He made those last night."

I laugh, unable to hold back my amusement. "You honestly think I'm going to believe you were fucking Carson last night because of a couple of hickeys? Anyone could have put those there."

She nonchalantly picks up her phone. "A picture is worth a thousand words. Here's a handful of them. What's that worth? Like a million?" Her words are chilling as she hands me her phone.

My heart stops. The Jack in my stomach swirls in a violent vortex as I look at the horrifying display in full color. Carson lying down, bare-chested, Misty in a black lace bra and thong on top of him. Her lips on his chest.

I swipe to the right.

Carson lying down, his hand on her thigh, his head turned toward her breast.

I swipe to the right.

Carson with a fully naked Misty straddling him. His head back, arms stretched to the side, her body arched in what could only be ecstasy while riding him.

My mind buzzes and I see stars. I need air. Right now. I hold her phone tight and run out of the bar, leaving my purse and my sanity. I've got my car keys clutched in one hand and her phone in the other. I don't know where to go or what to do. The hot burn of tears rushes down my face as I glance around in the darkness, not knowing where the fuck I am. My entire life is crumbling before me. Then my car comes into focus. I stumble toward it.

All I can see behind my eyelids is her body arched over

his. Naked.

I stash the phone in my back pocket as Misty comes screaming out of the bar.

"Wait. You can't leave. We're not done talking. You have my phone!"

"I don't care. I don't care about anything!" I cry as she reaches my car. My door is open, and she tosses my purse past me and into the car, and then holds out her hand.

"Kathleen, I'm sorry you had to find out this way. I really hoped he'd be the one to tell you," she says, sounding half human, almost kind. None of it makes any sense.

I grip the door as a bout of dizziness rushes over me. I brace myself on the car. "You can fucking have him! I'm done." The tears blur my vision as I tumble into my car. I put it into reverse, screech out of the parking lot, and head out along the road that follows the bay.

He's fucking me, and he's fucking you.

I slam my hand on the steering wheel and barely register the pain as it ripples up my arm. The tears are falling so fast I can't wipe them away quick enough. My head hurts, and a pounding starts behind my eyes. The vortex of Jack in my stomach spins in an endless acidic circle, and I cough and just barely avoid vomiting.

He's fucking me, and he's fucking you.

I press my foot to the gas pedal and push through the dizziness. The car lurches forward at a speed that seems to give me more control. I shake my head and swerve past a stream of rainbow lights. Car horns blare and I swear again.

He's fucking me, and he's fucking you.

I sob and cry out, screaming. I'm so tired. So tired of always fighting. More lights stream along both sides of my car, as if they are so close I can touch the rainbow. I roll down the window and the cold air blasts against my face. I close my eyes, feeling the darkness settling over me. More horns blare but they sound far away. Until the sound of metal hitting metal and a world of pain hits my head with a blow so hard I lose control and float into the ether.

Everything goes blessedly black.

CHAPTER SEVENTEEN

CARSON

"Wake the fuck up." A firm hand slaps at my cheeks, jarring the slosh that is my brain right now. "Carson, wake up." This time water is splashed on my face.

"Jesus..." I barely get the word out before nausea hits my gut. I tumble out of bed, running into walls and fumbling to the toilet, where I throw up.

"He's sick. You should go." I hear Misty's tight voice from somewhere in the other room.

"I'm not going anywhere. Kat's hurt. She needs him." Chase's voice. I hear Chase. Why the fuck is my cousin here? Why does my head hurt so much?

Kat's hurt.

I try to speak, but another bout of nausea rips through me and I heave over the bowl again. Whatever bit of food and water I had inside me comes out over and over again until I'm hacking up bile.

"You hungover?" Chase asks, handing me a wet cloth.

No man. I didn't even have a drink is what I mean to say. What comes out is, "Nah mah, I no drink."

"Sick?" He clasps my forehead. "Fuck, you're burning up."

"I no know. I no remember." My mouth feels funny and my head is dizzy. My tongue is swollen to double its size. Speaking clearly takes serious effort. The room tilts and sways as I attempt to stand up.

Chase's jaw tightens. "You need to get your shit together. Kat's been in a car accident. Four-car pileup on the freeway, and it looks like it's her fault. They're thinking DUI."

I run the wet cloth over my face and it feels like heaven. If I could crawl into the sink and let the water pour over me right now, I so would. Then a thought hits me. "Kat doesn't drink and d-drive," I stutter. "She Ubers everywhere." I get this out around the cotton coating my tongue and throat.

"Well, I don't know what happened. The doctors are trying to figure it out. We'll know more when the tests come back."

"Tests? What kind of tests?" Misty's voice is high-pitched and piercing my ear. I glance her way and notice she's bobbing Cora on her hip. I blink rapidly, seeing three of each of them streaming bits of color with every movement.

Chase crosses his arms over his chest and stares at her. "The kind that tells a judge how much she's had to drink and if she's on any drugs."

Misty's eyes widen and she nods. "Wow. I hope she's okay."

"She'll live." Then he focuses on me as I'm trying to put a long-sleeved shirt on. The holes are so much smaller than they used to be. Eventually, it dawns on me that I'm cold. My bottom half is completely naked. What? I haven't slept naked since Cora and Misty moved in. I'm always in sleep pants just to be safe. *Why the hell am I naked?*

The questions swirl around in my head, but I'm unable to hold on to any one thought long enough to make any sense of it. I'm so tired. My head is pounding so hard I lean against the wall and press my temples.

"You don't look good, man." Chase grips me by the arm and brings me to the bed, where he sits me down. Then he walks into my closet and comes back with a pair of boxer briefs and jeans. "Here." He tosses them on the bed next to me. Then he pulls his phone out of his suit coat pocket, brings it to his ear, and says something I can't make out through the ocean in my head. The waves are crashing so loudly I flinch.

I focus on getting my underwear on one foot at a time, and I gotta admit, it takes more effort than it ever has in my entire life. All I want to do is lie down, let the pounding in my head disappear, and then deal with the day—until I remember Chase said Kat's hurt. That's all the motivation I need to get my jeans on. I sway into my cousin when I stand.

"Fuck. You're not right."

Jack enters the room and wraps an arm around my shoulders. That's when I start to lose consciousness. I'm dragged through my house and into a car. The second my head hits the cool leather, I'm out.

★ ★ ★

I come to hearing my father's stern tone. "How is that even possible? My son doesn't do drugs."

I blink a few times, trying to open my eyes, but it's so goddamned bright and my eyelids are too heavy. I just can't. There's a pressure on my head that feels as though my head is in a vise.

"We're doing everything we can, for both of them," a voice I don't recognize says. "Just be patient. We'll get to the bottom of this."

Again, I try to come back to the surface, but the darkness takes me away.

★ ★ ★

Humming. I hear a pretty sound like a song, only it's soft and far away. It's a song my mother used to sing to me when I was little. I want to see my mother's face. So bad. I open my eyes, and I'm greeted by perfect blue eyes and straight blond hair. For a second, it's my mom. She's smiling, and I try to lift my arm to her face, but I can't move. Then my mom's face morphs into my sister's.

"Chloe," I croak, sounding like I haven't spoken in a year.

"Carson. Oh, thank God." Instantly, her hands are on my face, and she's kissing my forehead in quick presses.

The grogginess is trying to force me back down, but I push it back. I do a mental assessment, and my entire body feels lethargic. Heavy. Like I'd been asleep forever and am finally waking.

"You've been out for twenty-four hours, bro," Chloe says.

How the hell did that happen?

"What happened?" Then two words hit my memory like a jack hammer. *Kat's hurt.* "Kathleen!" I cry out and try to shift out and off the bed.

Chloe presses firmly against my chest to hold me down, but it doesn't take a lot of effort on her part. I'm sluggish as fuck and can barely move my arms and legs without using a great deal of energy.

"She's okay. They're treating her. The airbag gave her face a nasty beating, and she has a raunchy bruise across her chest where the seat belt held her in place. Thank God she was wearing it. The drugs though... That was bad on her system. Especially with the, uh...other thing."

Airbag. Nasty beating. Bruises. Other thing.

The words jumble around in my head until a doctor I recognize all too well strides into my hospital room. Dr. Dutera, the same doctor who has treated almost all of my friends and family at one crisis or another. He pushes his glasses up his nose and glances at me from head to toe before he comes over with a penlight and examines my eyes.

"Mr. Davis. Hadn't expected to see you here, and especially not like this. How are you feeling?"

"Like shit." No sugarcoating needed.

He nods and writes something down on his clipboard. "You got lucky. You didn't have as much Rohypnol in your system as your girlfriend."

"Kathleen was drugged?"

The doctor nods and checks a few things on the machine attached to the fluids being pumped through my IV. "Enough to know it wasn't a medicinal dose. Had it been any more, you both could be a lot worse. I'll be back later. You're here another day. Cops want to talk to you though. Anytime we find Rohypnol on the drug screen, we have to report it."

"The date-rape drug?" I ask, my voice betraying the shock.

"Yes, Mr. Davis. Try to rest and think about how you could have ingested it. There are no injection sites, so you must have eaten or drunk it," he says before he leaves.

"Were you and Kat together on Friday?" Chloe asks. "We figured the two of you had somehow come into contact with it together, and she left and you went to bed."

I scan my brain. "The last thing I remember I was sitting down to dinner with Misty early Friday evening. We, uh, were talking about her moving out, and then nothing. Everything goes blank after that. I don't remember finishing dinner, going to bed, and I sure as shit don't remember coming here."

Chloe's eyebrow rises in what I can only assume is speculation. "And Kathleen wasn't with you?"

I shake my head. "No. That I would remember. I think." I close both hands into fists, trying to remember what happened. It's all a big black hole.

"Misty," Chloe whispers and looks out the window. "That's weird. Kat left work on Friday evening saying she had to meet with Misty at a bar downtown. The way Kat explained it, they were supposed to have some type of come-to-Jesus chat with one another."

"But I was with Misty."

Chloe shrugs. "I don't know, but when I left work at seven thirty on Friday evening, Kathleen was heading to a bar named Bubba's to meet up with Misty."

Bubba's is the shithole where Misty used to work before I came back into the picture. "Fucking hell. I need to see Kathleen. Now."

"She, uh, doesn't want to see you." Chloe's entire face crumbles into an expression of misery.

"What?"

She rushes to continue. "I don't know what's going on. When they finally got her awake, she was crying, carrying on, saying you hurt her. You ruined everything. I believe her words were that you *betrayed her*."

Betray Kathleen?

I grind my teeth and brace against the mattress to sit up

straight. "I'd never in a million years betray her."

"I'm sorry. You do need to talk, but she's in no position. And Chase... He's got her on lockdown."

"Fucking hell. My goddamn cousin. Saint Chase. You tell Chase I want to talk to him. Now."

★ ★ ★

The door to my hospital room opens and Chase enters, my father hot on his heels. "Now, Chase, remember he was drugged and is in no condition for your wrath," my father says as they both enter. Chase's blue eyes are an angry blaze.

"Your wrath? I hear you have my woman in lockdown. Away from me. Hurting." The words seep from my lips, coated in anger.

"That's right. And you have some explaining to do before you're ever going to talk to her again." He throws down the gauntlet with absolutely no fear whatsoever. Whatever it is he thinks I've done, he's going all out.

Against me.

My best friend.

My fucking *blood*.

I grind my teeth and lift my chin to the sky. "Chase, tell me what's going on. All I know right now is both of us were drugged. I ended up in my bed. Kathleen ended up on the freeway in a four-car pileup. What the fuck happened?"

"You cheated on her, you fucking piece of shit." Chase's anger is so potent I can feel it pumping off him like an electric current in the small room.

"Chase, not that it's any of your business, but I'd never cheat on her."

"Oh yeah?"

"Yeah. I'd have my mother strike me down from heaven above before I'd ever fucking cheat on Kathleen. I love her. I want her as my wife. She's my future, Chase. My every... fucking...thing. You know she is. You know what the woman means to me. Has always meant to me. Now don't you dare look me in the face and spew this bullshit."

Chase shakes his head, and my father looks down and to the side. They don't believe me. An arrow to the heart couldn't have hit the mark better.

"Someone please tell me what's going on." I grind my teeth so hard I can hear it inside my head.

"You say you'd never cheat. Well, here's your proof right here." Chase holds up a phone I don't recognize and points the display at me.

I squint at the picture and see a mostly naked Misty straddling my thighs, her lips on mine, and me lying under her.

"No...no fucking way. This can't be me." If I weren't seeing this with my own eyes, I'd believe it was Photoshopped, but it's definitely me.

"It is you. I've verified that already," Chase says. "Keep clicking. There's several for you to choose from."

I swipe through the pictures and can't believe my own eyes. I just can't. "Chase, I don't know what to say. I don't remember this. Any of it."

"Convenient," he mumbles.

"Son. We make mistakes, and Misty is a beautiful woman..." My father starts to make excuses for what I can tell he thinks is me behaving badly.

"No. No. I would never. Not to Kathleen. Not to any woman. It took us forever to get here. Maybe it's from before.

When Misty and I hooked up over two years ago?" My voice sounds desperate, hanging on to any shred of hope I can come up with to explain what I'm seeing.

Chase tilts his head back and laughs. "Look at the fucking picture, asshole. Your daughter's sippy cup is sitting on the end table in the background. The same one that was on your end table when I picked you up on Saturday morning. Naked and in your bed. Misty was wearing a fucking skimpy-ass robe too. Now what more do you have to say for yourself? At least admit you fucked up."

I push the covers out of the way and off to the side so I can turn and get out of bed.

"Chase, I'm begging you on our blood and our honor as best friends. I was drugged on Friday. I don't remember anything that happened. Kathleen was drugged on Friday. Does she remember what happened?"

"No, but I'll tell you what it looks like."

"And that is?" I lean over the bed, cock my head to the side, and stare at my cousin with every ounce of humility I have. "I'd never hurt her willingly, man. You have to believe me."

Chase's eyes turn hard, and then something clicks as he takes in my defeated posture and gaze. His shoulders fall, and he takes a harsh breath.

"Fuck. It doesn't matter what it looks like. Only what it is. Kathleen doesn't remember anything after leaving work. She doesn't even know where this phone came from or whose it is. But the picture was the first thing Gillian saw when she pulled it out of the pocket of the pants the nurses handed us. She showed it to me, and Kathleen woke up and saw it over our shoulders and demanded to see it. We had no choice."

"Whose fucking phone is it?" I flip it over and glance

at the tiny crack in the right-hand corner. I know that crack. I've seen it before because my daughter did it last week while playing with her mommy's phone. She'd dropped it on the tile, and it cracked. I offered to replace it for Misty, but she said I'd done enough and not to worry. "Jesus Christ. It's Misty's. That means she met up with Kathleen after she had dinner with me."

"So, Misty saw both of you that night. She made you dinner and met Kathleen for a drink. She drugged you both."

I shake my head. Could it be possible? I mean, sure, she was angry about me telling her she had to move and of course the issue last week at dinner. But drugging us? That's extreme.

Chase grasps the phone again and starts squinting at the display and fiddling with it. After a few minutes of doing this, he sighs long and hard.

"I'm sorry, Carson. I should have given you the benefit of the doubt." He's frowning as he shows me the screen and a pic where he's zoomed in. I can see my face is completely lax and I'm unconscious. Even in the picture of her holding my hand to her leg, I'm loose-fingered. My hands are not gripping her flesh the way someone would while deep in the throes of passion.

The bitch fucking set me up.

"It's okay, Chase. I know what it looks like. I'd never hurt her. I need to see her. Talk to her."

He nods. "Let me go first. Tell her what we've put together. She, uh...has some news to tell you anyway. When she's ready."

Fuckin' hell. More shit being held back and another span of time where I can't go to my woman.

"Fine. Just make it quick. I'm there in an hour. I don't care if I have to check myself out against medical advice. I'm going to fix this. I need her, Chase. I'd be lost without Kathleen."

Chase closes his eyes and nods.

"Then you understand. Make her see. Tell her I love her and I want to see her."

★ ★ ★

Chase wheels me into Kathleen's room. The room is dim. Only a single light in the corner is illuminating the twelve-by-twelve-foot space. The moment I lay eyes on her, tears hit. It's only the third time I remember crying in my entire life. The first, when I told my mother goodbye as she died. The second, when I saw Kathleen in the hospital fighting for her life after the fire. And now.

I struggle to get out of the wheelchair and go to her bedside. "My God, Kathleen." It's three years ago, all over again. Her lying prone in a hospital bed. This time her face is messed up. She has monitors everywhere, two black eyes, a swollen nose, and a cut lip. She looks as though she'd been in a boxing match with Muhammad Ali and lost.

"Baby..." I whisper, and her swollen eyes open.

Tears instantly fall down her cheeks. "I'm sorry. I didn't know what to think." Her words crack, and I get into the bed with her.

"I don't think you're supposed to do that..." Chase says.

"Oh, shut up," Gillian says. "You did that to me the second I pushed out your twins, and you threatened to have the nurses fired if they crossed you. Leave them be. Are you going to be okay, Kat?"

She nods against my neck. "I am now."

"Come on, big guy. Let's have another chat about boundaries and other people's relationships," I hear her say as she pulls my cousin out the door.

"I'm not sorry I overreacted. Kathleen was hurting..." is the last thing I hear him say as they walk out of the room and down the hall.

I look down at Kathleen. "I love you so goddamn much, and I'd never cheat on you. You own my soul."

More tears leak out of her eyes, and she holds me around the waist and sobs into my chest. "It was so real. And then I didn't know where to go, what to do, and I was tired and groggy but still scared and devastated."

With a careful hand, I run my fingers through her hair. "I've been told there's only property damage from the accident. You were the only one who sustained any real injuries, and it's pretty good that you hit those cars, because your car was headed toward the girder over the bay." I swallow heavily and suck in a breath, smelling her hair, feeling her warm body alive and in my arms.

"I don't remember anything after meeting up with Misty and her telling me you were fucking her."

"So, you did meet up with her. On Friday." She confirms exactly what I'd already put together.

Kat nods against my chest as I tell my story. "I had dinner with her and then don't remember anything afterward. Chase says, in the pictures, Cora's sippy cup is on my nightstand. She put me in bed, stripped my clothes, and took those disgusting pictures. Then she must have met up with you and showed them to you. But I swear, nothing happened. Even the doc said I couldn't have functioned properly." I run my knuckles down her swollen cheek, needing to touch her, connect with her on this level. "Do you believe me?" I'm holding my breath.

"Yeah, I do. I'm so sorry I lost my mind. I should have

looked closer. Once Chase forced me to look at the enlarged images, I could tell you weren't even awake. You looked unconscious."

I chuckle, bringing some light into the darkness. "Because I was unconscious. Shit, I don't even know what to do now. This woman lives in my house. She's the mother of my daughter. That's fact. If she could do this to us, what could she do to Cora?"

"But what do we really know about her?" Kat asks the million-dollar question.

"Not much. Honestly, she never talked about her upbringing. All she's ever said is her parents are dead and she's an only child. No family to speak of."

"Seems suspect to me," Kat says and then yawns.

"You need to rest. Why don't you sleep? I'm here. An earthquake couldn't get me to leave this bed."

She rubs her hand up and down my chest soothingly. "There's something else the doctors found when they ran my tests."

A pounding fear hits my chest so hard I clutch at her body, holding her tight. I don't know how much more I can take. What more could she possibly have thrown at her now?

"Whatever it is, Kat, I'm here for you. We'll deal with it together. When we get out of here, you're moving in. I'm going to have you and my daughter in *my house*. Period. It's happening. So, whatever it is, it's you and me, okay? No running." I lean down and tilt her chin. Her lips tremble, and I try not to let her battered face anger me more. Not now. Not when she needs to share something serious with me. "What is it, Kat? Just tell me. I can handle it."

She swallows and pushes off my chest so she can look me

in the face. "When they ran the gamut of tests, they had to run all kinds of blood panels, and they found some of my levels were higher than they should be."

"What kind of levels?"

"Progesterone."

I shrug. "Sweetcheeks, I don't know what that means."

"Well, when they found that my progesterone levels were high, they did more tests. One very specific test and then an ultrasound."

"Ultrasound? Of what?"

She turns to the left, reaches for the side table, and grabs a piece of paper. "I wouldn't have believed it if I hadn't seen it with my own eyes." She hands me the piece of paper.

It's a baby sonogram.

"What is this?"

"It's our baby."

I glance at her bruised face, and the impact of what she's just said hits me like a category-five hurricane hitting the Florida shore.

"See here..."—she points at a specific spot on the picture—"it says we're ten weeks and a few days."

"Ten weeks..." I whisper and glance down at the blob. It's nothing more than a peanut shape with two tiny buds for hands and two buds for feet.

"Carson, say something."

"We're having a baby? You're pregnant?" I gasp, shock skittering through my veins, making my heart pump double time.

She nods rapidly and doesn't say anything more.

"How? You had the implant. We had this conversation before. Long time ago."

"Yeah. So long ago I was supposed to get a new one. The implant only lasts up to four years. I'm a full year past that. At the time I got my renewal card, I blew it off because I was in such a deep depression about my injury and not having you in my life. My future seemed so bleak, and I just...never renewed it. And it didn't register when we got back together that I'd need to...and..." She starts to shake in my arms.

I press two fingers over her lips. "Shhhh. You're working yourself up. It's not good for the baby. Oh my God, what about the Rohypnol? What did Dr. Dutera say?"

"He said the baby is fine. Obviously, we were all surprised by its appearance." She runs a hand over her flat stomach. I lay my hand over hers.

"We're having a baby," I whisper, allowing the awe to roll over me fully.

"Yeah," is her only reply.

"Oh my God. I'm going to be a daddy!" I smile huge, unable to control how much this news excites me.

"You already are a daddy." Kat nudges my shoulder playfully.

"Holy shit. I'm going to have two kids." At first, the thought fills me with joy, and then reality strikes. "I'm going to have two kids out of wedlock. Fuck. Kat, we have to get married. Like, right away."

She groans and lays her head back. "Not this again."

"Just promise me you'll think about it." If I have any say whatsoever, this woman will be wearing my ring before the year is out.

"How about we deal with Misty and her drugging us first and me getting out of here?"

I close my eyes and press my forehead to hers. We breathe

one another's air for a while. "Are you happy?" I ask her, afraid of what her answer will be.

"Are you?" She answers my question with a question. Typical evasive Kathleen.

I kiss her lips softly, being careful not to put too much pressure on her busted one. "Kathleen, having you in my life is the most natural thing in the world. You carrying my child is my dream. It's everything I've always wanted for us."

For a long time, she doesn't say anything. Then finally she adds, "You're my dream too. And I want this baby. I want you, me, our baby, and Cora to find a way to be happy and together."

The tears fall again. I wipe them away with my knuckles and kiss her softly. "One day we'll have that. I feel it deep."

Together we lie with our hands over her stomach. I can't feel our baby there yet, but knowing we've created life together proves just how much the universe is pushing for us. Now I just have to deal with Misty and get custody of my daughter.

For now, I let it go, close my eyes, and rest my head against the pillow, my hand over my baby and Kathleen's head over my heart. Nothing else matters but having this woman safely resting in my arms, carrying my entire world within her body, mind, and soul.

CHAPTER EIGHTEEN

KATHLEEN

Carson is a complete and utter wreck. It's been ten days since we came home to find his daughter and her mother gone. Not gone for the day, out and about at a park or a playdate.

G-O-N-E.

At the hospital, Carson was released before me. I have suspicions that he released himself against medical advice, because from the second he came to my room and the truth was revealed about our drugging, him being taken advantage of while unconscious, and me telling him about the baby, he hasn't left my side. While I was in the hospital, he was in the bed with me or in the chair next to the bed when the nurses were seeing to my medication and vitals. It was exactly where I wanted him, so I didn't complain.

Then we got home and found out Misty had cleared out her clothes, the baby's clothes and essentials, and her new car was nowhere to be found. Apparently, the day Carson was taken to the hospital by Chase, Misty had gone to the bank, cleared out her accounts, and taken a five-thousand-dollar cash advance from the emergency credit card Carson had given her. She was in the wind with approximately fifteen grand cash in her pocket. Carson had never taken a dime of the money she'd earned from working for Charles as his executive assistant, and the man was generous with his employees. With the way Misty lived in the past, that kind of money could keep her and Cora in hiding for a solid year.

Ten whole days and not a word.

To keep busy, I'm making coffee and puttering around the beach house. I don't have any idea what to do or how to make him feel better. We haven't made love since we came home, which has inadvertently put distance between us that I'm eager to fill. Only, I can't force him to feel good when he's lost in a vicious haze of worry.

The phone rings. I grab it before Carson and put it on speaker. Carson is quick to stand over the island and stare at the phone.

"Hello, Eli." I recognize the number and grip the counter for support. Every time he calls, a small bit of Carson's light flickers out. I know right now Carson wants to grab the phone and hold it to his ear, but we have a pact. No secrets, no matter what.

"Yeah, is Carson there too?" Eli's gravelly voice comes through the speaker.

"I'm here."

"I've got a lock on her," Eli says flat out. No lead-in, just straight to the heart of the matter.

Best six words we've heard in the better part of two weeks.

Elijah "Eli" Redding is married to my soul sister Maria. He's also a badass bounty hunter with loads of experience and countless takedowns. Apparently, he's magical at tracking people and bringing home the bad guy. Even people like Misty, who don't seem to have much to track. Eli also has his team running deep background on Misty Duncan, who on the surface was clean as a whistle. Probably because she wasn't always Misty Duncan. That was her dead husband's last name. Misty isn't even her real first name. It's a nickname. She was born Mystique Turner. What kind of name is Mystique? Her mother and father must be as wacky as her. Anyway, that's the last update we received from Eli's team.

"Where is she?" Carson says flatly.

"Sin City."

"Of course. No better place to hide. Bright lights, everyone with a shadow behind their eyes and a secret in their soul," I add unhelpfully.

"Got word from one of my men a woman matching her description is bartending at some skanky topless shithole called Jugz with a 'z.' Started a few days ago. Stands to reason. Close enough to get to quickly and seedy enough to disappear. Unless you know where to look."

I roll my eyes. Jugz? Really?

Carson leans over the phone. "When can you confirm it's her?"

"Headed there now with Dice, my best hunter. Davis Industries has a jet ready to go. Got Scooter, my tech, on the background. He's digging deep. Says he's close to breaking into something huge. Will call from the air, yeah?"

The veins in Carson's forearms bulge. "I know you said you don't want me there, man, but I gotta say, I want to be there." Carson's voice is like sandpaper over stone, scratchy and rough. He's keeping his emotions in check the best he can, but each day his daughter is gone, he loses a bit more of his sanity.

"You're in no condition, man. I got this. I'll make sure it's her. Keep eyes on her until I see the girl. Then we go in. I'll have them both on the plane back to you before you know it."

"Eli..." Carson's voice cracks, and he clears his throat. "Find my daughter. Bring her home." He closes his eyes and drops his head.

"Most important job I've ever had. You have my word I'll do it right." Then the line goes dead.

Carson grabs the cordless phone, flings his arm way back as if he's a professional baseball pitcher, and smashes it into smithereens against the opposite wall. He follows that up with a mighty howl. "Goddamn it!" His shoulders lift and fall with every labored breath he sucks in. His head falls forward.

I rush over to him and put my arms around him from behind. "He's going to find her. He's going to bring her home. He promised, and Maria swears he's the best in the business. *The best.* For Cora. He will find her. You have to believe."

Carson is no longer able to hold up under the weight of his misery. He falls to his knees, his fists on the tile floor. His entire body shakes, and a sob is torn from his throat. "I just fucking got her, and she's taken her away. My baby girl. My fucking daughter!" Finally, it comes out. He hasn't so much as shed a tear since finding out Cora was taken and Misty had skipped town. Instead he'd taken the anger approach, but right now he's losing it.

I go down to my knees on the cold tile floor next to him, wrap my left arm over his back, and lean toward his head. Tears slip down his nose, falling to the floor in tiny drops. The fear and anxiety has finally taken over. Instinctively, I push him so that he's sitting on his ass. Within a second, I crawl up into his lap, wrap my legs around his waist, and tuck my head against his neck. I hold him as tight as my arms will allow while he rocks and cries, letting it all go.

"Get it out, baby," I whisper. "Let it go, because I have a feeling really soon we're going to have our girl back. She'll need her daddy to be strong."

He nods into my neck, not saying a word, just holding me. I don't know how long we sit like this, but I'm comfortable just being there for him. The daylight shifts, and the sun sets over the ocean. I watch it while he rocks me. When the sun kisses the horizon, I lean back and lift his chin with both of my thumbs. The tears have dried, but the misery in his baby blues is gut-wrenching.

"Eli will find her. He will."

Carson nods but doesn't respond. His face is blank. Not even a glimmer of my fun-loving guy is anywhere in sight.

Slowly I kiss his lips. He barely responds with a pucker. Even that simple gesture of love is too much for him. He's lost, and it's up to me to bring him back. He needs to find his inner strength for Cora, for the battle ahead, and for us.

Easing out of his lap, I stand up and hold out my hand. He takes it without comment. I help him stand, and while holding his hand, I walk him toward his bedroom and into the bathroom. Once there, I undo each button on his short-sleeved shirt and slip it off his body. The golden chest I love is still beautiful with hard slabs of muscle, squared-off pecs, and abdominals. I slide both hands from his shoulders down the sexy hard male flesh in a blatant caress.

"Come back to me," I whisper and glance up into his eyes. He's just watching me, almost as if he's an outsider looking in and not a participant.

Seems I need to work a little harder. Watching his eyes, I tug at his Levi's, unbuttoning and then unzipping the jeans before pushing them over his hips. He steps out of them without a word. I glance at his package hidden beneath a pair of burgundy boxer briefs. Unfortunately, there's no movement happening...yet.

With eager hands, I slip my fingers around his waist, inserting them just under the elastic of his underwear before gripping the fabric.

"Come back to me, Carson." I push his boxer briefs down to the ground, where once again Carson steps out of them. This time when I look at his eyes, the light blue has darkened, a hint of interest sparking in his gaze.

As efficiently as possible, I lean into the shower and turn on the double heads, getting the large space nice and hot before turning around to continue my task. Using my good arm, I grip the fabric of my jersey top, pull it over my head, and toss it on the ground behind me. He blinks, his eyes going straight to my lace-clad breasts. An eyebrow rises, those blue eyes getting darker, his pupils widening.

There you go, baby. That's right. Look your fill.

Doing a little wiggle, I push down my skirt, letting it fall into a puddle at my feet. I kick it away and stand before him.

"Touch me. Come back to me," I say as softly as a prayer in the dark.

He blinks a few times and sucks in a large breath. It's like a window's been opened and he's just sampled a fresh breath of air.

Still, he doesn't touch, just looks. His fingers curl into his palms, creating fists. I don't know if he's purposely holding himself back or... Hell, I don't know what's going on in that head of his right now. I just know he needs to feel. Feel something other than worry, fear, and anger. He needs to feel loved, and this is the only way I know I can reach him. At least I hope I can.

With a flick of my fingers, I undo the front clasp of my bra—the smartest invention ever made, especially since I have the full use of only one hand. I shrug my shoulders until the lavender lace falls to the floor. Not even looking at his face, I shove down the matching lace bikini briefs and kick them away.

I take a breath, lift my head, and stare directly into Carson's eyes. I stand before the man I love, naked, giving everything I am in the hope it's enough to bring him back from the dark place he's entered.

Carson blinks, his eyes shifting, and the gaze I adore leaves my face to scan down my body and back up. When our eyes meet again, his are blazing hot pools of desire. I swallow but don't move a muscle. The only movement is the slight rise and fall of my chest with each breath I take, waiting, needing him to accept the gift I'm giving.

Finally, he speaks.

"You're so beautiful. I can barely breathe when I look at you. Sometimes I think you'll just disappear and I'll be alone again."

I wrap my arms around him and plaster my naked body against his. "Everything I am, all that I have, I'm entrusting to you. You'll never be alone as long as I live. I promise." My words are a vow, one I know I'll never break.

Carson's body trembles in my arms as he tucks me close, his mouth near my ear. "I'm going to hold you to that promise."

"Just as long as you always hold me."

"Always," he says before his mouth comes down to mine.

★ ★ ★

Steam billows around us as Carson moves deep within me. One of my legs is hiked up over his hip, the other holds me upright. He moves his hands all over me. From my neck, down my shoulders, and over my breasts, where he stops to give a delectable tug on both tips simultaneously. He continues his journey down along my hips, where he grips tight, digging four fingers into the fleshy areas, pounding harder. His thumbs span my lower abdomen. Using the full force of his hips, he presses deep and stays, his cock so hard, filling me so completely and deliciously I could die. He reverses just enough so he can caress those digits lovingly over where our baby is growing, seemingly mesmerized by the area.

"Gonna put more of these in you." His voice is a sex-roughened rumble. "Many more," he promises, pulling back out to the tip and ramming deep once more. I cling to his back and arch into the pleasure.

I'm incapable of responding to his delusions of grandeur in the kid department, because just then he moves one hand between us and uses his glorious thumb to swirl around my clit in dizzying circles. I cry out and shoot to the height of passion, tumbling right over the edge into the beauty that is Carson and me.

"Christ. Your pussy is so fucking tight when you come," he growls, taking my mouth and kissing me hard, elongating my orgasm to an epic degree.

"Need a taste of that," he murmurs and bites my earlobe. Quick as a shot his dick is gone, still hot and hard in front of me. I whimper at the loss, not exactly needing it after a blistering orgasm but wanting his thickness inside me all the same. The shower beats down on his back and now my front as he kisses his way down my body, paying special attention to both erect tips. He bites down hard on my left nipple until I hiss and grip his head, weaving my hands into his wet locks. Carson grins and looks up while sucking hard and biting the second one until I whine. He's rocketing my previously sated body back up into hyperdrive all over again.

"You're crazy, you know that?" I groan as he drags his teeth down the center of my belly and nips at the triangle of hair nestled neatly between my thighs. The action sends another spark of pain pleasure barreling through since I know exactly where he's going to end up.

He kneels in front of me and lifts my leg up and onto the tile seat that runs across the back of the shower. "Crazy in love with you. And after the past two weeks of hell, I'm going to lose myself in your magnificent body."

I close my eyes, letting the words slip dreamily over my senses. There was a time in the not so distant past where I wouldn't have believed a word of what he's saying. Now I know better. He doesn't see the scars as ugly or disgusting. He sees them as reminders of my survival. And because of them, I'm still here, about to be taken over completely by the man who loves me and will continue to do so until the end of time. I wholeheartedly embrace this to be fact, and the proof is growing within me. A piece of Carson and me. A child who will bind us together forever no matter what trials and tribulations life throws in our paths. We'll handle them together.

Carson nips and sucks at the tender skin of my inner thigh, bringing me back to the moment. I open my eyes and glance down, curling my hand around his chin. I lift my hand and then run my fingers and nails over his scalp until he groans.

His pupils dilate until there's hardly any blue remaining. I cup the back of his nape and lead him toward my open center. He grins and places a hand on my opposite leg, running it up the back until he's cupping my ass. He uses it as leverage and pulls me onto his mouth in a burst of fiery passion.

I cry out when his mouth covers the wet heart of me and his tongue dives deep. He alternates between lapping at my clit in hard presses and soft nips with his teeth to fucking me with his tongue. Shamelessly, I hold his head and grind against his face, allowing his nose and the scruff of his chin to penetrate me along with his talented mouth.

My second orgasm builds slowly, and I know it's going to be a doozy. Just when I get acclimated to his ministrations, he changes it up, inserting two fingers deep, hooking and rubbing along that intense spot hidden inside. He focuses on my clit with his mouth, sucking hard and long until my entire body sizzles with heat. Ribbons of electricity shoot straight up my body, and I go rigid, readying for the mother of all orgasms to hit.

Just when the walls of my vagina start to flex and squeeze, Carson's fingers and mouth leave my pussy, and I'm hauled up and flattened against the shower wall, where he drives deep. He's as hard as a steel pipe and so thick. I moan and cling to him as though my very life depends on it, sucking and biting on the sensitive skin of his neck as his hips relentlessly slam against me.

"Can't get close enough." He grinds his teeth as he tries to imprint himself on my body with his cock, hands, and mouth.

Our lovemaking is wild, savage, and so intense I have to blink back the stars shooting across my peripheral vision with the amount of pleasure roaring through every limb.

It's too much and not enough at the same time. "Baby, slow down, calm down. I'm right here." I dig my fingers into his back hard enough to leave crescent-shaped imprints in the skin of his shoulders while I try to get his attention and bring him back from the carnal, animalistic place he's slipped into. Under normal circumstances, I'd let him fuck the shit out of me, but this doesn't feel right. He's trying to substitute sex for his pain, and that's not possible.

Carson's body pins me up against the wall with his lower half, and his upper body shifts back. He cups my cheeks with both his hands. "I want to be closer," he whispers against my mouth, our lips barely touching.

"I need to be closer to you." He rests his forehead against mine, his body shaking with the physical strain of holding me against the wall and his need to come.

"Honey, we're as close as two people can get."

"I want to be lost in you. I want it all to go away." He presses his temple against mine and breathes into my neck.

The water is starting to get cold, and I shiver. "Let me down."

Without even a glimmer of a fight or retort he pulls out, still hard as a rock, and lets me slide down his body until my feet touch the ground. I turn off the water, grab two towels, and dry us both efficiently and quickly. Carson is barely holding himself up, his posture and facial expression showing defeat.

Naked, I lead him to his bed—our bed, seeing that I haven't left since being released from the hospital—and sit him back on it. "Get in."

He does so instantly, the lost puppy within him taking instructions and following them to the letter. It kills me that my normally strong, opinionated, focused man has been beaten down to this level.

Needing to comfort him, I crawl on top of him. His cock, now resting between my thighs, is still firm but not as hard as it was in the shower. I grip the comforter and pull it over both of us. Then I lift, grasp his cock, and slide right down it.

Carson moans, his head going back, chest arching up. His hands fly to my hips, where he holds on as I slowly and rhythmically make love to him. Nice and easy. With mouth, tongue, and fingers, I kiss his neck, chest, and nipples, thumbing them while I move.

"Kathleen..." He sighs and opens his eyes. They are filled with love and passion. Exactly what I need to see right now.

I lean forward and take his lips with mine. He opens his mouth immediately, welcoming me inside. Our tongues dance and swirl around one another playfully. Kissing Carson fills up the emptiness I've felt for the past ten days. His kiss makes my heart beat, bringing me back to life. While we kiss, I continue to ride him. Long drags up and slow impressions back down, grinding my clit against his pubic bone with every drive.

"You always know what I need," he whispers, thrusting his hips and stirring his cock in titillating circles.

"Hmmm..." I hum, enjoying his participation.

I am surprised that he doesn't take over. Usually when we reach the heights of our combined passion, he'll flip me over and take me hard, but this time he doesn't. He's content to let me love him.

Once a fine layer of sweat builds on our skin, I pick up the pace, pulling up and slamming back down. With every jarring thrust, I grind down until eventually I'm bouncing on his cock, hands resting on his chest, and he's pressing his hips into each downstroke.

"Yes, yes, yes," I scream out, lifting my head to the ceiling, every muscle in my body tense and hyperfocused. As the base of my spine tingles, my sex clenches hard around his thick root, and I go off.

Carson is right there with me, pushing up and grinding my hips down until he arches his body powerfully, elbows pressing into the mattress, and he plants himself deep and lets go. I dig my fingernails into his chest as my orgasm merges with his and his body locks around mine. He pulls me down flat against his body and wraps his arms around me. We both curve our heads into the other's neck and breathe through the succulent aftershocks of our lovemaking.

"Now we're close enough," Carson says into my ear before tunneling his hand into my hair, where he grips at the roots and tugs to get me to lift my head. Then he's kissing me. Long, luscious lip presses and tickling tongue flicks until we're both breathless from the effort.

Eventually, we pull away, and I rest my head on his chest while he plays with my hair.

"Thank you." His tone is indescribable. A mix perhaps of being sexually sated with a hint of longing. Not at all what I'd expect after a round of intense lovemaking.

"Uh...for making love to you?" I ask stupidly.

He grins and chuckles but continues to play with my hair as if he's deep in thought. I keep my chin on his chest, enjoying the beating of his heart and waiting for him to pull his thoughts together.

"For knowing what to do," he finally responds.

I sigh, not wanting to take credit for something I was completely clueless about, and frankly, rather scared too. "Honey, I didn't know what to do. Not really."

"You did. And you were right." This time his words are matter-of-fact.

"How so?"

"I needed to connect. Find a way to release all the anger and sadness that has been brewing in me since we came home. Loving you, you giving your love back, it's all I'm ever going to need to find myself again. Because without you, without our connection, I'm not me."

"Eli's going to bring her home," I remind him for what I feel like is the millionth time.

His arms wrap tighter around me. "Yes, he is. I can feel it now. I have the power of your belief to pull me through."

I rise up, resting my hands on his bare chest, and smile. "That's a really nice thing to say. Among all the other things too." I grin, push forward, and peck his lips in a simple kiss.

He sighs, curls an arm up my back, one hand going into my hair, the other wrapping around my waist, holding me close. "As long as I've got you, our baby, our future, Cora included, I'm going to be the happiest man alive. And I'm going to make sure you are too. I swear it. When this all evens out, it's going to be all about our family. The one we're making together."

His confidence is renewed, and I couldn't be more thrilled.

"Sounds heavenly," I admit, because it does. It's what we always wanted way back when we got together originally. If I hadn't been hurt and lost my way, we'd probably already be married with a couple of kids like Gillian and Chase or Bree and Phillip.

Now we just need to get Cora back, put Misty behind bars, and take full custody of Cora. It sounds so simple, but the most important things in life rarely are.

CHAPTER NINETEEN

CARSON

The phone blaring into my subconscious wakes me from the first real sleep I've had in two weeks. I glance at the clock and note it's five in the morning. Fuck.

I grapple for the phone on the nightstand. Kathleen wakes and sits up, her eyes sleepy and her hair a mass of tangles from the many times I ran my fingers through it while I made love to her. She gingerly drags the blanket over her naked breasts, and I have to blink back the desire that instantly hits me. Christ, this woman will be the end of me.

"Hello," I answer, staring at her sexiness.

"We got your girl." Eli's voice is a harsh slash through the fog of sleep and indecent thoughts about my woman, bringing me completely awake.

"Thank God. Babe, they've got her," I say instantly to Kathleen, whose hand flies up to her mouth. Her eyes water, but the tears don't fall.

A voice in my ear breaks through the happy moment.

"Carson. Carson. Man, fucking listen up," Eli commands.

"What?" I cringe and press the phone closer to my ear.

"We've got a problem, man. Misty gave us the slip."

I shake my head and run my hand through my hair, tugging at the roots. The prickle of pain clears my head further. "You just said you have her."

"No. I said we've got *your girl*. Your daughter."

Instantly my fear eases and relief soothes over the rest.

"You've got to come to Vegas and get her. Dice and I need to go after Misty."

I toss back the covers and shoot from the bed and into the closet like a rocket. "How did you get Cora and not Misty?"

"She left her."

Those three words send a knife to my gut. "She left my fucking daughter alone?" I roar into the phone.

Eli doesn't say anything.

"That fucking cunt! How could she? My God. Fuck!" I yell some more. "Where is she now? You have her?" I pace the floor of my closet, fire and ice heating and freezing my veins at the same time.

She left her alone.

"Yeah, man. I've got her."

"No, where is she right this second?" I clench my teeth, imagining my daughter left alone in a ramshackle apartment with no one there to take care of her. The vision rips through my chest and cuts into my heart.

"Right this second, Eli!" I'm losing control with every disgusting thing I can imagine that could possibly happen to my girl.

"In my arms. Not letting her go until I place her in your arms." Eli's voice is solid, and I focus all my attention on it like a lifeline.

My knees go weak with gratitude, and I brace my fist against the wall in the closet to hold myself up. Kathleen rests her hand on my back, a show of silent support.

"Christ! I'm getting dressed. I can be at the jetport in thirty minutes. Chase already has a plane at the ready. I'll call him to get the pilot. I can be there in...fuck. Two hours at the earliest. Please don't leave her," I plead.

"Not gonna leave my niece, man," he rumbles into the phone.

Besides his wife, Maria, that's the first time I've ever heard Elijah Redding lay claim to one of the girls or their children. Even though he's been at every function—unless he's out on a hunt—and participated in what the girls call "family dinners," I've never, not once, heard him throw down in this manner.

I swallow hard. "Eli, I owe you."

"You never owe family. Get here fast. Dice is on Misty's trail, but I need to be out there."

"What happened? How did she escape?"

"Fucking bitch went out the bathroom window. We were quiet, man. Didn't think she noticed us following her, but she must have. Dice took the back door of the rundown house she was renting, and I took the front. We broke in at the same time. I went straight to the room where I knew Cora was sleeping, and he went to Misty's bedroom. During that time she slipped out the bathroom window, and she was smoke, man. Just fucking gone. Not sure how she pulled it off, but I look forward to finding out."

"Jesus. I'm just glad you got Cora. I'm on my way."

"Good. Out," Eli says and hangs up.

I toss the cell phone on the shelf, pull out a pair of underwear and jeans, and put them on. I tell Kathleen everything. She agrees to stay home, knowing it is safer for her to be here than travel to Sin City and be anywhere near where

Misty is hiding. Eli has Cora now, so who knows what the crazy lunatic is planning. I can't believe she'd left our daughter behind when two unknown men had broken in. I thought she loved her more than that.

I finish getting dressed, grab my keys, call Chase to set up the pilot, and kiss my woman. I am off. I cannot wait a minute longer to hold my daughter. Kathleen had prepared a diaper bag with diapers, snacks, and clothes. She'd thought of everything. Even though Misty had cleared the house of the essentials, Kathleen had been steadily replacing everything. I think it kept her mind off the fact that Cora was gone. True to her word though, she always believed Elijah would bring her back. Thank fucking Christ for Kathleen. I know I am going to need her more than ever now that we'd be bringing home my daughter.

★ ★ ★

"Dah Dah!" Cora cries out, reaching for me the second her blue eyes meet mine. Her toothy smile is plastered on her face, and her eyes are alight with excitement.

I pull my girl against my chest and nuzzle her neck, her soft curls tickling my nose and chin. "Baby girl. My God, I've missed you." Her baby-powder-and-lotion scent hits my nose, and I inhale it deep within my body and soul. A piece of my heart opens and fills with such joy, I'm not sure I can contain the sissy-assed response overwhelming me. I power through and blink away tears as intense emotion crawls up my throat. Instead, I just hug her harder and swallow it down. I'll give in to it later once I've had a chance to process everything.

Cora smacks me on the cheeks, and I pull back to take her

in.

"Dah Dah," she says and lays a sloppy, openmouthed kiss right on my lips. I do not give a flying fuck. I kiss her back over and over until she giggles. Once I have my fill, she starts pointing behind me. "Eeeee." She's pointing her chubby finger at Eli.

"That's right, baby. He's Uncle E."

The huge man smirks while putting on his shoulder holster, adding his weapons, and covering it all with a worn leather jacket.

"Get her home. Tell Maria I'll call her when I can, yeah?"

I nod. "Yeah. I'll call her from the plane. Eli, I..."

"Not a word. I know what this means. And one day, there will come a time when I call in a favor in return. Cool?"

It has to be said, Eli is the epitome of cool. It makes sense why Maria hero-worships the guy. He is one. And I finally got to experience a dose of it myself. Now Maria and I have something in common. Forever. Eli saved my daughter and is going after her crazy mother so we can put her behind bars. Yeah, he's a goddamned hero.

"We're cool," I finally say, getting my emotions under control and putting out my hand.

Eli shakes it hard, using his other arm to grip my shoulder and give a squeeze of what could only be considered camaraderie. Then he lifts a large hand, places it on my daughter's head, and ruffles her blond curls. The word "Spicy" is tatted in blue ink running from the top of his wrist and ending in a loop of the "Y" at his index finger.

"Spicy?"

He glances down at his tattoo and grins. "Maria's the spiciest thing I've ever tasted. Need a reminder of my wife when I'm out on the job. Something easy to see so I always know what kind of fire I've got to come home to."

I nod, realizing how deep this man's emotions run. He may be a wall of muscle, with tatted-up arms and a scary growl—so different from his twin brother Tommy, who we lost three years ago—but he loves with intensity. Maria got herself the right man.

"Bye, munchkin. Uncle E's got work to do. Good times, girl," he says and then turns and heads out the door.

"Eeeeeeeee," Cora cries out and waves her hand.

He turns, grins at my girl, and winks. "Get her home."

"Will do. Be safe."

"Always am, man. Got something important to come home to." He grins and lifts two fingers in a quick wave.

"Yes, yes, you do," I mumble, holding my girl close. "Let's get you home, baby girl."

★ ★ ★

Once I get Cora settled on the plane and asleep on the couch next to me, I pull out my phone, planning to call Kathleen. But my phone rings in my hand from an unknown number.

Before I can say hello, someone is rattling off in my ear. "Dude, do you have your daughter?" says a voice sounding like a young teen's.

"Who the fuck is this?" I use a scary tone I don't even recognize, but between my daughter being kidnapped and her mother out on the run, I've lost all patience.

"Dude, it's Scooter. I'm one of Eli's hunters." He says this like I should know who he is.

Scooter. I let the name roll around in my head a few times

before it registers. Hunter, my ass. He's Eli's tech guy. Never enters the field, just stays behind on his computer, hacking away and drinking endless amounts of Mountain Dew and Red Bull, if I remember correctly.

"Yeah, I remember. And yes, I've got Cora."

"Wicked cool. But dude, I've got some shit news for you. I tried to call Eli to tell him first, because that's the way shit rolls around here, but he's not answering. I tracked him, and he's on the highway heading north. Means he's on the trail to meet up with Dice, who's a solid three hours ahead of him."

"All of this is very interesting information, but you said you had bad news?" I attempt to bring Scooter back around to the point of his call.

"Aw, yeah. Sorry to tell you, but your baby's mama is psychotic." He drops this little nugget as if he's just told me it's a breezy fifty degrees in the bay and to wear a pullover because of the chill.

"Tell me something we don't know, Scooter." I let all the air out of my lungs, my patience tried. I need to lie down with my daughter on my chest and just be still, listening to her heartbeat, not shooting the shit with some tech wizard.

"No, man. You don't get it. She's *clinically insane*. As in escaped from a mental institution."

A mental institution? "You're kidding."

I can hear the phone volume change, and then Scooter sounds louder but farther away, like he's in a tunnel. He's probably put me on speaker.

"Says here she was diagnosed at age fourteen with a brain tumor. The tumor was benign and stopped growing a year after she was diagnosed, but it presses on the part of her brain that deals with being able to discern reality. Apparently, the tumor ate through her paracingulate sulcus, a part of the brain that controls judgment. Fucked-up shit," he whispers.

I hear him tapping away and try to remain patient while I wait for him to continue.

"Shit, dude. Says before she was diagnosed, she tried to kill her boyfriend, who she believed was cheating on her. The boyfriend's father caught her with a knife in her hand, standing over her boyfriend's bed after she'd broken into their house. The dad happened to hear music playing in the kid's room and was going to turn it off before he settled in for the night. Took her down, and she was arrested. She was assessed by a pediatric psychologist and underwent more testing. That's when they found the tumor."

"Jesus Christ," I mutter, and Scooter continues to level me with more bad news.

"Says here the boy's family didn't press charges, which they should've, because fuck!" He continues tapping on the keys. "Fucking fuck."

My worry ramps up a hundred notches. "Scooter. Focus. What?"

"Shit, dude, she went on to marry a man named Jared Duncan right out of high school. And a year into the relationship, she sliced him up something horrible. Slaughtered him in his sleep. They found her rocking herself in the bathtub, covered in blood. Chick had some type of psychotic break. She was arrested, found unfit to stand trial due to insanity. Then they locked her away in a high-security mental hospital, where she didn't speak. Meaning, she didn't utter a word for over a year. Eventually, she started talking at some point during her five-year stay there before she escaped three years ago."

I breathe through the fear and swallow down the vomit

pooling in the back of my throat. She's so much more screwed up than I thought. "Does it say how she escaped?"

A flurry of clatters come through the line as I wait.

"Duuuuuuude. She killed two guards. One with a toothbrush that'd been filed into a sharp point. She stabbed it up through the guy's nose right into his brain. Whoa, brutal. She offed the other one with the first guard's gun. Scary bitch. Gives me the willies." He makes a burr noise, like he's cold.

"How did she fly under the radar?"

"Shit happened in Wyoming. In California, anyone can stay off the radar. I've got no employment for her under any of her legal names. Looks like she probably worked under the table until your father hired her. Looks like he didn't do a background check on her and listed her as Misty Duncan with a false Social Security number. That's why we couldn't find any real information on her. Bitch stole someone's number."

I grind my teeth. "Fucking hell."

"Dude, I gotta go. I've got to reach Eli or Dice. Give them a heads up on how crazy this chick is. Glad Eli got your daughter. Later."

"Later," I reply, but the line is already dead.

I sit back and pull my sleeping daughter up and over my chest so her legs are straddling my waist. She doesn't so much as stir as I make her comfortable against my chest, where I can feel her heartbeat and hold her close. "No one is getting to you ever again, baby. It's going to be me, you, Kathleen, and your sister or brother from here on out. I'll not allow that woman anywhere near you."

With my daughter safely on my chest, grounding me, I call Kathleen and tell her what Scooter said. Once complete, I call Maria and give her a heads up about Eli and thank her.

She assures me it's all Eli's idea, not hers, and he's doing what he needs to do for his family.

Family.

There is a lot of that going around. For the first time in a long time, while I hold my daughter close and think about the woman I'm going to marry and have another child with, and all the extended members, including Kathleen's soul sisters and their men, I'm finally content. I'm exactly where I'm supposed to be, and nothing can take that away from me.

Nothing.

★ ★ ★

A week goes by with absolutely no sight of Misty. Eli and his man Dice have scoured Nevada and have people looking in Oregon, Idaho, and Utah. Eventually, I tell Eli he needs to get home to his wife. He can't keep looking for Misty when she's got a shitload of cash and some type of unmarked vehicle. We all need to move on but stay vigilant. With her history, we're hoping she disappears.

"I don't know, man. Not feeling calling off the hunt."

"Eli, you have no leads. You said it yourself, she's smoke."

He makes an animalistic sound and picks up Cora, who's steadily tapping him on the leg and reaching her arms in an up motion. "Munchkin," he says to her while placing her on the counter in front of him. He puts something into his leather jacket pocket and then pulls out a little pink box. Seeing this huge, rough-looking guy pull out a pink anything from his jacket is shocking, never mind the fact that he leans forward with it and shows it to Cora. Eli flicks open the lid with one finger and up pops a ballerina spinning in a circle to music.

"Auntie Ria bought this for you. See, she's a dancer like her."

"Pwitty." Cora looks in complete awe at the ballerina spinning.

Eli smiles, all white teeth and happiness. He's a lot less scary when he's smiling.

Cora kicks her legs and tucks the box near her chest. "Dow dow." She wants down.

Eli chuckles, picks her up, and puts her to the ground. He surprises me again when he holds her in front of him while he's crouched down at her eye level. He runs his hand through her golden hair and kisses her forehead. She leans forward and gives him a slobbery cheek kiss. He doesn't even flinch. Guy is cool as fuck.

Once she's free, she toddles out of the room with her new treasure, screaming, "Kiiiittttyyy," calling for Kathleen.

I shake my head and smile. "Thanks, man."

He harrumphs. "Thank Maria. She's the one who picks out that shit."

"So, when are you going to uh...build your family?"

Eli grins wickedly. "I try every night."

I laugh hard and lean over the counter. "Okay, let me rephrase. When's the wife going to allow you to knock her up?"

His shoulders slump. "Been asking that for a year. Says she's scared she'll lose her clients. Me, I could give a fuck. We're not getting any younger, and I want to see a little girl with those eyes and that dark head of hair."

I nod. "You know Kathleen is pregnant. Gillian's pregnant. Use that to your advantage."

A light shimmers in Eli's eyes. "Fuckin' A. Need to have a chat with my wife. I'll keep you posted, yeah?" Eli says, walking toward the door.

"Sounds good. Thanks, man."

With a lift of the hand, he gives his standard two-fingered salute. "Later."

Kat enters the room as the door shuts. "Eli left." She frowns.

"Yeah, Sweetcheeks." I grin. "Think he's going home to nail Maria."

She giggles, puts her arms around my waist, and lifts her chin toward my face. "Honey, they're always banging."

I grin. "This time, I think he's going to talk her into falling in line with her friends." I lay a hand over her belly. It's still flat, since she's only just over three months, but it's hardened in a way I know my baby is right there under my hand. Fucking bliss.

Her eyes grow round, obviously taking in what I just said. "Eli wants kids?"

"Yep. And I think he wants them bad. He's good with Cora." I kiss her neck, running my nose up the column and saturating my senses with sunshine and coconut.

She purses her lips. "He's good with Gigi's twins too. They love hanging out with Uncle E."

I nod and continue to bathe myself in her essence until a little bundle of wild pounds against my legs. "Ice keem," Cora says, slapping Kat's and my legs.

Kathleen giggles. "I made the mistake of saying I wanted ice cream and thinking maybe we could go get some."

I look down at Kathleen and Cora, both in their pajamas and already settled down for the night, and glance at the clock. "Babe, it's eight o'clock. We need to get her to bed."

Her shoulders fall and she frowns. "But I really wanted ice cream." Then she rubs her stomach where our baby lies. I can see what manipulation the next six months is going to bring. I look from her hand to her face. She pouts, and I roll my eyes.

"Fine. You two stay here. Snuggle up on the couch, and I'll go out and get the ice cream."

Kathleen kisses me fast and hard and then leans over and grabs Cora's hand to lead her to the couch. She's gotten a lot stronger over the past three months, but she's still not comfortable lifting Cora from the ground just yet. She can easily pull her out of her crib with one arm, but normally she leads Cora to the couch and lets her crawl into her lap. I know she's working hard every day continuing her physical therapy. Even working on it at home with hand presses and small weights.

Yesterday, when she was in our bedroom sitting on the edge of the bed, I saw her lift a seven-pound barbell with her injured hand. I didn't say anything, but I witnessed the smile on her face when she gripped the bar and held it up to her chest. She'd closed her eyes and smiled the sweetest, most satisfying one I've seen in a long time. It was pride, and I fell in love with her all over again.

Whistling, I grab my keys off the hook on the wall, hit the garage opener, and get into my car.

CHAPTER TWENTY

KATHLEEN

"Get up, you bitch!" An angry voice shreds into my dream of Eli and Maria playing at the park, pushing a little girl with long dark hair and icy-blue eyes on a swing set. "Get up. I don't have a lot of time."

I come to with something cold and hard pressing into my temple. As I blink away sleep, I notice two things at once. Misty is standing over me, and a gun is pressed painfully against my head. As if on autopilot, I sit up. The gun follows me, but I don't care. I look to my left, where Cora had fallen asleep. She was so snuggly and warm I nodded off holding her against my side. She's not there now.

"Where's Cora?" I ask with zero concern for my own safety.

Misty snarls. "Like you really fucking care now that you're going to be pushing out your own Carson mini-me."

I'm certain my eyes go wide, because Misty keeps talking. "Yeah, I know you're pregnant with his child. Of course you are. You couldn't stop at stealing my man, my future husband. No, you had to steal Cora's daddy too." She swings the gun around before pointing it directly at my face.

I swallow down the fear and forge ahead. "Misty, where's Cora?"

She snorts and runs a hand through her mangy hair. The woman is a mess. Normally, she's clean, dressed to the nines, makeup on, and not a hair out of place. She'd always put herself together as though she needed to be perfect. Right now, that person is not here. In her place is a woman wearing dirty jeans, and her stringy blond hair looks like it hasn't been washed in a week. She has shadows under her eyes and is at least ten pounds lighter.

I'm aware of her mental status now, and it's clear this woman is no longer in touch with reality, if she ever was.

"My daughter... *My* daughter is fine. I put her to bed like a good mother does. Unlike you, who can't even lift her into her crib. What do you think you're going to do when your child comes, huh?"

How would she know that? She must have been watching us. *For how long?* The thought sends a shiver of disgust through me. Still, I ignore her taunts and breathe easy for a moment, knowing Cora is safely in her crib. She can't get out yet, so no matter what happens here tonight, she'll be safe. Carson will get to her.

"Uh, I don't know what I'm going to do." I'm stalling to keep her talking. If she's talking, she's not shooting me.

The phone rings and the noise makes Misty flinch. Her hand wraps tighter on the gun. I shift to the side as she shakes her head, puts one hand to her temple, and winces. The phone rings two more times, and with each ring she seems to get more agitated, bouncing from foot to foot. Her eyes are large and wild, pupils so dilated all I can see are black, empty holes of rage.

Another ring and she pulls at her hair, opening her mouth in a silent scream when the machine picks up.

"Kathleen, Carson told me you were home..." Chase says on the machine.

I glance at the phone longingly, wishing I could run to it and tell him to call the cops.

"Fucking shut up!" she screams at the phone. She points her gun at it and shoots. The gun's blast rips through the room, and the answering machine explodes into little pieces when the bullet hits its target.

I wrap my arms around my belly to protect my baby and try to run for it when she's not paying attention. Cora screams from the other room.

Misty follows me into the hallway, hot on my heels. "You get back here, you bitch! You're fucking dead! You hear me, homewrecker? You're dead!"

I run as fast as I can and make it to our bedroom, where I know my cell phone is charging on the end table. I just barely grab it when I'm pulled back by my top and smashed upside the head with Misty's gun. Blood sprays from my face as I fall to the bed and scramble across it to the other side. I lift a hand to my face and find my cheek is split open and blood is gushing out.

Misty points the gun at me, her back facing the doorway. Cora is screaming at the top of her lungs. The situation is dire. I know she's going to kill me and leave my dead body for Carson to find. This would utterly destroy him. I can't have that happen. He can't see what she's about to do to me.

Suddenly I come up with an idea. "Misty, I'm sorry I, uh, stole your man. He's really not in love with me."

"You think?" Her hand shakes wildly as she points the

gun at me.

"Still, you don't want him or your daughter to find me dead in *your home*, right?"

Her face contorts into a menacing glare. "My home. *My fucking home.* The one you took away from me!" she screeches. "He was going to kick me out on the street!"

Technically not true. He had an apartment lined up for her, but I'm not in any position to argue. I have to keep her talking, and I need her to get me out of the house and away from Cora and Carson. He'll be home soon, and I don't want him caught up in this. Cora needs her father.

Our baby needs us both, a little voice deep inside my head mutters. The pang of guilt rips through me, but I have to hold on to what I can save right now. Getting away from Cora and leaving this house is priority number one. I don't want this insane woman anywhere near Cora and Carson.

I swallow down the bile that's creeping up my throat. "He told me he loves you. That's when I went after him," I lie. "He doesn't love me. This baby isn't even his. I had sex with someone else." Another lie. Whatever it takes to get this psycho to take me far away from here. "So you see, you need to just take me. Get out of here, and come back and get your daughter and man."

Misty's eyes lighten, and a small smile overtakes her lips. I can tell the wheels are turning in her head. She lowers the gun, and her face softens. She's considering my suggestion. I breathe a sigh of relief, but it's too soon. Out of the corner of my eye, I see a figure enter the room on silent feet.

Chase.

No! I shake my head, close my eyes, and pray Chase won't do anything stupid. I should have known better. His gaze goes to Misty's hand holding the gun, and he walks up silently behind her.

Please no. God, don't. Don't.

My heart stops beating as I watch him get closer to her back. The room is dead silent. I can't even hear Cora screaming anymore. Misty's eyes flick to me and then to the picture hanging over the bed. I follow her line of sight and see reflected in the glass with sickening clarity Chase creeping up behind her. Her eyes widen, and she turns around as fast as a spinning top, the arm holding the gun rising instantly.

Chase lunges at her, grabbing the gun with his hand. The sickening sound of a gunshot blast reverberates through the room. Chase's body jerks once, but he shoves Misty back, his hand now holding the gun. Misty falls to the bed as Chase stumbles back, blood spreading on his white dress shirt. He falls to his knees, the hand not holding the gun clutching at his belly. In a nanosecond, he lifts the gun just as Misty finds her footing and stands. Her face is maniacal and she snarls, screaming out while pushing forward and lunging for the gun.

Chase squeezes the trigger once, catching Misty in the chest, and then fires a second time, the shot entering directly over Misty's heart. Her body jolts and falls back to the bed, eyes open and lifeless.

I dash over to Chase as he falls to his back. The bloodstain on his shirt is bigger than a dinner plate already and pouring out from his abdomen. His body jerks as he coughs. I rush to his side and fall to my knees, using both my hands to put pressure on his wound. It's the hardest I've ever pushed my injured hand. Still, blood is oozing over my fingers, warm and slick.

"Chase, Chase, honey stay with me. Please, please, stay

with me." Tears spill over my cheeks. "We need help. Hold on, please!"

He looks at me, his eyes filled with agony. "Gillian, the kids..." He gasps and winces. "My reason."

"Yes, Chase. Gillian and the kids, they're your reason for living, so live! Don't give up! Don't give up!" I'm yelling and pressing harder on his wound. "I need to get you help!" I scream to the empty room, thinking I need to get to my phone. Call someone. Anybody.

That's when Carson runs into the room. "What's going on?" He drops the bag he's holding. "Oh my God! Kathleen! Fuck, Chase!" He falls to his knees by my side. "Are you okay? The baby?" His voice is stern and assessing.

"Fine, fine. We're fine, Chase. Call the police. Now! He's been shot in the stomach."

Cora is still screaming in the other room.

Carson runs to the phone, calls it in, and before long sirens are blaring. Time seems to stretch, ebbing and flowing wildly. Carson has Cora in his arms just down the hall, not where she can see her mother dead or Chase on the floor bleeding out. When the paramedics finally arrive, Chase is unconscious and barely breathing.

"Back away, ma'am. Let us do our job."

"I can't let go. He'll bleed to death."

"Ma'am, we've got this." A big paramedic grips me around the biceps and physically pulls me off. "We've got him. Let us help him." He sets me aside and goes to work. The scene as they work on him floats through my conscious mind as if in a dream.

Finally, they are on the move, and I follow them to the ambulance, blood coating my pajamas, arms, and hands.

"Kat..." Carson says, broken. "Baby..."

"I've got to go with them," I say, swiftly slipping into my flip flops at the door as they maneuver through the entry.

"Sorry, ma'am. Against protocol for a GSW. You'll have to meet us at the hospital." The paramedic jumps into the back of the ambulance and slams the door so fast a gust of air hits me.

Carson puts a hand on my shoulder and squeezes. "The cops need your statement, and you need to change before we go to the hospital," he says while looking down at my blood-soaked clothes.

That's when I start to shake. A small tremble in each limb turns into a full-body shudder. My stomach twist and turns until vomit roars up my throat. I rush to the nearest bush and empty the contents in several body-racking heaves. A female cop holds my hair back and soothes a hand down my back as Carson stands helplessly to the side, calling out kind words while holding Cora tight.

This is pathetic! I lock my fear and anguish down. I need to be present for Chase. He saved my life, my baby's life. I owe him everything. I'll keep it together until I know he's going to live. I wipe away the tears and the moisture coating my mouth and vow not to lose it again. I'll be strong for him, for all of them.

That's when I start to pray.

★ ★ ★

The only sound in the room is the ticking of the clock, a low murmur from outside in the hospital corridor, and my sniffles. I grip his hand as tight as I can with my gnarled one, but he doesn't so much as flinch. He always comments on how the strength in my hand is getting better, patting the top of it while gifting me with a tiny curl of his lips. Right now, nothing. Just me and him. I'm not sure where Gigi ran off to. I expect she's resting, since they finally kicked her seven-month-pregnant ass out. After four nights of touch and go, she and the baby need it. Hell, we all do.

Only, I can't sleep.

Every time I close my eyes, I see Chase falling to his knees, blood pooling red on his stark-white dress shirt, his eyes widening and his lips firming while one of his arms comes up, the track lighting glinting off the gun. One shot, then two, right into Misty's chest. Then he falls back, his mouth opening in a silent scream, but nothing comes out.

Then I wake up. Every night. I slip out of Carson's warm arms—we're sleeping in the guest room for now—being as quiet as possible. I change into yoga pants and a sweatshirt and come here. To the hospital. I need to make sure Chase is alive. That he's still breathing.

When he breathes, I breathe. Usually it's just me watching through the blinds outside of his ICU room as Gillian and Chase sleep. Tonight though, she's gone. So I've slipped in to sit by his side.

It's weird to see him unmoving. Completely still. On an average day, Chase is such a large presence. When he enters a room, everyone notices. His magnetism is that strong. People watch him. Women devour him with their eyes. Men are either scared of him or revere him. Not now. Now he's lying silently, sleeping, his abdomen wrapped heavily with gauze and his chest bare. I watch him breathe. Every time his chest lifts, mine does as well. With each inhalation, a piece of me settles, relaxes, allowing me to survive another day.

A warm hand curls around the cap of my shoulder. "Hey, honey, it's late. Three in the morning. What are you doing here?" Gigi whispers, even though Chase hasn't woken up yet. They have him on a respirator and under heavy sedation so he doesn't feel the excruciating pain a gunshot wound to the gut entails. She pulls a chair directly next to mine and sits in it, facing me. She grabs my other hand and holds it in both of hers.

I suck in a breath, and for the first time since it happened, my eyes fill with tears that fall over the edges of my lashes. "I love your husband," I say with my heart in my throat and my fear spilling from my lungs.

"I know." She blinks prettily, her green eyes so soft and welcoming in the dim light of the hospital room.

With every ounce of shame and pride I have inside, I repeat what I'm trying to say. "I really love him." I squeeze her hand as best I can, trying to make her see. To understand what he did for me, for my baby, for Carson and Cora. I'll never ever be able to repay that. Never. And this doesn't include all he's done for me over the past three years. I can't lose him.

"I know," she repeats.

I swallow, and the depth of my feelings comes out in a rush. "No, Gigi. I love him...like...like he's my brother." My voice makes the words sound scratchy and hard to get out.

"Honey, he *is* your brother," she says simply, matter-of-factly, and pulls me into her arms. I go willingly.

"He could have died. And it would have been my fault." My voice cracks, and I choke on each word, but I need to tell her. To admit the horrible pain that is swallowing me whole. "I could have lost him and you at the same time." I hiccup through my tears, my body trembling violently as she holds me.

Gillian's arms tighten around me. "There's nothing in this

world that could take you away from me. And Chase is too strong to leave this earth without one hell of a fight." She runs her hands through my hair. "And sweetie, he made a choice, one I'm very thankful for. Had he not taken that chance, you and the baby would be dead. Misty would have killed you. There's no question in my mind."

"But Chase could have died, and it would have been my fault." I sob against her neck, the shame flowing over me like a tidal wave.

Gigi holds my hair and pets my back. After allowing me a few minutes to wallow in my misery, she finally speaks. "Do you blame me for your burns? For losing the ability to use your hand fully?" Her question is as soft as a prayer but hits me as hard as a hammer.

In fact, the question flashes straight through me like a lightning strike. I push back and focus on her eyes. "Goodness, no. What happened to me was the direct result of a madman. You are not responsible for Danny. Have you thought that for the past three years?" My mind whirls with the possibility that my best friend has carried this tremendous weight all these years.

Gillian ignores me. "Misty was a mentally ill woman. She quite literally lost her mind and her ability to judge what was real and what wasn't. You are not responsible for her actions."

"But..." I try, and she cuts me off.

"No. Kathleen, I've not thought you blamed me for what Danny did. Not for a long time. At first I did. I worried all of you blamed me for what happened. But I worked through it with Dr. Madison when the situation went down. And it sounds like you are going to need to as well."

I nod and let my head fall forward.

"Chase is going to be fine. The doctors say he will make a full recovery. Sure, he'll need to be babied, but he's got four women and a host of house staff falling all over themselves to help him." She pats my hand the same way her husband does when he's trying to get a point across to me. "He's going to be fine. Knowing you are alive, the baby you're carrying is okay, is all he needs to motivate him."

I take a long, slow breath and glance at him. He's sleeping. And he will have years and years to continue razzing me.

"You know, Kat, Chase would do anything for his family. And you're part of that. Not only are you family through our bond, the two of you are close. Friends in a way the rest of us are not. That's special, and I want him to have such a special connection. He'd have been devastated if you and the baby were hurt."

She is right. Chase puts family above all else, and he was happy about the baby. Ecstatic, even. The more Davises the better, according to Chase.

Gillian's phone buzzes from within her cardigan pocket. She pulls it out and lifts it to her ear. "Hello?" A soft grin overtakes her lips. Her gaze flits to mine. "Yeah, she's here. I'll send her home to you. Yes, she's okay, just checking on the big guy again."

Again? She knows.

Her lips turn into a slow smile. "Yeah, I think she's worked through something that was keeping her from resting. I'll make sure she leaves in a few minutes."

"You knew?" I ask when she ends the call and puts her phone back in her pocket. "How? You were asleep."

She stands up and pulls me up with her. "The nurses told me. I had to approve you coming into the ICU. How do you think you got in every night?"

Huh. It hadn't entered my mind. I was just thankful when I pressed the button and told them who I wanted to see, they automatically buzzed me in.

"Honestly, I didn't question it. Are you mad?"

"That you came and checked on my husband? That you love him and me so much you couldn't sleep until you saw him alive? No, honey, I'm not mad. I'm grateful to have you in my life. Grateful for your love and friendship. Family is everything, and you're my sister." She pulls me into her arms, and I let the tears fall again while I hold her.

She keeps me close until our tears have dried up and I'm ready to go back home.

★ ★ ★

Carson pulls back the covers when I enter the room. "How's he doing?"

I shrug, pull off my yoga pants and sweatshirt, and slip into bed beside him in only my cami and undies. "Gillian says he's going to make a full recovery."

"Of course he is." He pulls me into his warmth and holds me close. "Are you okay?"

"Yeah."

"Why do you keep leaving my bed to go to him?" His voice carries a hint of something I never expected from him.

Jealousy.

"I...I need to see him breathe." I split myself open wide and let all of my worry spill out.

"You feel responsible?" He holds me close. I rest my head on his chest right above his heart.

"Yeah."

"But she was my mistake. Not yours. I'm the one who fucked up." The way his voice sounds, this is something he's been carrying around with him for a while as well.

I sigh and nuzzle into the smattering of soft chest hair. "We both messed up, but we're fixing that. And besides, now we've got Cora, and our baby on the way."

Carson runs a hand down my back over my waist until he tucks it around me. "You have to marry me before this baby comes."

"Okay."

"Okay?" Surprise and awe coat his tone. "That's it? Just okay?"

I shift my shoulders and sigh sleepily. "No reason to wait. Just as long as Chase walks me down the aisle."

"That could take a few months," he whispers.

"Then we have time." I'm not at all concerned with his need to rush a ceremony.

"Where do you want to get married?"

"On the beach in front of our house. Just close friends and family. Barefoot. Ocean. The girls and a flowy white dress designed by Chloe," I mumble, imagining it already.

"Sounds perfect. There's just one thing left." He lifts and scoots to the side of the bed, opens the nightstand drawer, and pulls out a box. I can barely see what he's doing in the moonlight, but he opens it, claps it shut, and something sparkly catches the light. "Give me your hand."

I lift my left hand over his chest. "Are you going to ask me?"

"No."

"What?" I push up as he slides a ring on my finger. Of

course, it's a perfect fit.

"No. I told you. This is it. No going back, no pushing, no running, no anything. You could have died. We could have lost the baby. We are not fucking around. You are marrying me the second Chase can walk you down the beach. End of discussion."

Holy fucking shit. Carson has never been so forceful and serious in his entire life.

"And furthermore, the next time you slip out of my arms and our bed, you kiss me goodbye and tell me where you're going. After what's happened in the past few months, hell, the past few years, you owe me that much. So, if you're going to slip out to ease your conscience by checking on my cousin and his wife, you give your man a heads up. Okay?" He lifts my hand and kisses the ring on my finger.

I lift it up to the moonlight and smile as streaks ricochet out in all directions. It's a perfect oval diamond with two matching ovals on each side. I've never seen anything more beautiful.

"The big oval diamond is you, right in the center. And the two diamonds on each side, that's you accepting Cora and me as your family. The three of us until we bring home our newest member. Until death do us part."

"Until death do us part." I slide over his body, straddling him so that my heat is centered over his. He groans, cups both cheeks, and grinds into me. "I love you." I lean forward, seal my mouth over his, and set about showing him just how much I love him, this ring, and our future.

EPILOGUE

KATHLEEN

"What is it with you *chicas*?" Ria asks, hands on hips, shaking her head, rocking a royal-blue skintight dress she could have stolen right out of Sofía Vergara's closet. She's standing off to the side of the mirror catching my gaze through the reflection, her eyes an icy-blue as usual.

I'm also in front of the long mirror in my new bedroom, the one Carson added on to our beach ranch house so we didn't have to sleep in the room where Misty died. That room is now a game room for the guys. Right this instant though, I'm looking at myself in my wedding gown. It's a breezy, flowy white silk that covers one shoulder completely, hiding my scars. The other arm is bare, showing all skin. The bodice is cinched together with intricate beading, emphasizing my seven-month baby bump, not at all trying to conceal it. Carson and I are excited about our growing family and want the world to know it.

I run my hands down my belly, settling the little kicker inside. He or she wants me to move, and by the way the kicking gets harder, I can tell my little one is very insistent. The only time I get any rest from the soccer player inside me is when I'm moving around. Apparently, rocking the baby to sleep through movement is in my very near future.

"In what way?" I ask while Bree places sprigs of baby's breath and a fresh brilliant-orange Gerbera daisy in my hair in the small sweep we've pulled to the side. The rest is falling in long curling waves down my back the way Carson likes it. One bonus about being pregnant—my hair is growing like a weed and is three times thicker than normal.

Maria points at my belly and then gestures to my entire body. "Isn't it obvious? Hello, pregnant and getting hitched."

Gillian fluffs out the bottom of my dress. "So what?"

"I just think it's funny that I'm the only one who did things right." She grins cockily.

"Oh, is that so? Says the woman who married her boyfriend's twin brother!" Bree laughs manically, and Ria pouts.

"*Cierto.*" True, she admits.

I chuckle and swish from side to side. "You have to admit it is kind of funny that all three of us got married while pregnant."

"Technically, I didn't know I was pregnant at the time, so it doesn't count." Gigi flicks her long red waves over to one side.

"Doesn't matter. You were pregnant. So was Bree when she and Phillip eloped, and now, here you are, very pregnant and getting married." Maria's confirmation is not helpful.

I frown. "You calling me a hoochie? You calling all of us hoochies?" I put my hands on my much fluffier hips and cock my head for emphasis.

She grins. "*Si el zapato calza...*" she says in rapid-fire Spanish.

"Shut your mouth. If the shoe fits... What the fuck ever. I had sex one time. One frickin' time and got pregnant," Bree huffs. "Gigi was kidnapped and missed her birth control pills. And Kat... What happened to you, Kat? I forgot." Bree frowns and taps her lips with one finger.

"My implant ran out."

"Oh yeah, her implant ran out... Wait. You let that shit run out?" Bree accuses.

I roll my eyes. "Bree, rant. Maria, continue. Or better yet, don't. Just because Maria's afraid to get pregnant and be responsible for another human being besides herself doesn't mean we are."

Maria's mouth opens and her entire face contorts into a fiery demon. "That is not true! If it were, we wouldn't be expecting right now." She crosses her arms over her ample breasts, and her eyes widen to the size of small saucers.

All three of us stop fiddling with my dress, lose the wind in our bickering sails, and stare at Maria. Her mouth twitches and her eyes water.

Three voices split the air at once.

"No fuckin' way!" Bree squeals and jumps up and down.

"Oh my God, Ria!" Gigi cries, her hands clasping and going to her chest over her heart.

"Holy shit!" I whisper, not believing what I just heard.

Maria swallows while all three of us stare at her, mesmerized. I'm not sure any of us believed this day would come. The day Maria broke down and gave that man of hers a child. She loves children, sure, but she's always been so focused on her career and enjoying her relationship. Every time the subject came up, she would change it immediately, stating they had all the time in the world.

"Maria..." I don't know what to say.

Bree, on the other hand, does not have a problem

speaking. She practically flies over to our soul sister in her hot-pink slinky tank dress and tackle-hugs her, squealing with glee.

Gigi loops an arm around my shoulders as we both tear up and wait our turn. Only Bree has no plan to let our sister go, so we make our way over and wrap our arms around one another in a group huddle. All three of us express our excitement over the fact that our kids are going to grow up together, and we're going to spend the rest of our lives as one big happy family.

Our girl-hug session is broken up by a booming voice. "Everyone ready to get this show on the road?"

I pull back first to see Chase standing just inside the bedroom in black dress slacks, a linen button-up, and an orange Gerbera daisy matching the one Bree put into my hair pinned to his shirt. He looks alive, tan, and healthy. In his arms is a tiny bundle of love wrapped in a blue blanket. Gillian leaves the huddle and wraps her arms around her husband's waist, leans up as he leans down, and kisses him softly on the lips.

"Everyone ready downstairs?" she asks, eyes focused solely on her husband, love shining all around them.

"Yeah, beautiful. Will you take Clay so I can get the bride-to-be handed off to my cousin?" He grins and kisses her one more time.

"Yeah," she says dreamily, putting her hand into the hair at his nape, tugging him forward, and kissing him with a bit more depth than the previous two pecks before finally pulling back. She then takes their three-week-old son into her arms.

The girls shuffle out, and Chase walks over to me and sets both of his hands on top of my shoulders. We look at one another in our reflections in the mirror as I assess myself one more time before becoming Mrs. Carson Davis.

"You ready to become a Davis?" He smirks.

I put my hand over one of his. "Damn straight. Take me to my man."

He chuckles, hooks his elbow with mine, and leads me through my house and out across the porch to the private beach. A path has been created out of flower petals, and our beautiful gazebo is decorated in a mixture of orange daisies and other wildflowers. Swags of fabric fall down each side, providing the most beautiful arch. At the top step are the preacher and Carson.

His eyes are as blue as the sky, and his smile is bigger than ever before and filled with so much love it makes me stumble. I want to get to him faster. Chase holds me up and grins as we walk up the two steps it takes to get to the entry of the arbor and the man I'm going to spend the rest of my life with. Chase hands me off to Carson, who holds both of my hands.

"You're beautiful," he whispers only for me.

"You're sweet," I counter.

"You're everything." His voice is filled with unending emotion.

"Everything I am is yours."

CARSON

"Baby, you were amazing. I'm in awe of you," I tell my wife after experiencing the most death-defying act known to man. How a woman survives childbirth is a mystery.

Kathleen sighs, petting our son's cheek with her thumb. Yes, Maria was right, as usual. She sure knows how to take the fun out of the we-want-to-be-surprised game with our first child. Still, I can't be mad right now. I'm looking at my wife and our son. Twenty-one inches and seven pounds of perfect human being.

"He's perfect," Kat says, tears clogging her throat.

"Yes, he is."

A knock sounds at the door. "It's time to introduce him." I make sure she's covered from her first nursing session, which went surprisingly well considering she's new at it.

Kat swallows and looks at the door nervously. "Do you think he'll be happy?" Her caramel-brown eyes flicker with worry.

"Only one way to find out." I know this is going to floor the man entering the room.

"Everyone decent? Can we come in?" Chase asks, Gillian tight to his side.

Kathleen chuckles. "Come in, guys."

Kathleen adjusts herself, sitting up in the hospital bed. Chase comes to her right side first, Gillian a few paces behind him. He's always eager to hold the babies. The man is a baby magnet, and I have a feeling he's going to have a very special connection with this one. At least I hope so. My little guy is going to need all the love and strength of his family.

"My, my, why look at our little bruiser," Chase murmurs, getting close.

Gillian leans over Chase's side to get a gander. "And a brunette with blue eyes like his Uncle Chase. What's his name, or does he not yet have one?" Gigi asks, petting his foot.

Kathleen clears her throat, and I tighten my hand on her shoulder, giving a squeeze so she knows I'm here for support.

Gingerly, using her newfound strength in her injured arm, she lifts the baby toward Chase. "I'd like you to meet Chase William Davis the Second." Shivers ripple down her arms and sear into my hands. Tears begin to fall down her cheeks.

Chase's eyes whip up to me, to Kat, the baby, and back to my wife. "Kathleen...Carson...I don't... I-I don't know what to say." He's clearly shocked by this gesture.

Kathleen puts her hand over his, which is cradling our son. Gigi puts hers on his back, silently crying what I can only believe are tears of joy.

"If you hadn't risked your life that night, he wouldn't be here. And neither would I. This is our gift to you for making such a sacrifice." Kathleen struggles through what I know she's practiced a hundred times over the past few months since we made the decision.

Chase shakes his head. "Not a sacrifice, Kathleen... Carson..." Again, his words are stilted and thick with emotion.

She places her hand on his cheek. "Thank you," she whispers. His eyes fill with tears, and one spills over the edge. It's the first time since Aunt Colleen's funeral I've seen him shed a tear. To see this powerful man filled with such emotion and allowing it to be seen is something I'll never forget as long as I live.

Chase swallows and clears his throat. "I'll strive to be a good role model and show him and both of you how honored I am by this gesture. He'll want for nothing," he says with finality.

"Oh no!" Gigi shakes her head, and it falls forward against his back. "Another one bites the dust. Good luck, guys. He'll be buying your kid every toy, car, house, whatever it is. It's now his. You should have thought of that before you dropped this kind of bomb," she jokes, lightening the situation.

Chase is not at all fazed by it. He lifts the baby toward his face, nuzzles his neck, inhales deeply, and kisses his forehead. "It will be me and you, Chase-ter. I'm going to teach you everything there is to know about money and how to control the universe with it. Isn't that right?"

I roll my eyes but can't suppress the smile as my cousin carries on.

"And look at your Auntie Gigi. Later, you'll understand how gorgeous she is. I'll teach you how to secure your own babe. Yeah..."—he paces around the hospital room—"me and you, kid. My namesake. Not a more fitting name. Just me and you..."

Gillian leans over and pulls Kathleen into her arms. "The gift that keeps on giving." She laughs.

"Yeah, kind of the point." Kat chuckles too and hugs her friend tighter.

"Nothing's ever going to reach this level of awesome. You realize that, right?"

"Best sister ever!" Kat grins, and the three of us chuckle.

"He may never let you have your son back." She hooks a thumb over her shoulder at Chase, who does not seem at all eager to bring the baby back.

I walk over to him. "That's enough. Give me back my son."

"He's my namesake. We're bonding," Chase rumbles and holds the baby closer.

I put a hand out in a hand-him-over motion. He grumbles and carefully transfers the baby to my arms.

The door opens, and Bree and Phillip enter, all smiles. Maria and Eli are behind them. Chloe pulls up the rear with my dad. Cooper will be here soon, and Craig and Faith are flying in with the kids in a couple weeks when things are settled.

Everyone greets my son, Kathleen, and me with well wishes, hugs, and pats on the back. Each girl cries when they hear we've named the baby after Chase. The laughter ensues when Kathleen asks Maria what she's having. She pets her four-month-along bump.

"*No lo sé*," she admits, and everyone stops laughing.

"Wait a minute. With every single one of us you could tell what we were having before we had it, but you can't on yourself?"

Maria shrugs and Eli grins, putting his arm around her. "Guess it doesn't work in reverse. We have an appointment to find out Monday."

The rest of the group laughs and carries on until it's clear Kathleen is tired and the baby needs to nurse. Plus, I want to spend time with my whole family alone.

Just as everyone is leaving, Chase and Gillian's nanny brings Cora into the room. I hand off baby Chase to Kat before picking up Cora and settling her on the bed next to Kat. The nanny leaves silently.

"Mommy, dis my baby?" she asks Kathleen.

Once Misty had been out of the picture for a couple months, Cora instantly switched to calling Kathleen "Mommy." Neither one of us asked her to do it. We never stopped her. And Kathleen has never shied away from the role, much to my heart's content. She's shown nothing but love for Cora since the minute she met her.

She runs her hand through Cora's blond hair and taps her nose. "Yep, honey. This is your baby brother, Chase."

Her nose crunches up. "But dat's Uncle Chase's name."

"I know. We named the baby after him. Isn't that great?"

She nods and leans forward and kisses his forehead. "Hi, Chasey. I your sister, Cora. Say Cooooorrrrrraaaa," she drawls out. She waits a moment and looks up. "Nope, he no say it yet."

Both Kat and I laugh. "No, honey, because he can't speak. It will be a long time before he learns how to talk the way we do."

"He tired. Look, he closed his eyes," she says with glee, as though she won the lottery by guessing what he needs.

"Yep. How about you lie with Mommy and Brother and rest awhile."

"Okay." She leans against Kathleen and focuses on her brother quietly.

I press against Kathleen's side, a boulder of emotion so big pressing on my chest, I'm not sure how I'm going to get it off, or if I ever want to.

"Kathleen, how did we get so lucky?" I kiss the top of her head and stare down at our beautiful son and daughter sitting on the bed, Cora petting his wispy brown hair, proving that we did in fact name him well. He may even end up looking like my cousin.

Kat is silent for a moment, just staring down at our son. Then she looks at Cora and then back up to me. Her brown eyes are so soulful, and I plan to spend every day of my life looking into them.

She smiles softly. "There's only one logical explanation."

"And what's that?" I lean down and press my forehead against hers.

She responds with her lips touching mine so we both can physically feel her answer.

"It's fate."

THE END

ALSO BY AUDREY CARLAN

The Calendar Girl Series

January (Book 1)	July (Book 7)
February (Book 2)	August (Book 8)
March (Book 3)	September (Book 9)
April (Book 4)	October (Book 10)
May (Book 5)	November (Book 11)
June (Book 6)	December (Book 12)

The Calendar Girl Anthologies

Volume One (Jan-Mar)	Volume Three (Jul-Sep)
Volume Two (Apr-Jun)	Volume Four (Oct-Dec)

The Falling Series

Angel Falling

London Falling

Justice Falling

The Trinity Novels

Body (Book 1)

Mind (Book 2)

Soul (Book 3)

Life (Book 4)

Fate (Book 5)

The Lotus House Series

Resisting Roots (Book 1)

Sacred Serenity (Book 2)

Divine Desire (Book 3)

Limitless Love (Book 4 - 1/16/2018)

ACKNOWLEDGEMENTS

To my husband, Eric, you know how much this series means to me. Thank you for always being there for me when I'm out of my mind with worry or fear that the readers won't connect with my words the way I hope they will. I love you.

To my soul sisters, Dyani Gingerich, Nikki Chiverrell, and Carolyn Beasley...this is the end of the series but never the end of us. Our bond knows no bounds. I'd like to think that after reading this five-book series you know how very much I love and adore you. This series is my legacy of friendship to the three of you. I'll always love you more.

To my editor Ekatarina Sayanova with Red Quill Editing, LLC...there will never be another editor I connect with so completely. I wish all authors could find what I have. Thank you.

Roxie Sofia, you make me laugh and my manuscripts shine. I'm so thankful to have your critical eye on my projects. I really enjoy working with you.

To my extraordinarily talented #TEAMAC, Heather White (aka Goddess) and my personal assistant Jeananna Goodall, it has been a crazy journey to this point. Thank you for having my back in all things.

Ceej Chargualaf, I can't tell you how much it means to have you pre-reading my books. Your enthusiasm is infectious and gives such spirit to my muse. I'm sorry you had to wait so long in between chapters where I inevitably left you hanging.

You are such a good sport and a loving, kind human being. I love having you on my team.

Ginelle Blanch, Anita Shofner, Tracey Vuolo, my fantastic beta readers... I hope this book gave you all the resolution you needed in this series. It's been a long time coming. Thank you for being there when I needed you.

To the Audrey Carlan Street Team of wicked hot Angels, together we change the world. One book at a time. BESOS-4-LIFE, lovely ladies.

ABOUT AUDREY CARLAN

Audrey Carlan is a #1 *New York Times, USA Today,* and *Wall Street Journal* bestselling author. She writes wicked hot love stories that are designed to give the reader a romantic experience that's sexy, sweet, and so hot your ereader might melt. Some of her works include the wildly successful Calendar Girl Serial, Falling Series, and the Trinity Trilogy.

She lives in the California Valley where she enjoys her two children and the love of her life. When she's not writing, you can find her teaching yoga, sipping wine with her "soul sisters" or with her nose stuck in a wicked hot romance novel.

Any and all feedback is greatly appreciated and feeds the soul. You can contact Audrey below:

E-mail: carlan.audrey@gmail.com
Facebook: facebook.com/AudreyCarlan
Website: www.audreycarlan.com